Take Down Request

Take Down Request

James Krake

CONTENTS

Blood Spot

2140/06/05

Bastion was a city overgrown on itself, spilling out the sides and tumbling to the ground. Shimmering spires of photovoltaic cells still struck toward the sky, but beneath the distribution web of the twentieth floor was an almost organic heap of structures. While autonomous trams and maglev trains could fly from tower to tower in the sky above, the work of traversing labyrinthine ground floors fell to humans like Clyde.

There was an art, and a danger, to carrying goods through the lowest strata of Bastion. He was less likely to find a working elevator than to clamber up a welded down step-ladder. The lack of safety railings didn't matter to Clyde, his hands were full with Ajitatsu chocolate bars. Someone had ordered a box to yet another mass-produced apartment block somewhere attached to the serpentine boulevards of the city.

Weaving through crowds of shoppers and drinkers was little relief, as people continually bumped into him. He merely cranked up the volume of his music through his neural implant. While other people listened to the ambient advertisements flooding out of storefronts, he drowned it out with a stream of live-mixed synth electronica delivered straight to his auditory cortex. He ignored the crowd and he was gone from their minds the moment he was out of their sight.

And he was fine with that. When his uniform made him part of the background, that usually meant he didn't get into trouble.

As he rounded through one flight of rusted steps after another, he wondered if the DJ was even human or just a corporate-backed piece of machine imitation software. After almost sixteen hours on shift, the idea that he might be indulging the capital property of a trust fund kid, probably all the way up on the eightieth floor, made him want to smack the grin off the possibly-non-existent punk.

He didn't have the attention to both search up the DJ's personal information as well as follow the WPS map to his destination though. The map never seemed to know the latest info when he had to move so close to the ground floor, constantly updating with last second re-routes. Bridge connections across train lines were nearly random and the pre-fab shanty walls that squatters liked to shift around were definitely random. The computer system tried to catalog the labyrinth that was Gamma, but even the government struggled to know who to tax and how much to tax them.

Luckily for him, he knew he would eventually be in a sane neighborhood. His company kept their own list of addresses. Anyone in an unregistered domicile would have to go to a postal suite instead. When he found himself in a standardized hall, with residential doors evenly spaced, he at least knew he was delivering to someone with a job and that meant it was very unlikely he was going to get jumped.

Clyde knocked where his map told him too. "Candy man's here."

The music inside, some kind of saxophone rock, paused and he realized the moaning hadn't been recorded. The resident yanked the door open, shirtless and sweaty. He had his hair bleached and standing on end like lightning had struck him. He was as thin as a lightning rod too. "Fuck yes, I forgot I ordered these," he said, reaching for the box.

Clyde jerked it back and held out his tablet. "Thumbprint first."

A blonde snuck out of the bedroom and threw her arms around the resident, using his back to cover up. Nuzzling against him, she asked, "What's going on, babe?"

"Candy," the man said, and stuck his thumb in his mouth. He greased it up with drool and scraped it off on the wall as a means of cleaning it. When he jabbed the touchscreen, the print validated and payment went through.

Clyde turned the tablet around and almost gagged. He didn't want to put it back in his pocket, not still dripping with the guy's spit. He couldn't spot a public bathroom from where he was and he tried to remember if there was one around the corner. He was about to just wipe it off on the side of his denim pants when the couple popped the lid open.

The foil wrapped bricks of chocolate didn't lay flat in the box. The girl reached in and ripped one open, devouring it with moans reminiscent of before Clyde had arrived. What laid beneath was the resident's fixation: unlabeled pill bottles. "Thanks for the lift," the guy said. He grinned and slapped his hand on Clyde's elbow before popping the cap off and walking inside.

"Come on babe, let me–" the girl kicked the door shut with her foot, cutting her sentence off and giving Clyde only a glance at her backside.

"What the hell?" Clyde said. A box of chocolate was one thing to be walking around with, fifty credits worth of goods at most. Drugs were an entirely different realm. They warranted hazard pay for one thing, and that risk very often was realized. Clyde was a big guy and could take a risk or two, but he wasn't getting paid for that.

The door deadbolt slammed home and he took a few steps back. His navigation app happily chirped about a job well done. It pinged a fresh route for him, asking him to continue through the apartment building. It wanted him to head down two flights and across three towers so he could meet another coworker for another handoff. It treated him like a dancing puppet in an old German clock.

He declined it.

The app freaked out, but he submitted an emergency occurrence and the package he was supposed to get was rerouted somewhere else. He neither knew nor cared as he headed for the nearest train station to head back to the office. While the station scanned the ID in his jacket, he called up his boss. It went to voicemail and he left a message, "I gotta report contaminated goods, or something like that. This is a talk in person kind of thing. Okay? I'm heading back now. If you know what I'm talking about then you should know I ain't cool with this."

A pack of cityboarders blasted by him, flying across the maglev rails. They whooped and laughed, snapping pictures or filming, getting their kicks by letting the train nearly nudge them in the back. It scared some of the onlookers, and the kids just hollered louder.

Clyde watched with impassive eyes. They weren't doing anything he hadn't done when he was their age and he wasn't impressed. If they wanted reactions, they should have been higher up in the city, where the wind was stronger and the people livelier. They were wasting their time as far as he was concerned, or maybe they had just lost a turf war. The important thing was that they got out of the way when the train started moving again, with him aboard it.

The car was packed, but somehow everyone found room to stay away from him. He took a seat on a mid-facing bench, spread his legs, planted his elbows on his knees, and thought about his job. Most distribution in Bastion was done through autonomous shuttles. Door delivery was an added fee because the average walk to a post office took five minutes. Of course, plenty of people paid for it regardless. Food was a common need, and finding people carnally engaged was hardly uncommon. Especially with chocolate deliveries.

He didn't know if that added up to enough money that Ajitatsu was actually profitable though. He tried to remember how many packages he delivered in a day, to average that across how many employees Ajitatsu had in his department. Clyde could simply look up the sale price of a chocolate bar and he tried to remember how many bars were in his average delivery, but he could only take a guess at what the production cost of each was. Even his most liberal guess came up short though. Not just his own wage but the local warehouses all had rent. Paying it all legit just felt like a stretch.

Market share and marketing was hard to quantify, but he couldn't imagine they would accept losing money on door deliveries. Cash flow was another consideration. Ajitatsu was a food additive company, not a true mega-corp. Banks liked to see turnover.

In his gut, he could only believe they were doing door deliveries to transport illegal goods, to move them around without EVE taking a direct scan. Those pills had been opioids most likely–not many drugs were still prohibited–and he had been complicit in the business.

He could only imagine what his mother would say. He couldn't imagine telling her either.

Clyde stepped off the train at the bottom of the Ajitatsu tower. Deep in Missou, but Gamma was the same everywhere. It was dirty, dark, and full of people he didn't trust. One of those people was a cityboarder who leapt off the junction line above him without a word. Clyde saw the shadow and jerked his head up. The fiberglass board slammed into his face and snapped his nose.

Pain blurred his vision. He hit the ground and the kid landed on top of him. The clench in his chest was all he could think about. He couldn't breathe. He was groaning as his senses came back. Blood poured out of his nose and back through to his throat. His first halting breath became a sputtering cough as he threw the cityboarder off of him. The anti-slip grating dug through his jacket, biting at his flesh as he spat out blood. The grating was vibrating. People were running towards him. The world clicked together and his adrenaline spiked. The kid hadn't fallen.

He was getting mugged.

"Oh, you quaz ass mother f–"

Something caught him in the head. It didn't hurt so much as jerk him around and he heard the noise of bone on bone. The next kid fell, whining in pain and clutching his shin. Clyde's nostrils flared as he felt the heat across his scalp. The kids were idiots, too young to know better, but he wasn't going to let them off.

The first one, the cityboarder, was still scrambling to unbuckle his boots. Every frantic jerk changed the whirring electro-magnets. Then Clyde was on him, lurching from the ground up. He grabbed the cityboarder by the jacket and hammered a fist down. The kid's mouth was soft and bloody.

A third one grabbed him by the foot and jerked him back. Clyde was a big guy. He didn't move much. He rolled, slinging his boot into the newcomer's leg. Hard, but not enough to knock the kid down. The kid who had booted him in the head ran back over and tried to stomp Clyde. He caught the kid's foot instead, throwing him on his ass. He followed it up with a slam of his fist between the kid's legs–very soft.

Something wrapped around his throat. Firm and covered in plastic–the cityboarder's jacketed arm. He could feel bicep and forearm squeezing. Before he could pry it off his throat, the third kid started kicking him in the side. Slam, slam, slam, until his breath was knocked out again.

The world went black.

Clyde was face down, gasping. The floor vibrated with pounding feet again. "Shit man, they got your credit chip." The unfamiliar voice brought a pang of panic. Clyde shoved himself up, burning every bruise the kids had given him. His rise lurched. The kids were nothing more than a blur of multi-colored jackets; gone into the city as fast as they had come.

Clyde checked his pockets. They'd taken his credit chip and his corporate tablet. At least his phone was still in his jacket. "Son of a bitch!" he shouted, the noise high and pinched. He stood up and stumbled to a dark window. He scowled and peered at his reflection, then snapped his nose straight again and sneezed the blood out.

Two dozen people had watched him get mugged. He could see them in the reflection too; how they all just walked away once the show was over. EVE called his phone as he shuffled into a public restroom. "Mr Bondsman," the AI said, her voice calm and compassionate. "I'd like to inform you that your mugging was successfully recorded by station se-

curity. Their likenesses have been recorded and the information transferred to all local security forces. Please rest assured that they will be
brought to justice."

Clyde laughed and ran the tap. The water was cool, but his split flesh
burned.

"Do you need an ambulance?"

"I ain't paying for EMT," he said, toweling off. He looked at himself
in the mirror again, and watched blood drip from his nose. With a sigh,
he got some toilet paper to wad up like tampons. He could still feel the
trickle of blood down his back. It wetted his jacket and soaked into his
t-shirt. Only thing he could do was hold a wad of toilet paper against
it. There was an apothecary between the station and the office, so he
stopped inside. Liquid Bandage was stocked.

He gritted his teeth when the check-out machine rang it up at thirty
credits. He tried to pay it anyway and then remembered his credit chip
had been stolen. He logged in through his neural implant and had to
sort through half a dozen payment reminder alerts just to pay. None of
them had overdue fees yet and his paycheck was processing, so he put
them out of mind as he squirted the goo into his hair where it felt tender. The bleeding stopped as it hardened like a plastic scab. The packaging and the bloody tissue he shoved down a trash chute.

He was still itching when he walked into the Ajitatsu breakroom.
To call it an office was a misnomer. There were no desks, no cubicles
or computer stations. There was an assembly room so the staff leaders
could prattle on about quarterly targets, as well as lockers and the smell
of smoke. No one else was in the office when he arrived–midnight
wasn't a shift changeover for anyone–and his boss hadn't responded to
the message yet.

Clyde took his jacket off and tried to clean it up in the bathroom.
Blood had dried all over the collar. The material was stainproof, but he
left it soaking in the sink regardless. His t-shirt was another matter. It
was part cotton and had gotten blood down the front and the back. No
amount of soap or scrubbing did anything, so he queried EVE on ways

to remove blood. She provided an article explaining that his saliva could dissolve his own blood, so he tried sucking on his shirt.

It tasted like soap, but the blood stain did fade.

"God damn it." He only had one other t-shirt left at home. After a moment of staring at the pink-tinted water, he put the shirt back on, wet or not, and opened his locker. He had half a dozen dead nicotine vapes rattling around the cubby shelf. He tried each in turn, eventually finding one good battery and one good oil cartridge.

Unlike his coworkers, he didn't smoke it in the breakroom. He stepped out to an obsolete little balcony. It had once been a walkway, but the growth of the tower had cut it off in one direction, and the bridge in the other had been removed for a new train line. The only thing keeping it from being a deadend was a rusted ladder going up: a joke of a fire-escape if he had ever seen one.

He leaned against the railing, half-chewing the vape and half-smoking it. He could see down an alley of the city. Hundreds of walkways, dozens of train lines, thousands of people, and every few moments someone went zipping by on a cityboard. He cranked up some music through his neural implant, switching to metal as he wondered if there was such a thing as too loud for a neural implant.

Things were supposed to be different for him. He was a veteran. He had made it, hadn't he? Everyone who did their service and got an honorable discharge was supposed to have life on easy afterwards. They got corporate jobs and moved up through the floors. They merged into the machines of industry and profited from it. They weren't supposed to get the shit kicked out of them by punks. They weren't supposed to be used as drug mules for opioids, or worse: CZAR.

Clyde was biting the vape so hard his teeth hurt. He could feel the plastic straining, deforming as he stared at the city with glassy eyes.

Then someone grabbed him by the shoulder. Their fingers dug into his shirt, pushing him forward slightly. His vape flew from his mouth as he spun, adrenaline spiking again. He nailed the guy before he even thought about it and then he was standing over the crumpled body of Mr Hill, almost as bloody as Clyde had been and twice as mad.

"What the fuck, Bondsman? You beg for double shifts and then you attack me? What the hell is wrong with you?" the older man shouted, covering his bloody mouth as he got back to his feet.

It felt like all the energy in Clyde's body knotted together and sank through his gut. He watched Mr Hill make up his mind even before Clyde said, "That was an accident."

"Get out!"

2 ▍

Unwanted Visitor

2140/10/16

Elliot's so-called vacation had started two days prior and he was already wondering if he would have to take more time off to recover from it. Amara's [Zom-Fortress] competition team had turned their week of practice into a reality show. Not that they weren't putting in hours practicing, but every minute they weren't playing was either spent sleeping or making gimmick content like teaching one of them how to cook better, or a gluttonous eating competition of said food.

Not one to be in front of the camera, that left Elliot scrubbing pans and picking at leftovers of some kind of egg soufflé which would have been delicious if he hadn't watched one of the other streamers eat two kilograms of the stuff.

I need a drink.

"Any leftovers?" one of the streamers asked as he wandered into the kitchen. It wasn't the glutton, nor was it either of the chefs.

It took Elliot a moment to place the name, and he said, "Some, getting cold though. Help yourself, Nelson."

The man, about Elliot's age and apparently with a bigger audience than Amara, swiped a pinch of soufflé on his way to the fridge. Nelson was a skinny fellow with a patchy beard he didn't trim. His face had a reverse-raccoon stripe from constantly wearing cityboarding goggles. His brown irises seemed to jump out of his face to point at Elliot, with an intensity that Elliot would have assumed would drive off viewers.

"I've been meaning to ask, Mr Luck-E's Husband... what exactly do you do for a living?"

Elliot flipped the faucet and started filling the dirty pot with water as he side-eyed the streamer. Nelson cracked open a beer, looking at him expectantly until offering the drink. "Thanks," Elliot said as he took it and wetted his throat. After Nelson got a new beer, Elliot said, "I work security. Not exactly a glamorous job."

And not exactly a lie either.

"Oh, for one of the mega-corps?" Nelson said, leaning on the counter and nodding. When Elliot didn't deny it, the streamer asked, "Ever killed anybody?"

Is this guy on a hot mic?

Elliot narrowed his eyes and nodded. "I've had to shoot some people, yeah."

"In self-defense of course, at least I assume," Nelson said.

"When you've got a crazy guy on top of you with a knife that he thinks belongs inside your lungs, you don't have much of an alternative."

Nelson's eyebrows rose. "Sounds like a story."

"It is," Elliot said, but he put his beer down and put his attention on loading the dishwasher.

Before Nelson pushed the subject, another set of footsteps entered the kitchen. Elliot recognized the cadence, but when he heard his wife's tone, he turned around. "Hun," Amara said, in a honey-sweet voice. "You have a visitor."

I didn't tell anybody where I was going. I guess it could be Ram.

Elliot held up his hand at the appropriate height. "About this tall, dark hair, just got out of service?"

Amara crossed her arms. "Blonde."

Elliot cocked an eyebrow and adjusted his hand. "This tall?"

"I didn't know you had these kinds of friends."

"I have coworkers," he said. Elliot slapped the faucet shut and strode toward the door. He paused and gave his wife a quick hug, but she didn't reciprocate. When he made it to the front hall, he realized why. It wasn't Ram and it wasn't Cinder. It wasn't any of the women in his department.

The blonde would have been half a head shorter than Elliot, if not for the heels she was wearing. Thigh high socks left a band of skin beneath her pleated skirt which swayed with the steady swing of her augmetic cat tail arching from her backside. Beneath her jacket, her neckline plunged deep enough that Elliot could see the bullet scar he had given her two years prior.

Her face lit up with a dramatic smile. "Mr Blackstone! You are here. Or, rather, I should say you're still here. I saw you on one of the streams and—"

Elliot marched past her, tore the door open and hauled her out of the homestead. She was laughing as he slammed it shut behind him. "What the hell are you doing here?"

Seraphina was from IID, Internal Investigations Department. The last time he had seen her, she had been in their undercover division, but that had been two years ago. The last time he had seen her, she had been unconscious in a Californian ICU. Aside from the scars, she didn't seem the worse for the wear. To say she turned heads was putting it mildly.

The woman from IID casually sat on the walkway railing, letting the wind flutter her hair as she grinned at him. "What other reason would I have than work? I'm a busy girl, Mr Blackstone. But I was just delighted to see who I would be working with after all this time."

Elliot sneered as a train flew by beneath them, the air roaring. "I don't work for IID."

Seraphina clapped her hands together. "Actually, I'll be working for you!"

"I'm on vacation."

She lolled her head to one side, still grinning. "So I saw. Working yourself to the bone for... was that your wife? The woman who glared at me just like you're glaring at me now? Not very nice, is she? But, more importantly... they don't know you're a jannis, do they?"

"Is that a threat?" Elliot stepped closer to her, his hands balling into fists. The fact that she was certain he wouldn't do anything infuriated him.

"Come on now, Mr Blackstone. If I wanted to threaten you, we both know what I could be saying."

"If you've got work for the department, take it up with Cinder. I'm on personal time. Hell, I'm on psych time for that matter. I never got my break after getting the shit kicked out of me a few weeks back."

Seraphina giggled. "Cinder knows all about it."

"She has plenty of other people she could assign whatever this is to."

Sera spread her legs and planted her hands between them, perching on the railing so she could lean toward him precariously. "You're the head of the virtual crimes department in South Missou though. What we've got fits the bill and is top priority."

"Says who?"

"Your Vice-Commander."

"Bullshit."

"Check your phone, you luddite. You know, you really should get an implant."

Elliot patted his pockets and came up short. With a scowl, he remembered he had left it on the kitchen counter.

"Or," Seraphina said as she slipped off the railing and stood up beside him, "you could just believe me and join me for a drink? Cinder is on her way already."

I say no, and she'll cause a mess for the stream. I say yes, and my wife will be pissed. What a lovely way to start working together.

Elliot looked back at the door. They were high up in the city, and it was security rated but that did not mean the door was thick. Anyone standing on the other side could hear the entire conversation. He looked back at Seraphina. "If Cinder doesn't show up, me and you are going to have a problem."

"Oh, maybe now I don't want her to show up. I kind of want to know what you'll do to me. Our last time together was so intense, you know?"

I should have left her to die.

Seraphina had a booth reserved down on the adjacent boulevard. A nightclub had scooped up all the real estate behind a swath of storefronts, making a tunnel of booze and music colored by sweeping colored lights. Elliot could only guess how many back entrances it had. For all he knew, the other tables had international spies and criminal syndicates brushing shoulders. Most people were just locals getting a drink, creating a facade for meetings like his.

The worst they would have to hide would be a bit of adultery.

Seraphina lit up a cigarette the moment they sat down in their private cubby. Her smoke was wafting between them before Elliot had even ordered a drink. He grimaced as the waitress double checked Seraphina's age. Despite being older than Elliot, she looked and dressed like a teenager. The bewilderment on the waitresses face just made Elliot sneer more.

Seraphina leaned on the table as soon as they were alone. "Hey, you wanna hear a joke?" she asked.

"No," Elliot said. He wanted his uniform, even his cloak. It would have branded him as an MP, but that would have been better than this.

"Come on, it's funny," Seraphina said, tucking one foot up on the booth beneath her. The club was not the kind of establishment that would mind a bit of dirt. Spilled drinks and sex were a bigger concern.

Elliot was reasonably certain he could hear someone making both messes behind him. Something about their one sided conversation forced itself into his imagination, and his only distraction was Seraphina as they waited for Cinder. "Fine, what?"

She snickered and tugged a half-pack of cigarettes from her skirt. "How many seconds are in a year?"

"Three hundred and sixty-five times twenty-four times sixty times sixty."

Seraphina lifted her head up and smirked at him as the organic cigarette smoldered. It flushed her face orange against the purple glow of the club. "Nope."

Elliot wanted to check his phone. He didn't even know how long he would have to wait for Cinder to arrive. His wife was probably wondering where the hell he had gone. "Sorry, you pedantic bitch, three hundred sixty-five and a quarter times the rest."

Seraphina laughed. "Still no. Want one?" She tapped a cig out for him and held it out.

"I don't smoke anymore."

"What? Why's that? You'e got plenty of insurance. The fuck do you care about cancer?"

"The wife doesn't like it."

There's an unfortunate correlation between it and killing people.

Seraphina nearly threw herself on the table, sucking on her cig and exhaling the alluring smoke as she asked, "Mr Blackstone, before today I didn't know there was a Mrs."

"Can't imagine why you would know. Don't act like we're friends."

Seraphina suckled on her cigarette and asked, "Does she know you're a murderer?"

Elliot wanted to kick the table into her gut. If it weren't bolted down, he might have. "That's none of your business."

"Au contraire, we're going to be working together, Mr Blackstone. Don't you think I need to know these kinds of things?"

"No. And I already have a partner. She's a lot better than you are."

For a moment her smirk vanished, then it came back. "She? My my, I wonder what she's like. How about her, does she know–"

"Shut your mouth before I shut it for you."

Seraphina paused, meeting his gaze with her cool, sapphire eyes. She sat back in her seat and snuffed out her cigarette, left it smoldering like incense between the two of them. "Twelve."

Elliot dragged his gaze off the vice stick and asked, "Twelve?"

"There are twelve seconds in a year."

Elliot let his breath out. "Oh, for fucks sake," he said as Seraphina laughed.

He had his face covered by his hand when the club music burst into their booth with a shower of static. Cinder strode through the audio isolators–far out of date but functional–and slapped a chair down at the end of their table. She must have made a scene strolling through in full uniform, her blonde hair almost radiant in the disco beams. "Blackstone, what's got you down?"

Seraphina burst out laughing again as Elliot composed himself. "What's got me down," he said, "is that I'm here instead of on vacation with my wife."

Cinder spotted the half-finished cigarette. "You mind?" she asked, glancing at Seraphina as she picked it up.

"If you wanted a pack, I could have brought you one from the Isles," she said, offering to relight it.

"I have my own sources. I just need something right now because, Bastard's Blood, the goddamn vice-commander is tracking this one."

"Which one?" Elliot asked.

Cinder leaned back in her chair and crossed her legs. She inhaled like she wanted to burn her fingertips with the ash. "Chase."

Elliot winced. Vice-commander Chase was the most ruthless ladder climber in all of Bastion. Rumor had it that he had let the government experiment on his own daughter to not get a bad mark on his profile. "Who got shot to get his attention?" he asked.

Cinder finished off the cigarette and snubbed it out again. "No ones been shot yet. The killer is using a micro-blade. And the man in question isn't dead yet. Are you familiar with the Heartsteel corporation?"

"Should I be?

"Private security forces," Seraphina said. "They're to police what mercenaries are to soldiers."

"Their CEO had a death threat slapped onto his office window," Cinder said.

Elliot frowned and started searching for info on his phone, only to remember he didn't have it. "So what, he's like a congressional donor or something? A candidate? If he's the CEO of a security company, can't he protect himself?"

Cinder scoffed. "He's the premiere speechwriter for the Buffalo Party. Way more important than a donor. You can get money anywhere. Packaging talking points is irreplaceable."

"I thought those were machine generated?"

"Some are. Less than you would think. Point is, someone declared war on the guy."

"Cinder, you still haven't gotten to the part about why you've brought me in for it. I thought I was your VR guy?"

Seraphina planted her elbows on the table and grinned at him. "Come on, Mr Blackstone, isn't it obvious? You're the best at this."

At killing CEOs, maybe.

Cinder was tapping in a drink order, a bucket of beers. "Blame her," Cinder said. "She made the request direct to Chase."

"Why?" he demanded. "I can't imagine why you would ever want to see me again in your life."

"Catching up for old time's sake," Seraphina said.

Cinder arched an eyebrow. "Do I need to know what kind of history the two of you have?"

"No," Elliot interjected. He took a breath and stifled his anger. The boiling rage that had been tamped down had been seeping out of him after so many years. She had put a crack in his defenses, but he buried it again. Like filling an underwater pipeline, he poured in sand and smothered it with numb indifference. "We met in California years ago. It's history now. Isn't that right?"

Seraphina flicked her tail from side to side, swatting the air as she watched his eyes. "The past is passed, baby. If it ain't the present then it's history. It's just been so long since we've seen each other, I couldn't help myself. I wanted to poke and prod and see how much you haven't changed. I'm so sad I missed your little indiscretion."

Cinder took out her phone and offered it to him, photo gallery up. "Don't let it affect the job. Three people are dead already and EVE doesn't have any leads. She didn't even realize there was a pattern until yesterday. Working for Heartsteel isn't good for your life expectancy. Their employees get jumped all the time, but these are different."

Elliot reached out and flipped through the set of photos. The first was an overweight man, his skin splotchy with either bruises or disease: his head had been cut off. The next was face down, face a mask of agony. His clothing had been split down the back and blood seemed to pour out from his spine. The last was a woman missing half her hand and lying in a puddle of blood pouring from her throat.

"Micro-blade?" he asked.

"That, or magic," Seraphina said, and slipped from the booth to take the bucket of beers from the waitress.

"There are two key similarities," Cinder said. "Each were killed with a single cut from a micro-blade, and each of them–despite being in public–died without the camera seeing what happened. Each were fine one moment and dead the next."

"Well, it's not like he's stopping time, right?"

Cinder pulled a beer bottle out of the bucket, before Seraphina sat down, and cracked it open. "It's that, or this killer found another little oversight in EVE's surveillance. That's the actual expertise you bring to the table, Blackstone. That's why I need you."

Elliot almost didn't take the offered beer, then thought better of that and took two. "I'm on vacation for the rest of this week. Let someone else work on it. I can consult when I get back." He cracked open the first one and knocked it back. Both women politely watched as he drained the entire bottle.

Cinder said, "You're really learning a thing or two from those streamers, aren't you?"

Elliot wiped his lips off and set the empty bottle down. "Earlier today, I watched a grown man chug raw eggs to win a bet. However, I learned how to drink beer in bootcamp, same as you."

Cinder laughed. "You don't want to get in a drinking contest with me, Blackstone. I worked in the Cambodian jungle for six months. Beer was the only sanitary thing to drink. And you know what, if you catch this guy I'll get you promoted and take you out drinking. You and Ram."

Seraphina grinned. "So her name's Ram?"

Cinder shoved Seraphina off the table. "I'll make it worth your while even if you don't want the raise. For tonight, I'll send you the data and let you look it over on your own time. The killings were all in public, so there's not much of a crime scene to investigate yet."

"Yet?" Elliot asked, cracking the second beer.

She swirled her beer with an expression both forlorn and frustrated. "Those three were all with the company for a while. They were acclimated to it, real company people, but they were low on the totem pole. With that and the threat, I think the guy's plan is to work his way up from bottom to top. By threatening the CEO, he was threatening all of Heartsteel. He's going to kill again if we don't catch him. I've added you to the database for this. Take a look at it, will you, Blackstone? I don't want to make this an order."

Elliot stared at his own beer. It was cool in his grip, condensation running down to meet his thumb. The prospect of a promotion without getting moved tempted him. It would do right by Ram too. He had to move up from E rank if she was to have a career in the VRC with him. Then he wondered what she would say about police resources getting pulled to protect the political elite again. "Send me the data. I'll go over it when I can, but I'm logging this as half a work day."

Cinder clicked her tongue and finally took Seraphina's offer for a fresh cigarette. "For someone who puts in as much overtime as you do, you're a stickler for PTO, aren't you?"

Elliot finished his beer and rose. "Yeah, I think I am. Now, if you don't mind, I'm going back to my wife. And you–" he jabbed a finger at Seraphina, "are not to fucking show up unannounced again."

Cinder puffed and asked, "You went in person?"

Seraphina lounged in the booth and threw her arms across the back. "I did. I watched the egg chugging on stream, you know. It was both impressive and disgusting. But, come on, what choice did I have? He had his phone turned off!"

"You didn't even try to call me."

She stuck her tongue out at him. "You wouldn't have picked up even if I had."

"No, I wouldn't have," he agreed, and turned his back on them. The moment he walked through the isolation field, the storm of music assaulted him. The smell of alcohol and sweat, the way the floor swayed beneath the dancers. He had to turn down a girl wearing a latex bunny suit trying to offer him a "thank you for saving the boss" kind of dance. The exit nearly eluded him, just one more light in the flashing chaos.

"Blackstone!" Seraphina shouted. She stood just outside the audio-isolator with a grin fit for her cat-like implant. "Make sure you pick up when I call you. If I get bored, I might just reach out to Wyatt and catch up with him, for old time's sake."

Elliot felt his body chill. People bumped into him as he stood stock still halfway through the club and stared back at her. He said nothing as she waved and sat back down to drink with Cinder.

"This goddamn bitch. I should have left her to die."

3

The Bottom Rung

2140/06/06

Clyde came home smelling like smoke. Not tobacco smoke, but the trademarked and scented odor of cigarette that emitted from his vaporizer. He would have preferred the cotton candy flavor–and been able to lie about it easier–but the vending machine had been empty. The smell of stress-relief was a small trace amidst the cornucopia of scents that was his family's home.

Synth-log sizzled on the stove, kernels of fat crackling and oozing into the oil. A can of wine seltzer fizzed, spewing the scent of champagne into the air. Those were the good scents, from the kitchen, along with the gush of steam that came out of the boiling pasta pot. The bad smells came from the living room. From the musty air of the bathroom because his younger brother hadn't left the door open again. From the overflowing trash bin spilling microwave meal wrappers onto the floor. And mostly from the greasy intake of tainted air out of the Epsilon substructure.

There were no windows in Clyde's home, so the smell festered.

"Welcome home, Clyde," his mother called, snatching up her drink as she abandoned the stove to give him a hug. He hadn't even mumbled a response when she held him at arm's length and glared at him. "What happened?"

"Got jumped by some punks. I'm alright. Hey, Johnny! Did your nose stop working? Or do you just not care about the trash?"

"Don't need a nose in VR, bro," his brother shouted back from their shared bedroom.

His mother hadn't stopped glaring. She fussed and touched his cheek to turn his head and look at the bruises and scrapes. With a click of her tongue she asked, "Okay, but what actually has you bent out of shape? What's got you smoking today?"

"Nothing. It's fine. Just another day of work, you know how it is."

His mother planted her hands on her hips and stared at him. The wrinkles in her face were more plentiful every year, but she had a way of making them look hard as stone. Other people, older people, seemed to fade away. Their skin became paper and drawn over from the inside by thin veins. The only wear and tear on her showed in the creeping purple beneath her eyes, stubbornly ignored because she had one more year before Johnny could get drafted.

Clyde sighed. "Got in a fight with my boss. I think I'm going to need a new job."

Her mouth tightened and she nodded. After taking a quick sip of wine, she ran back over to the meat pile. Some of it had begun to stick to the pan and she scraped at it with more force that she really needed. "What was the fight about?"

Clyde wetted his lips and paced behind her. "It was an actual fight, Mom. Sort of. I was on edge because of kids that jumped me. Got lost in my own head, you know, and when he surprised me I just kind of hit him."

She glanced at him from the corner of her eye. "Son, you might be a vet but that doesn't mean much if you get charges stuck to you. A criminal who served is still just a criminal."

"They're not gunna press charges." He sat down on the counter, the one clean spot in the kitchen. A dozen boxes of ordered goods, economy food, and mismatched appliance repair parts had conquered all the table space in the kitchen. Finally, he spotted the jar of pasta sauce and cracked it open.

His mother took it from him with a shake of her head. "I could have opened that," she said as she fished out a bowl from the dishwasher. "What are you going to do for another job?"

Clyde's hand itched to pull the vape out of his pocket, but he didn't. "I'll have to figure something out. Not sure what the job system will say about me needing a new job. EVE's the one that put me with Ajitatsu. Maybe I need to get away from the corpos altogether. Everyone always seems to get pulled into Rommie Blocks or a Phoenix Tower or something like that. I bet if I go walking in Delta I can find someone hiring. I'm a big guy. Reliable. I can find something."

His mother slapped the scoop into the bowl and jabbed the button to kill the stove. When she spoke, the irritation didn't come through though. "Babe, I don't want you thinking you can just walk in somewhere and get work. If you did that, a guy like you, they'd be trying to give you some kind of bullshit. You're a big guy. You're strong. You even served your time. There are bad people out there. If they see you vulnerable they'll try to take advantage of you."

"Mom, I'll be fine. We've got some savings. I'll make sure I at least have something even if it's washing dishes."

She crossed her arms and shook her head. "I know you will, but I don't want you reaching too low either. It's bad enough you never got higher education. If you start working with felons, you'll get treated like a felon."

Clyde turned his head up to stare at the waning light fixture, the crystals slowly turning yellow. He wondered what the punishment was for being a drug mule and if he rightfully was a felon already. "I'll do it right. Once Johnny gets out from service, none of us will have to worry about money anymore. Everything's going to be great this time next year."

His mother shook her head and started scooping out the pasta. "Set the table, will you?"

"Sure, just as soon as I do something about this smell. Actually, Johnny! Set the damn table." Clyde slipped off the counter and started picking up the trash. He crammed and stretched the bag–almost tore it pulling it free of the can–and headed back out to the alley he called a home street. The strip of air wasn't even outside. It was a three story promenade along the inside of a residential tower none of the corps wanted to own. Street lights crossed the terraced walkways and kept it in perpetual gloom no matter the time of day or night.

It wasn't a cheery place to live, but that didn't mean he expected to find a corpse sprawled out next to the trash chute.

Clyde stood next to it, holding a sagging sack of half-rotten kitchen waste, and wondered how a camera hadn't seen it yet. The cameras out near the train lines were usually scuffed, broken, painted over, or otherwise disabled, but everyone in his neighborhood knew to do their illegal business in their own homes or not at all. But, the landlord was cheap and didn't spend money on redundant cameras. Someone had hung a sheet out to dry across their balcony, half covering the camera–probably not on purpose. Backup systems were wi-fi, but when he checked with his neural implant nothing pinged on the guy.

Which meant that the system of last resort was him.

"Aw, fuck." he stepped over and crammed the bag down the trash chute before kneeling down. He was no detective, but he knew how to check a pulse. Before dialing up EMT, he nudged their head over and pushed his fingers into their neck. The body was still warm and their curly hair had stuck to the floor. They had on some kind of black mask. Holographic to the extreme, like their face was nothing more than a black hole sucked in on itself. An anonymous pit. The mask hadn't protected them from getting the back of their skull split open though.

He didn't find a pulse, not in their throat nor on their wrist. The mask resisted, but came off and revealed a normal, forgettable face beneath. He tried to think of ways to confirm they were dead, and was pretty sure doctors only checked for pulses. Pupil dilation wasn't something he could do without a flashlight. He sighed and pinched their nose.

"Get your hands off of him," a woman said.

Clyde froze. He hadn't heard any breath from the body, not a single twitch of muscle. His attention pivoted up, tracking from boots, to cargo pants, to tight little waist, to a tank top and then the same black mask as the corpse. He asked, "This your friend?"

"He needs a doctor. I'm not asking. Get your hands off him." She pulled a pistol from her back pocket and pointed it at the floor. It was a slick thing of machined steel. Very intimidating to the average person, but he saw the twin barrels. That meant it wasn't a real gun, just a self-defense toy. He was pretty sure he recognized the model from some advertisements. It could break his skin and make a mess of him, but not kill him.

"Girl, he doesn't need a doctor. He needs a crematorium. The guy's dead."

"Fuck off. No he's not. He just got hit is all. He needs a doctor," she said and started to lift her weapon.

Clyde drew himself away without taking his eyes off the toy gun. She didn't point it at him, and he gave her enough space to feel comfortable getting on her knees herself. It didn't take long for her to check his pulse, to pull out her phone and shine a light in his non-responsive eyes. When she pounded a fist on the ground, Clyde did not say, "I told ya. Sorry about your friend. Did he live around here?"

"No," she said, and rocked back onto her ass. She hugged her knees to her chest and buried her face in the gloom of the alley. "I'm the one that lives here."

Clyde winced and rubbed the sweat off the back of his neck. "He must have been your friend, then."

The girl didn't say anything, and the longer she sat huddled on herself, the smaller she seemed. "Not anymore."

"Are you going to contact the police?"

"I would get arrested... ah, don't worry about it. Nothing is coming after me. We settled everything already."

"I wasn't worried about anything," he said, and glanced back at his home.

Eventually she lifted her head and looked at him, despite the mask. "Do you live around here?"

"No, I go into someone else's neighborhood to use their smelly trash chute instead of my own."

She laughed. "Fuck. Goddamn it... could you–sorry–could you help me get the body outside? I don't want to drag him, you know? If the police find him on a public walk no one here will get bothered."

Clyde hesitated, and then found himself carrying the man back out the neighborhood door. He took his shoulders while the masked girl took his ankles and the two of them put the body down right outside the door. He made sure to use his coat to cover his fingerprints, which made it more difficult, but the two of them managed.

When they were done, she sat down against the railing and tossed her mask off the side. She was gorgeous. Maybe her nose was a bit too round at the tip, and her eyes were a bit too red from fighting tears–both of which clashed with the dangerous punk aesthetic–but it didn't break the impression of beauty.

She didn't look up at him as she mumbled a thanks and said, "I'll explain to the police that I found him. Keep your head down, neighbor."

"Thanks," Clyde said. He didn't know anything about the two of them, whether they deserved it or if they would be dangerous to him later. Part of him wanted to comfort her, but the majority of his mind was afraid of her, so he shut the door and walked back home. His mother asked what had taken so long and he lied about the delay. To his luck, as he sat down for dinner, he got a message from Ajitatsu that warranted all the shock, confusion, and surprise he was feeling.

They asked if he wanted to participate in their labor reassignment program.

4

Kicked Out

2140/10/16

The whole flat was starting to take on the smell of sweat and bodies and bad food. They couldn't open the windows, despite being high enough in a tower to have windows, because of privacy concerns. Besides the never-ending need to cook, the flat needed to be doused in cleaning chemicals and multiple trash cans needed to be cycled out to the chute. There was no end of work for behind the scenes.

Amara still stopped him before he could even reach the kitchen. "So, where'd you go?"

Elliot scanned the hall. The apartment was quieter than he would have expected it to be. Everyone else must have been in simulation. They might have been running exciting and popular events that very moment, but in the flesh they may as well have been asleep. He still kept his voice down as he answered, "They're trying to call me back into the office."

She crossed her arms and didn't move from the doorway. After a moment, she asked, "So, she's a coworker? Are you going to leave?"

He found himself wanting a cigarette, a beer, or both. Chemical distractions for his brain to keep the frustration away. "I don't want to, but it seems likely."

Amara looked like she wanted to start swearing, but she said, "I thought your boss was all for this?"

Elliot shook his head and gestured, pushing through and the two of them stepped into the kitchen so he could crack open a beer. "She was," he said, rummaging around until he found a lager. "Until things got political."

"Is this about that Congressman you had dinner with?"

"No, Ghos has nothing to do with this. It's internal. The politics are in the command chain. I'm going to do what I can to not go, but... you know how it is, don't you? I've got a vice-commander telling me to do this. If he pushes it, I'll lose my job if I don't go."

"That's bullshit," Amara said.

Elliot spread his arms and shrugged. "That's how it's always been."

"Like getting sent to California for three months and coming back broken? Is that just how it goes? Do you just accept that?"

She still thinks I got sent there. Bastard's Blood.

Elliot dropped his arms and hung his head. He didn't know what to say so he kept his mouth shut. Their silence was interrupted by a message to Amara. She mumbled something about needing to get back into the game and he mumbled something about tidying up some more.

She stopped at the door and asked, "So that was just a coworker?"

"She's a fucking hazard is what she is."

When he came back in from the trash chute, ready to turn his mind off and scrub the counters clean, one of Amara's teammates caught him in the kitchen; Nelson again.

"Are you really her husband?" he asked.

"Yes, I am. Is that a problem?" Elliot knelt down beneath the sink and got the chemicals. He started on the opposite side of the kitchen as Nelson, where spilt egg yolk had been hardening.

Nelson watched him, and after too long of a pause for polite conversation, he said, "I've known Luck-E–"

"Amara. Or are you recording right now?" Elliot asked, staring over his shoulder at the guy.

"I've known Amara for a few months now, and she never mentioned having a husband. I guess she did mention that she was taken, but not married. It's not like she's out there luring in men for money, but I always wondered what the deal was."

"Some people keep their private lives just that: private."

"And some people like to know when they have a fucking jannis in the same room as them," Nelson said, and when Elliot turned to face him, Nelson whipped something across the room at him.

It caught Elliot flat footed, and hit him in the chest. His badge clattered to the floor. He glared at the streamer and sized him up again. Nelson was thin but not in the wiry kind of way. Nelson was a keyboard warrior, a VR-lifer, not the kind of strung-out and hardened guy that lived in Gamma, one wrong look from a fight. Nelson had designer clothes–and not just from partnership deals–which matched his upper class aloofness. Nelson was a reflection of a punk and nothing more.

Elliot asked, "You went through my stuff?"

"Yeah, I did. And I'm glad I did. What the fuck interest does the government have in us? How the fuck do we warrant a sting operation?"

There was a table between him and Nelson, and he was lucky for it. Elliot grabbed the edge and squeezed, anchoring himself from going over there and putting hands on the streamer. "This isn't a sting operation. It's exactly what we said it was from day one. I'm here to help my fucking wife. We didn't make a goddamn announcement about my day job because twats like you have this kind of reaction to it."

Nelson snorted. "For a married couple, you sure don't get along."

Elliot held up his hand and stuck up his ring finger and the wedding band on it. "I don't have to explain myself to you. Now, you can either drop this entirely and pretend you know nothing about it, or I can arrest you for theft. One word from me and your bail hearing will be the last thing a judge gets around to ever doing."

Nelson scoffed. "And to think there are some people who don't realize why you fucking uniforms are hated. Drop of a hat and you abuse your authority. Why don't you get the fuck out of here before I make a scene of it? If that is your wife, I should get her dropped from the team.

Not telling us something like this is bullshit. If it gets to her fans there will be a shitshow, you know that? For all of us."

I should have him arrested. But that would screw up the [Zom-Fortress] thing. I could beat his ass, but that would get Amara kicked off the team. He's not going to let me just ignore this. I can't think of any other immediate option. Wait a minute–

"Didn't you go out with the waitress from Peasant Food?" Elliot asked.

That caught Nelson off guard. He stood up straight and stuffed his hands in his pockets. "How would you know that? Did you run a background check on me or something?"

Maybe I should.

"I have my sources," Elliot said. Nelson was the one who had asked Ram out and never gotten a second date because she thought he was crazy. He had arguably made an ass of himself, as far as internet perception was concerned. "I think you need to think a little harder about who you're fucking threatening, don't you?"

"I don't know what you're talking about."

"I have a recording of that entire date."

Nelson was struck silent, his face consteranted with the effort of remembering each and every line he had said over a week ago. Anything could be taken out of context if the other side had the emotional advantage. But, before Elliot could drive it home, the two of them were interrupted by Nick The Giant squeezing through the doorway.

"There a fight going on or something?" the rotund mountain of a man asked on his way to the fridge. When he cracked open a beer, the entire can vanished within his fingers.

Elliot said, "No."

Nelson said, "Yes."

Nick drank the entire can of beer and shrugged. "Well, clear it out of here. We're going to be catching up on viewer comments and revealing the mystery challenges."

"The what?" Elliot asked.

Nick pointed at a board with a few dozen sticky notes lined up beneath their names. "The unlucky among us are going to be doing a bunch of shots. So, no fighting. No bad energy. No bad mojo. Take it the fuck outside if you have to."

Elliot looked back to Nelson and cocked his head. "If you want to take this outside, I'd be happy to."

"Nah, man," Nelson responded. "I can survive the PR damage of bad flirting. I'll lose some female viewership, but I'm not attractive enough to get their donations anyways. So I'm calling your bluff."

Elliot restrained himself, calmed himself, and picked up his badge before Nick caught sight of it. "We're not done here," he said, and left the flat with his travel bag.

From the train ride back to his apartment, he sent Amara a message explaining just what had happened. He drafted it six times trying to fit the nuance and make sure she would understand it correctly, and then he didn't hear back from her. That wasn't unexpected. She rarely looked at personal messages while live, and he had no idea how long it would be until she was off-stream again.

He didn't turn the lights on when he got home. After a moment standing in the darkness, he turned and slammed his boot into the door so hard he thought he might have broken the frame. Stewing with a dozen half-formed ideas of frustration–most of which were just recirculating through his brain and pretending to be new ideas–he sat down in the gloom of kitchen appliances. He drummed his fingers on the table and checked his phone for a response.

Rationally, he knew the best case scenario was for Amara to smooth things over. To keep a lid on things. Anything he did would be damaging.

Before he knew it he had his police uniform on again, his gun strapped to his hip and his badge on his chest. He made it all the way to the door, hand on the handle, when he realized what he was doing. "Bastard's Blood," he grumbled and marched back to his bedroom. He stripped it off. He kept the gun but put it beneath a casual jacket. It was a leather piece that barely fit him anymore because he had bought it when he was seventeen.

Barely knowing what he was going to do, just that he couldn't sleep, he headed out to Bastion and got on the first train that arrived. He didn't watch the display screens and got off when most other people were getting off. His attention kept swinging back to his phone, checking for a response that never came. He was messaging Mikey to catch a drink when the din of people began to roar in his ears.

Not the casual mass of human life, the mumble and chatter of millions of people diffused through the buildings. He heard the noise of tens of thousands of people fighting for elbow space, packed from wall to wall and squeezing between each other as they tried to talk over the noise of advertisements. A menagerie of holograms flew through the air. Dragons tussled with birds while half-naked women called out to shoppers. The names of stores were a race-to-the-bottom for attention grabbing, not one of the big corps in sight. Each was trying to re-sell the latest in tech releases, to push refurbished equipment, recovered retro classics, unforgettable VR experiences, the latest merch of the greatest idols and stories.

Elliot had gotten off in the holy site for all things tech. He was surrounded by the absolute best in neural implant installation, maintenance, updating, overclocking, and nerve-mapping. He had wandered into Neo Akihabara and would have turned around and gotten right back on the train had it still been there. The boulevard was a shopping center of epic proportions, and one that had its share of memories for him. Stranded by the train, he found himself wandering with the crowd until he spotted a cafe he vaguely recognized. Amara and he had had a date there once. He just couldn't remember when.

He remembered it had been fun though.

So he grabbed a table, pulled up the evidence database Cinder had linked him to and started going over murder documents.

5

Labor Reassignment

2140/06/21

"You're asking to work at a tech support call center... despite not having a technical background?" The manager—fat and with greasy hair past his shoulders—leaned his head forward to stare at Clyde. The expression might have been more incredulous if the man hadn't trimmed his eyebrows till they were almost missing.

"You and I both know that ninety-nine percent of tech support calls don't require a technical background to fix. Telling grandma how to reboot her PC is something anyone can do," Clyde said. He stood with his hands together, one squeezing the other wrist to keep them there. He felt like a fool, wearing a buttoned shirt that hardly fit him. Whenever he inhaled, the buttons strained, but he couldn't afford a new shirt.

The manager kept noticing it too, like he thought one might come flying at him. He leaned back in his chair, making the old plastic creak. He gestured about the room, walls of glass like a box separating them from so many cubicles of headset wearing phone operators. "Mr Bondsman, if you would, could you tell me why we here at Reboot-Resume still have jobs?"

He furrowed his brow. "Because people need help understanding some of the stuff they buy. That's why they call you and pay by the minute."

The manager folded his hands across his belly and nodded. "True, true. But it's the twenty-second century. If we can build EVE, don't you think we can manage a chatbot able to troubleshoot their problems?"

"Nobody would pay money for a machine though."

The manager shrugged. "That's pretty much the point. Hell, we have competitors that are trying to bankrupt us with their own pseudo-AIs, but here we are. The thing is that we understand that people are calling for the human element. Some people? They don't even have a real problem. Every once in a while they call up just to talk to somebody that will think about them. We're like a cheaper version of phone-sex. You understand?"

"No, I don't. You help people with computer problems, don't you?"

"Yes, plenty of people get their problems solved by us, but what we are offering is something you can't find just by searching your question online, you see? Our clientele don't just want their problems fixed, they want their hand held through the process and frankly, from chatting with you and your background, you don't have the skills to do that."

Clyde fought the scowl from showing on his face. "Sir, I think you'll find that I can be plenty pleasant to talk to. That won't be a problem."

After a moment, the fat bastard just laughed at him. "Kid, I'm trying to let you down easy here, maybe point you in a better direction. Fact of the matter is that a vet without a job? It's very suspicious. I'd understand if Ajitatsu had filed your termination as some kind of disagreement over working conditions or something. Maybe you were drinking on the job, that I'd understand. Hell, I've got liquor in my own desk. But nothing? It's never good when there's no reason listed. You're a kind of risk that Reboot-Resume can't take. You understand, don't you?"

And so Clyde left his tenth interview without success. Standing halfway to the train station, he dug a nicotine vape out of his pocket and tried to suck on it. He realized it was dead empty as he stared up at the underbelly of Bastion's commercial district. The nearest vending machine declined his credit chip. His credit was so low in his bank account he wasn't allowed to withdraw it for luxury items. The only thing he could do was pound his fist on the side of the metal box and hope something would fall.

Nothing did.

"Need a smoke?" a woman asked. Not just any woman, but his neighbor. She leaned against the wall and crossed her arms. She had on the same outfit as when they had moved the body, but different colors. No void mask though.

"Yeah, I do."

She bought him one, and–as he bent down to get it–said, "I hear you're looking for work."

"Who told you that?" he asked. He cracked the seal and sucked hard till the flavor went from cotton candy to singed tar. "Your drug lord or whatever?"

She rolled her eyes. "From your mother, Clyde."

He sighed and ran a hand through his curly hair. "I guess that's what I get for not telling her about you."

She rolled her eyes. "Don't worry, I didn't mention how we met. Look, you helped me out and you need work. I can hook you up. At the rate you're going, you're going to be doing something like working at Soc-Merc, scanning chat logs to find pedos."

"No, thanks."

"What? You like the sound of that?" she asked.

He scowled and he did have another option. He could accept Aji-tatsu's offer to get him a new job. He just didn't want to because they were brushing him under the rug. They might pay well though. "I do, yeah. And I don't appreciate being stalked like this. We're neighbors, not friends."

She sighed and shrugged. "Alright, alright, it's not like I can twist your arm... but, you took the mask. You had better be careful with that."

He had almost forgotten he had stolen it off the corpse. He didn't even know what to do with it, just that criminals and weirdos liked them. "What's the deal with the masks? I see them all over the place but no one ever selling them."

She smirked and wiggled her eyebrows at him. "That's because if there was a distribution system, EVE would shut it down. She'd track back to the maker. She'd figure out how to see through them and then none of them would be worth a damn. You want a mask, you gotta get one. Either someone gifts it to you, or you steal it. No traceability. You got yours, so welcome to the club. I should tell you, though, that it doesn't do much to help you if you're all alone."

"And here I thought the point of being anonymous was to have privacy."

"Privacy doesn't have to mean isolation. Good luck with the job. If you find yourself pinched though, you know where to find me, alright?" the girl said, and started walking back to the train station.

"Wait," Clyde said, and she turned. "Don't you need to tell me your name?"

"Zarah," she said, and vanished into the crowds. Between one blink and the next, her brown hair was lost in the flow of the city.

Clyde leaned back against the vending machine and sucked on his vape again. He stared at the crowd, trying to pick her head out and thinking about her offer. She was criminal, without a doubt. Working for a gang didn't mean he had to work with them forever though. They wouldn't send hit squads just because he wanted to go clean. He sat there wondering what kind of work they would have for him. The shills would claim the work was like any other job. Some of them were officially organized as labor unions.

Of course, there was a chance they'd use him as a CZAR mule, a thousand times worse than the pills he had been moving for Ajitatsu.

Three years in military service and he had encountered blighted once–discounting the training footage. One time and he had filed for discharge immediately after. It was granted. One time and he had nightmares for a year about the gnashing teeth and the black blood. Down in Gamma, hardly anyone believed the government line that one bad trip on CZAR could turn you into a blighted, but Clyde did. He didn't want to be anywhere near CZAR.

For a moment, he held the vape out in front of himself and stared at it. He hadn't been able to afford a five credit smoke stick. Because he had just covered rent on the apartment, he didn't have enough to feed himself and there was no way he wanted to go begging his mother for a loan. He knew she'd give it to him, but he didn't want to imagine what she would do to tighten her belt.

Clyde booted up his neural implant and dug into the government support systems. He called up EVE at the job support line and said, "I need a fucking job."

"Good afternoon, Mr Bondsman," the AI responded, her voice as clear as if the two of them were in a room together. "My records indicate that you are currently on administrative leave from Ajitatsu Corporation."

"They fired me."

"They may have said that, but until your termination is formally processed, there is nothing I can offer you."

He sucked on the smoke stick again and said, "Come on, EVE, you help complete fuckups get work, don't you? That's the grand government promise, ain't it? Work for anyone who wants it, and cheap food for those that don't? I see these fucking politicians every year talking about how they keep the prices down on the slop slime bullshit garbage they squirt out and call food. I ain't a fuckup, so why can't I get a job?"

"With your record, Mr Bondsman, you could always re-enlist."

He hung up on her and shoved off the vending machine. He marched past bars and clubs he couldn't afford. He passed by staircases up to shops too rich for him. He didn't even board a train because his ride pass was almost expired.

And on the way, he called his old boss.

"Mr Bondsman, to what do I owe the pleasure?" his old boss asked, his voice still pinched and nasally.

Clyde could almost see the bandages across the man's broken nose. "You know this ain't a pleasure for me either. Just tell me what the hell this labor reassignment thing is."

"It's more than you deserve, you brute."

"You were using me as a drug mule. You're lucky I haven't reported you to the police."

"Go ahead and try."

"Maybe I will."

"If you're going to ruin your chances at climbing the ladder, be my fucking guest."

Clyde stopped himself. "Why don't you run that by me. How does accidentally breaking my manager's nose get me a promotion?"

"Not at Ajitatsu it won't. You're done here. It's other corporations that might want you. Fact of the matter is you still showed up on time and met your quotas. Down here at the bottom, that puts you solidly in the top quartile. Shit, you know as well as I do that most of your previous coworkers were just trying to get through probations of one kind or another. So, what happens when we need to bounce someone like you, there are other companies willing to hire. Now, for violent outbursts from assholes who can't control their tempers–"

"Reflexes," Clyde corrected.

"The options are limited," he continued. "But lucky fucking you, you bastard, there's one that still wants you and is willing to give us a kickback to take you off our hands. You see?"

"What company?"

"They're called Heartsteel. You probably haven't heard of them. They do business to business security. You wouldn't have run into their muscle unless you were ever in a boardroom or something. Maybe a factory floor."

Clyde stopped right in the middle of a bridge. The people around him shoved past, knocking him into the railing, dumbfounded. "Security?"

"You've got military background and you're a big guy. Why are you surprised? Now, do you want the job or not?"

His heart was racing and he could feel phantom sweat across his palms and his neck. He tried to dry his hands with his hair, but his head kept reeling as stress metamorphosed. "Yes."

"Then fill out the form online. They can interview you next week. Hope to never see you again, Mr Bondsman."

Clyde slid down the railing and sat on the bridge. People nearly tripped over his feet, but he ignored their complaints. He had a job lined up, a way forward that would keep his family taken care of easily, until Johnny enlisted at eighteen.

He just had to survive a week until then and–glancing at his stretched out shirt–make a good impression at the interview.

6

Tattoo Parlor

2140/10/16

Abi-chromatic was a type of alcoholic drink that performed a certain chemical reaction over and over again, swinging back and forth like a pendulum. The result was the change of color of the drink every ten seconds or so, along with the flavor. Back in the twenty-first century it was considered a chemical marvel to find an unstable chemical equilibrium. A century later it was a commercial product that bars loved because they could control the pace of re-fills based on the oscillation of acid in drinks. Only a madman could drink a bi-chromatic when it was blue, even if it looked like it should taste like blue raspberries.

Elliot would have loved to keep his melting attention on his own bi-chromatic for the rest of the night, getting refills here and there, but someone decided to rob the bar while he was sitting there. Elliot was at the bar, hunched over a drink and looking at a near-dead phone between sips. Drinking it only at peak-sweet rather than sour was a very attention consuming process, and while some people liked not knowing what they'd get as they talked with people, Elliot had no one to talk to.

He did not like sour drinks.

The fact that someone was trying to cause a fiasco in Neo Akihabara was even worse than the mere fact that his own drink was getting ruined by some punk with a gun. The serving staff didn't even know what to do. Nobody shot up a bar in Neo-Aki. There was barely anything to even steal. Elliot knew they had to be more interested in the commotion—it was three people in void masks, each swinging around their own firearms. He could tell from a glance that only one of them had actual bullets. The other two were only sporting self-defense poppers. Tasers would have been more effective, but the average buzzed shopper didn't know the difference.

Elliot knew the difference.

While the guy in charge was shouting, "The top shelf! In the bag. I don't give a fuck about your bullshit money. I want the liquor!" Elliot kept his head down and queried the QRS team. They were five minutes out. Guns were coming in ablazing, but they weren't as fast as guns in the bar.

He was off duty and didn't want to pull his gun. Pulling his gun meant shooting the guy in charge. There really wasn't a way to arrest him when Elliot was outnumbered, and they were obviously just making a commotion. He was drunk too. Then EVE sent him a message, "Do something."

His phone ran out of battery and he groaned. A neural implant couldn't run out of power. The things ran off the user's own blood. They fed off blood sugar and ran for free, according to the advertisements. Other advertisements said that a neural implant was like a free weightloss supplement. Either way, he only had his phone and there was no charge left on it.

He groaned and glared at his bi-chromatic. The drink was near the end, clinging to the ice cubes and changing color erratically and inconsistently. Half would be pink while the other half was blue. Every sip was half-sweet and half-sour. No good as far as he was concerned, and he couldn't order a fresh one while the bartenders were busy getting robbed.

The guy in charge, probably a veteran criminal of some sort, noticed that Elliot was the one person at the bar not trying to slip out to the alley for the smoking section, and came strutting over. Elliot couldn't read the man's expression because of the void mask, but the criminal puffed out his chest and shouted, "Don't you got fucking ears? Shouldn't you be running? Or do we got a certified nutcase over here?"

Elliot was too drunk to care that he had a self-defense gun almost shoved in his face, and was confident the mask-wearing thugs could see that he was drunk. It would hurt to get shot with the popper, but it wouldn't kill him. What he didn't do was tense his muscles. He didn't move towards the guy. He didn't react to the underlings hopping over the counter to scoop up bottles of imitation whiskey and cackle at the workers. Elliot just pulled his gun and shot the leader in the hip.

The report of the gun shocked the entire club. Even the people running away flinched and turned around to see the criminal howling in pain. No one seemed to know what to do as the thug fell to the floor, gripping his hip and trying to stop the squirt of blood.

Elliot stood up and kicked their weapon away as he looked at the hole he had put in his own jacket from the tangled fire. "Bastard's Blood. I've had this jacket for almost twenty years and this is how I fuck it up? A triplet of idiots?" He didn't even bother pointing the gun at the others, just leveled it at the head of their leader on the floor. If the one with the actual gun had moved to aim at him, he would have fired.

They didn't bother fighting to protect their friend. No honor among thieves. The subordinates took what they had in their hands and bolted. Elliot couldn't shoot them without pointing his sidearm away from the guy who clearly had been in charge.

He just sighed and looked down at the man cringing across the floor, kicking over bar stools as he gasped in pain. "Who the fuck are you?" Elliot asked, kneeling down to peel the void mask off.

A brown-skinned woman sneered back at him. That was a surprise to Elliot because nothing about her body frame had been feminine, but that kind of mistake was common enough with baggy clothing.

"Who the fuck are you? You got any idea who you just shot?"

He shook his head and checked that the other two weren't about to shoot him. "No, I fucking don't. I'm Officer E11107 of the Southern Missou Police Department. Who the fuck are you?"

That took the wind out of her sails. She went from scowling to wincing. Her hands unfurled over her head as she melted to the floor. "Uh, wasn't expecting a jannis to be here."

He huffed a breath and shook his gun at her. "Don't you people think it's reasonable to call me a police officer in situations like this? Like, goddamn, I've got a gun to your face. I wouldn't get in trouble for shooting you right now. Why are you insulting me?"

"Sorry, Mr Officer Sir," she said.

Elliot turned the void mask over and saw the voice changer stuck to the inside. "You stay right there. QRS is on their way."

She just stuck her hands up and babbled for mercy. "It was just a little something something. A smash and grab. You know? We weren't going to actually hurt anybody."

"Save it. Do I look like I'm in the mood for bullshit?"

They shut their mouth. Elliot checked his pockets but he didn't have anything resembling handcuffs. He settled for enlisting the bartender to fetch the popper gun and empty it out. He sat there, keeping his firearm pointed at the would-be thief, sipping a lager until the QRS team arrived. One officer marched in, his steel-clad boots thumping the ground as he checked over the situation and barked orders to the civilians.

He recognized the voice. "That you Fools?"

"It's Essay now," Officer E55444 responded. "I got promoted about a week ago. Did your phone just die?"

Elliot pulled out his phone and clicked buttons to no response. "Guess so."

"Bad luck that. You really should get a neural, you know? Anyway, Boss says she wants you down at the tattoo parlor," Essay said as he rolled the thief over and cuffed her.

"Why's that? I'm on vacation."

"There's a body."

Elliot headed over to the tattoo parlor and found the body in question. It was brawny, tawny, and in two pieces. The majority of the victim was laid chest-down across a work table with bandages covering fresh ink. It looked to Elliot like they had just finished their dragon art piece and had been letting the ink settle when someone had cut their head off. That–along with a chunk of the table–was on the floor.

Essay's new boss was evidently Officer B35513 "Bess"–never Bessie–Hyun. Professional but without many accolades because she tended to linger after QRS actions. Cinder never complained, so she never changed. She should have been able to handle a killing without Elliot. "Don't you got some luck, huh?" she said, carrying her helmet under one arm and pointing at the head with the other.

"Why do you say?"

"That's part of your case, ain't it?"

I don't have a... Cinder already assigned me the Heartsteel case, didn't she?

"I wouldn't know. My phone is dead."

"Well, get it charging, or get a neural implant. When my boys called this in, we immediately got a priority message that you were the presiding officer."

Elliot sighed and squatted down next to the head. Blood oozed out, still fresh. "This must have happened just a minute ago."

During the armed robbery across the street.

He glanced around the parlor. His eyes could barely make out the layout because every door, wall, and shelf was laden with stickers of designs and happy customers. He could barely see the shadows and contours. "Where's the artist?" he asked, moving from the one table to the back.

"We've got him out front, says he stepped outside when he heard people shouting and when he came back the guy was already dead."

Elliot opened the door in the back–the deadbolt tumbled to the ground, cut in half–and found himself looking at an alley staircase. Wedged between walls and half-forgotten, it was a rusty snake through the tower leading up and down, with no cameras in sight. He sighed. "So, the corpse... he worked for Heartsteel?"

"Yeah. Name is Glenn Clarkson. Apparently they had him stationed over at the Sigurd Chemical Plant. Guess they'll have to find a replacement."

Elliot shook his head. "Get a forensics sweep in here, would you? The killer must have come in and out through here. If he was stupid, he might have left fingerprints or something. Someone is going to have to interview the artist alongside the camera footage, check his timing. And that someone isn't going to be me. I'm on vacation. Tell Cinder to get someone else to do it."

Bess whistled. "Sure, I'd be happy to tell her that you said that."

Elliot rolled his eyes. "I'm not afraid of her."

But, maybe I am afraid of Chase.

7

Temp Work

2140/06/23

Zarah promised him that the work wasn't illegal. She even went so far as to say that he was just covering work for people who were needed elsewhere. He had to be paid under the counter on a private credit chip, but they were willing to pay in standard credits–no strange crypto currencies needed. She gave him that little taste of truth, just enough that he could gauge his distance from it and deny any responsibility.

So, she sent him to a dry cleaners in Delta. The place stank from steam, machines puffing away and vaporizing chemicals. He had never seen so many suits and dresses before in his life, all on a spinning carousel. The Dawn-Dromat billed itself as a one stop shop and half a dozen kids worked cleaning shoes. Some of them even seemed to be genuine leather. It kept them busy rubbing and polishing, taking layers of grime, dirt, and oil away.

They didn't trust him with helping the kids. Cleaning rich people's shoes was valuable work for the outfit–whoever's outfit it was–and the kids had all been trained for it. One pissed off customer with the right connections and the place could get raided out of spite. That was a risk they couldn't take.

So the only thing Clyde had to do was stare at the order screen and fetch whatever numbered parcel it told him to fetch. It should have been easy work. All he had to do was hang up the clothes, or deposit the shoe box, in a metal turntable and spin it around for the customer. It would have been easy if the numbering system had actually been ordered, or if anything resembling intelligence had been used for the scheme. They could have included something in the number that would have at least told him if he was looking for a hanger, a box, or a package. That would have told him where in the storage racks to even look.

Instead, they had apparently done everything in their power to confuse and obfuscate, which not only wasted his time but made him wonder just what was in the packages that felt heavier than a pair of shoes. He wondered who was standing on the other side of the wall using the customer computer to ask for those parcels. All he knew was they had the right password and the records weren't kept.

He told himself to not think about it, but music could only be so mindless. After the first day, he was ready to quit, then Zarah handed him a chip with two hundred credits on it, along with a pack of beer. Drinking on the bench outside his family's home–the alley was supposed to be a micro-park just like the roof was supposed to simulate the sun–he came to think that the work really wasn't that bad. Cold beer stirring around his guts and watching Zarah chit-chat with their neighbors went a long way towards smoothing over the rough spots.

It was the second day when he started getting headaches.

The fumes were getting to him in more ways than one. Rifling through the clothes, not the ones being ordered up for delivery but the suits that had just been cleaned, began to irritate his fingers and palms. The chemical residue bit into his skin no matter how much he scrubbed his hands clean in the bathroom. He found his head light, his heart rate elevated, and a feeling of anxiety creeping in.

When it repeated on the third day, he shouted at the kids to crack a window. They laughed back, saying, "There are no windows. Where do you think we are, quaz?"

When work lulled to a stop, he went searching for vents. A dozen of them dotted the ceiling and he tried to fiddle with all of them. As if the architects had played a cruel joke on him, the vents were either disabled or, if they did have cool air flowing, the panels did nothing. Zarah caught him trying to get some air and asked, "Looking for a spot to smoke?"

His eyes darted to the door, but she hadn't used it. The latch clanged like a gong to prevent people from sneaking in. Somehow, she had materialized from within the cleaners. "I was under the impression that if I needed a smoke, I could just step outside for a minute."

She shrugged. "You're not wrong. That's not why I'm here though. Jared said you were messing with the system?"

Clyde frowned. Jared was one of the shoe cleaners. Clyde gestured at the racks of clothes. "You realize some of these have been hanging here for five years? Who the hell is going to come pick up a five year old dress?"

She shrugged. "Might be a bit out of fashion, but so what? We have the space, don't we?"

"Do you realize how much time I've wasted sorting around them looking for these random numbers?"

She cocked an eyebrow at him. "Is that why you've been moving everything?"

"I've been sorting things. Trying to order them so I can find what I'm looking for instead of running around every time."

Zarah laughed at him. "Clyde, you're only here for a week. Don't get hung up about it, alright? We have it that way for a reason."

"Only a week, huh." He glanced around the cleaner and stepped closer to her. "At least I know I'll be seeing you around after, right?"

Zarah didn't smile. "Is that your way of saying you want to see more of me?"

"I think I would, yeah."

She shook her head. "We only just met, Clyde."

"Right, sorry. Was easy to forget with you running around confident and in charge."

She grimaced. On her way out, she said, "Just keep your head down and stay out of trouble till you get that real job. Okay?" She left through the front door, letting in a cool blast of late summer air. The deadbolts clanged.

Clyde kept his distance from her after that. He kept his mouth shut, listened to the same seven rock songs on repeat, and he fetched the parcels the machine told him to. Only on his seventh day did he cause trouble.

Zarah had gotten into the shop somehow, and left from the front door. The kids had been there and hadn't said anything. They hadn't shown one lick of surprise at her appearance. Part of that could be chalked up to them expecting her, perhaps over a private channel, but that meant they knew there was a way in and out not officially monitored.

Clyde found the door behind a rack of dusty cloaks. The things were decades old at minimum, and all of the same fashion. He didn't recognize the logo on them, so the company was probably defunct; he figured that had happened around the time the police had adopted cloaks for winter wear. The age of them made them a perfect setpiece to roll in front of the backdoor, on perfectly greased wheels no less.

It wasn't locked. There wasn't even a handle on it. With no latch, the kickplate could pop it open with ease, which he guessed was to prevent fingerprints. The hall beyond was a cramped staircase, squeezed between structural supports and pipes, rusted grating led up and down with echoing feet. It smelled like Gamma; a rot of stagnant air.

"Moving through," someone said, and nearly shoved the door into his face. They squeezed by and glared at him from behind a void mask. "Don't forget to cover your damn face, idiot." A moment later they had slipped down two stories and turned a corner.

Clyde put a hand to his sweaty chin. He had a mask back at his home and he wondered what other places were connected. The tunnel was cramped and winding, it split like the branches of a tree, but it couldn't get out of the tower, not unless it went all the way down to Epsilon.

Sneaking around the dark of Epsilon was not something to do lightly though.

He knew perfectly well that there were kill-zones in Epsilon. Whether they were government, corporate, UAAF, or gang related, nobody knew. The only thing confirmed were the sentry guns hard mounted into the foundation of the city. Once, he had met a man who—drunk—claimed to be the one that went down and scooped up the spent brass. He had said other people went down to burn the bodies.

Clyde shut the door and backed away. He almost forgot to slide the cloak rack back in front. Zarah noticed the difference in his posture when she handed him his last credit chip. "Did something happen?" she asked.

Clyde rubbed his thumb across the sliver of silicon that had his pay and shook his head. "Just that the interview is tomorrow, you know? I'm finally going to know why these people want to hire me."

Zarah put a hand on her hip and shrugged. "Well, good luck. If it doesn't pan out, we can find more permanent work for you."

He flinched back and grimaced. "Sorry, but I think that wouldn't be a good idea for me... If the interview goes bad, they gotta release me in the system, you know? So EVE will be able to set me up someplace else."

"She might give you a job on the wrong side of the city. You really want to ride a commuter for an hour every morning just to go scrub toilets?"

Clyde shrugged. "I'll have to make it work somehow," he said, and slipped out of the cleaners. On the walkway out, he glanced back at the unassuming front, just one splash of color and lettering in a mosaic of others. He crossed a bridge to the opposite tower and leaned on the railing, scanning floor after floor. There were franchises and chain stores. Apartment blocks slotted between restaurants. The advertisements and nameplates were all set to different intensities, like a blurry haze of light—some old and dying, others recently replaced.

Then he saw, here and there, the people with masks on. They came and went not from all the stores but only a select few. Nearly a random selection of connections, but surely all with the same backdoor crawl-space that EVE couldn't see into. He couldn't even imagine what they needed something like that for. Delivering drugs across the city was apparently as easy as sneaking them into boxes of chocolate and having dupes hand-deliver them.

You'd have to be off killing people if you really needed that level of anonymity.

8

All Nighter

2140/10/17

Ram threw back her coat, planted her hands on her hips, and demanded, "Mr Blackstone, what the hell are you doing back in the office?"

Elliot had on his spare shirt reserved for emergencies, such as spilled coffee right before legal meetings or if he had just inadvertently spent the entire night working on a nightmare case and his co-workers were about to see him in a Chaos Splash t-shirt. He still liked Chaos Splash's music, before their drummer overdosed and their lead singer had his vocal chords tightened for a permanent falsetto, but the office was not a place for personality. Most people didn't even have pictures of their family at their desks.

He cracked open his third Zeus and sipped. The jolt of energy the drink promised had begun to feel more like a sticky tremor, but it kept his eyes open. "It's been a rough night."

She looked him over again. "I can see that," she said, and took the seat next to him. "What happened?"

His chair creaked as he sank back into it and gestured at his computer screen. Half a dozen photos of the latest murder were pulled up, along with schematics and database windows. "Just a regular day in Neo Akihabara. Nothing to lose your head over."

Ram winced at the pictures and scowled at him. "Is that really something to be joking about?"

"Humor is a great way to get ahead in life. It can fast track you on promotions."

"Mr Blackstone, that's awful."

"Sorry. I've been up all night. It's starting to give me a bit of a headache."

"How many of these do you have ready?"

"My list isn't that long, but if you're going to just chop me off at the end here…"

"That one's not even a head joke!"

"Well the rest of those puns are all variations on oral sex jokes, and that just wouldn't be appropriate."

Wyatt stood up from a few cubicles over and said, "Did the guy take 'giving head' too literally?" The older officer laughed until he saw Ram cross her arms and glare, then he vanished behind his cubicle wall again.

I wonder what he'd have to say if he knew Seraphina was back in town, or that she's alive for that matter. Need to figure out how to broach that subject.

Elliot drank half of his energy drink and stared at his wall. The report EVE had on Glenn Clarkson was uninspiring. The man was a thug with a stalled out investigation against him by some journalist. The reporter alleged Glenn broke his arm, but he'd be lucky to get a settlement out of Heartsteel now. Frankly, part of Elliot was fine with a vigilante taking thugs off the street, but he kept that thought to himself. He almost kept it from himself. "Technically, I'm here because I was basically a direct witness to a murder, but…"

"And the reason you weren't at the gamer party pad?"

"I got kicked out by your ex-… by the guy you went out with from the restaurant."

She hesitated, then recoiled like he had puked on her shoes. "Nelson? Oh, God, really? He actually is on your wife's team?"

Elliot looked over at his computer. The analysis wasn't done but he couldn't wrap his head around the last steps. Just trivial requests and queries and yet the computer screen resembled an abstract mosaic to his beleaguered mind. "I need food. Want to go to the cafeteria?"

Ram recovered from her shock and asked, "There's a cafeteria here?"

The cafeteria in question wasn't unoccupied, but the people inside were not using it appropriately. While the auto-cooking machines still worked, and even had two whole settings, the tables were no longer distributed evenly through the room so police officers between shifts could fuel up. Half a dozen recluses avoiding QRS duty had collected tables like children making fortresses and laden them up with binders, laptops, and unmarked evidence bags. They secluded themselves into corners and did quiet work that no one else quite understood. They didn't cause any problems and they kept their paychecks with the understanding that if one of the higher-ups really did force them out on QRS duty, the useful officers would probably get injured.

The noise of the auto-cooks actually turning on drew everyone's attention, but Elliot ignored their gazes. His account had a certain amount of free meals left on it from before his demotion, so he plugged in his order and told Ram to do the same. She hesitated and picked up one of the syrup bottles. "Is this stuff still good?" The date was technically still in the future, but she tried to spot a worker regardless.

"The selection ain't great. They only have shelf stable stuff. You can get oats, pancakes, or waffles. No butter, just margarine to go with the syrup. If you're lucky, there's some honey sitting around but the bottles have usually crystallized."

Ram stared at the computer screen for the auto-cook like it was a surprise test at school. "I think I can see why so few people come here."

"Carryout on the way in is usually easier," Elliot said as he grabbed a tray and walked over to the end. A moment later, the auto-cook spat a steaming waffle onto his plate and he heard the hiss of water jets cleaning the insides. He liberally doused it in the maple-flavored corn syrup as Ram followed behind him. She had gotten three pancakes, which she poked with her finger. The sponginess evidently wasn't to her prefer-ences, so she added a double helping of butter-substitute. She caught up with him as Elliot tried to find a table he could snag.

The only one available was next to the window. He was stealing chairs for them when Ram saw what was outside. "Is that a park? We have a park here?"

"Privatized," Elliot said, and sat down to dig into his breakfast.

Ram looked between him and the field of genuine green grass. "Pri-vatized? By who?"

"Our bosses. They made it a play park for the families of the com-manders and vice-commanders. Have a seat and enjoy the view."

Because you're probably not going to enjoy the food.

His waffle was dry and half-burnt. The so-called syrup helped, but mostly just made him regret not buying real syrup when he had been at the convoy from the Isles. "So," he said. "You didn't tell Nelson what your job was, did you?"

Ram shook her head and washed some pancakes down with her cof-fee. "Not until after we had met up. It was actually really awkward. He had been grinning the whole time he was rambling, and then he got real serious afterwards."

Elliot nodded. "He thought I was a plant. I think he has some kind of paranoid schizophrenia or something. Literally, the only thing he had to go off of was that Amara and I weren't making out with each other, so he slipped into our room and searched through my stuff until he found my badge."

"Isn't that, like, a huge breach of trust? If I were your wife, I'd have him kicked off the team! Like, Bastard's Blood, yeah he came out of it with your badge but she just has to accuse him of trying to steal her panties or something. You can do that in bootcamp, but he's a damn adult!"

Elliot planted his elbow on the table and his chin in his hand. The shadows were creeping across the grass, flushing it with light and warmth. "The problem is there'd be blowback on her for not telling them about me."

"I'm sorry, but it's kind of weird that she hid that from them too."

Elliot pushed his plate away. "She should have told them, but the way I see it, she has to make a deal of it now and take the damage or Nelson is just going to hold that over her. Those kinds of privacy scandals sting more in the moment but... damn, I've been up all night waiting for her response and gotten nothing."

After a moment of looking at him, more than she needed to eat another of her pancakes, Ram asked, "I know you're a workaholic, but I was wondering what drove you this hard. The sun coming up is usually a bad sign if you haven't slept yet."

"On the bright side, at least Cinder will understand when I don't pick my phone up for the next eight hours," he said.

I need to get ahold of Amara, but maybe when I'm sane in the head.

"I'm sure she can put that murder on someone else's agenda," Ram said.

Elliot groaned. "The problem is the rat hole the killer used. They sent drones through it, mapped it to thirty-two separate storefronts."

Ram whistled. "So, let me guess, the possible number of suspects was a few hundred?"

"Three hundred and forty-one... But, the good news is this isn't the first related killing. If it's one person, then we can cross reference the possible people, profile the guy, and grab him."

"How do you know it's a guy?" Ram asked, grinning playfully. "A micro-blade is just as dangerous in the hands of a woman."

The database had one silhouetted picture of the suspect. "I know it's a guy because he showed up outside the CEO's window to declare war. But, it's time I throw in the towel though. I'm headed home."

"Sleep well, Mr Blackstone, and hopefully the situation with your wife gets sorted out soon."

Elliot found himself thinking about the murders more and more. It was someone with a grudge. That meant it was someone who had been wronged, who thought they were in the right. He needed an investigation into Heartsteel if he was to understand why someone wanted a bunch of them dead, but he didn't see how he could get that kind of warrant. The only reason he had been brought in was because of the electronic anomalies obscuring the deaths.

That, and because Seraphina had asked for me. Why now though? Why bring me in this time? Is it something she knows about the case? Or did she just think this was a good time to mess with me?

9

The Last Interview

2140/06/29

Clyde couldn't take his eyes off the button in front of him. The woman had E cups at the least and her shirt was about two sizes too small. It only came together through the sheer force of the button, threatening to pop off if she ever inhaled too much. She wouldn't, he knew that. The corporation had her dosed on diazepam or a derivative, giving her an inhuman calmness as she asked, "Can you tell me about the altercation that led to the termination of your previous employment?"

Clyde's foot jittered, nearly beating on the floor beneath the table. He turned away from the woman's smile. "It was an accident. The guy—Mr Hill—snuck up on me. When he grabbed my shoulder, he scared the piss out of me."

"And that's why you...?"

The table didn't have his resume on it, but it wasn't empty either. The corporation had set out more distractions than just the woman. His eyes slid over the things: steaming coffee, a nicotine vape, and a little stack of chocolates. "You've never—have you ever lived down in Gamma?"

"I'm sorry, I can't share any personal details about myself, Mr Bondsman."

"Right, of course not."

"You can have one, if you'd like."

He hadn't taken his eyes off the chocolates. Her words made him tense and smooth his hands down his pants. "No, thanks. Down in Gamma, though, it's not very safe. I mean, the corpo-blocks can be alright, but the only people who sneak up on you, they aren't your friends. It was just reflex."

Her smile stayed as still as a painting. "Just a reflex."

Clyde grinned back at her. "Did him a favor really. Knocked that snaggle tooth out of his mouth. Insurance gave him a proper tooth to replace it."

"The Ajitatsu Corporation didn't see it that way, or they wouldn't have terminated you."

His grin vanished and his mouth went dry. "No." In the corner of the interview room was a camera, one glossy eye fixed on him. Whether the Ajitatsu lawyers were on the other side, he'd never be able to know. "But, the parting was amicable. I was tired of the job anyway. Hand deliveries are punk work. Dangerous too. I'm a veteran, you know."

"Yes, your record shows you served your two years and were discharged without problem. Top marks in all training categories, but not enough to get you scouted."

"Deployment wasn't for me. I didn't like being so far away from my family. Look, I think I'd be a great asset to Heartsteel. You won't find a more qualified man for the job. I'm recommended too."

The woman folded her hands together on the table and leaned in. "I think it's wonderful that you care about your family so much, Mr Bondsman. We here at Heartsteel think very highly of that mindset, but we take a broader look to it. Everyone in the company is like family, and when our security forces are hired to protect someone... well, we would need you to treat that someone like you're protecting your own mother."

"Of course." Clyde jerked his head up and down. "Yeah, absolutely. I did plenty of security detail. I know the deal." His sergeant had loved to put him as the VIP guide—to put him between the guest and the blighted. They loved his twitchy reflexes when monsters were on the receiving end rather than staff supervisors.

"But, no accidents."

His laugh was as dry as a cough. "Luckily, I've never met a VIP that wanted to touch their bodyguard."

She smiled at him and silence lingered. She must have been getting instructions through her neural implant. After what felt like minutes, she spoke again. "Our on-staff psychologist has looked over your files, did you know that? She gave a tentative diagnosis of anit-social personality disorder."

Clyde's grin set into a line. His foot started tapping again. "It's against guidelines to make a diagnosis without meeting the patient."

"It's preliminary only. We at Heartsteel believe these sorts of diagnoses are false positives, more often than not. Rather than something innate to you, we believe it's learned behavior from your environment. Like you said, Gamma is a rough place to live outside of corporate housing districts. If you were to join the Heartsteel family, you would be moved into a corporate housing district, though. You wouldn't have to worry about getting mugged at night. Outside of working hours, your biggest concern would be which restaurant to eat at, or what video show to watch."

"Sounds like a dream." The words were like sand in his mouth. He didn't even have money to be robbed of at the moment. The chocolate called to his empty stomach but he kept his hands in his lap and tried to stop his foot from tapping.

"But, you understand that this olive branch is a tentative one. If you attack someone in the Heartsteel family we can't offer you a second chance. Mr Bondsman, you're already on your second chance."

"I know."

"Well then, we don't need to go over your qualifications again, and Ajitatsu has already informed us that you are available immediately. Do you have any questions for us?"

He swallowed. "The apartment I would get. How big is it? Would I be able to bring any of my siblings?"

There was a hint of a twinge in her smile. Some emotion almost broke through the drug-induced mask. "I'm sorry, but the basic level housing units we offer are only fit for one individual. After three months, you can apply for a family unit as part of your employee evaluation, at which time you may qualify for a two person habitat. If you have any children, educational boarding can be provided at a cost garnished from your wages. I assure you that we have the fastest internet in all of Bastion, direct fiber optic communication."

He nearly told them he didn't care for virtual reality. He barely stopped the words from coming out; no point insulting their offer. He folded his hands on the table like she had. "Okay then. Three months isn't too long. When will a decision be made on moving forward here?"

"A decision will be made in the next twenty-four hours. Is that all of your questions?"

Nothing else about the job mattered. "Yes."

She rose, her chair scraping across the plastic tiling. "Thank you for coming in, Mr Bondsman."

He jumped up and stuck out his hand, but she turned away and slipped out the back. Clyde put his hand down and glanced up at the camera. It stared back at him. The door back to the waiting room was behind him and he nearly headed out. His willpower wavered with a question, 'Maybe they want to see I can be tempted?' It stopped his foot. He turned around and picked up the dish of chocolates, dumping them all into his pants pocket.

Other would-be employees scowled at him when he returned to the waiting room. They were rough men, some rough women too. Clyde gritted his teeth as he walked past them, returning their glares with his own. Most of them glanced away, pulled their jackets tighter, or tucked their feet beneath their chairs. A few smirked and he tried to remember their faces.

He hoped he'd never see them again.

Heartsteel's virtual mascot popped up in the hall, dancing across a floor to ceiling display screen as she said, "Thank you very much for your interest in working for the Heartsteel Corporation! If you don't hear from us within three business days, please understand that we aren't able to give personal rejections to every application and we wish you the bestest luck elsewhere. Thank you again and have a nice day!"

The mascot gave him pause without him realizing it. Young, bubbly and bouncing along beside him with an open smile the interviewer couldn't have dreamed of; and this was the computer program. She looked about the same age as Clyde's younger sister, who had just gotten drafted. He sighed because he wouldn't be seeing her again for a year.

Instead, as he walked out to the fifteenth floor train station, he called his brother. Wind whipped him, cutting between the towers and the Missou wall. He was looking up at the gray sky, wondering if a storm was coming, when Johnny picked up. "Hey, Clyde. What's up? I'm gaming."

Through his neural implant, the kid's voice came through perfectly clear–totally unlike a phone. Clyde shook his head. "Not much, Johnny. What game are you playing?"

"[Dynasty Conquest]. I'm kind of getting my ass kicked."

"Don't swear over a game."

"Well, I am getting my ass whooped."

"Then get better so you don't have to swear about it."

"Whatever. Are you coming home tonight?"

The train pulled in, segment after segment of steel and glass with dazed commuters. Clyde joined them. "Nah, I'm just checking in before the night shift. You know how it is. Is everything good? Getting your homework done in time for games?"

"My grades are fine, Clyde. Hey, can I catch you later though? The game's waiting on me."

Clyde sat down as the train peeled around the corner, diving into the heart of Bastion. He stared at the map as he said, "Yeah, sure. Just tell Mom I said hello."

"Right, talk to you later bro."

The call ended as abruptly as it had started and he was left alone in the train, amid the crowd of people. He hunched over, folding his hands together and staring at the floor. There was no night shift for him to go to, so Clyde rode the train into the center of Bastion and slipped off a station before Liberty Stadium. He slipped into the boundary between the heart of the city and the sole of the ghetto.

Close enough he could hear the echoes of shoppers, drinkers, and advertisements, he wandered across the bridges and down stairs. He slipped from the fifteenth floor to the tenth and then the fifth. Like river flotsam, he washed up in a forgotten snag. With a dress and leather store on one side and a psychic reading store on the other–their market appeal synergistic enough that Clyde suspected they had the same owner–he shouldered through a boarded up door. There was no sign on it, not in English anyway, but it had the subtle markings of a speakeasy.

The bouncer inside patted him down and found nothing, letting him meld into the darkness. The owner had a scratchy jazz record looping in the back and half the seats were empty. "You here for whiskey or water?" the bartender asked as he took a seat.

"You don't have beer?"

"Tapped out."

Clyde reached into his pocket and squeezed his credit chip, trying to remember how much was left on it. "How expensive is the whiskey?"

The bartender crossed his arms. His mustache rolled down his face in a frown. "It's ten credits for a drink."

"I can have one then," Clyde said, setting his credit chip on the counter.

The bartender plugged it into his register and then got him a glass of amber swill. It looked like oil and smelled like cleaning chemicals. The burn on his tongue wasn't too bad. The bartender leaned against the back counter, arms crossed once more, and asked, "I thought Ajitatsu paid pretty well."

Clyde glanced where the man was looking and saw the corporate logo on his jacket shoulder. Frustration welled up in the back of his throat, worse than the whiskey. In his mind, he rehearsed half a dozen excuses and then just said, "They fired me today."

The frown vanished from the bartender's face. "Well that explains why you look like your girlfriend just dumped you for someone else."

Clyde laughed. "Not quite."

The bartender got him another whiskey. "On the house. Private access code is there on the left of the bar." He pointed to some login info scrawled across a refrigerator door and excused himself to the back of the speakeasy.

While Clyde connected to the internet the bartender flipped through old vinyls, eventually picking one out and blowing some dust off. Clyde didn't listen much to the new music, it was something from the twenty-sixties with a bit of Creole Revival. He connected his neural implant to the speakeasy's router as just one more anonymous drinker. Then he started searching for a new job; one that might actually hire him.

Hours later, sipping through his fourth whiskey, he got a call. His eyelids had been weighed down by the liquor and the night and he almost didn't recognize the name. It was the cheery voice that caught him. "Hi there, Mr Bondsman! This is Silver from Heartsteel."

Clyde blinked and looked at the bar clock: one AM. "You're a bit outside of working hours, aren't you?"

The corporate mascot laughed. "That's one of the perks of being a computer, Clyde. Your file indicated that you'd still be up and we figured that you'd want to know as soon as possible that we're offering you the job!"

Clyde took a moment to process the words. The change in his expression caught the attention of the bartender, who arched an eyebrow at him. Clyde slammed the last of his whiskey and jumped to his feet. Fumbling out his credit chip again as his heart raced, he asked, "What time do I have to be there?"

10

First Partner

2140/10/17

Sleep devoured Elliot's day and provided little relief. He had the energy drinks to thank for that. While he was out, his wife got around to messaging him. "Don't make a scene, I'm talking it out with Nick." That left him in limbo, unable to go back, unwilling to go back to work, and recently burned for going out on the town. Autopsy reports on the tattoo victim weren't in yet either. Not wanting to abandon his vacation day, he called up Mikey d'Angelo.

As the sun was setting, he showed up to a reservation at a murder mystery speakeasy. The place sold three types of tickets as well as decent dinners: players, background, and viewers. The tickets were priced accordingly of course. Elliot arrived at the establishment in a button up shirt with no tie, because the recommended attire was business casual. All part of the ambiance. The girl at the front, a tiny thing in a sequin dress who looked like she had missed the draft, smiled at him when he approached. "Should be a table for two, under the name d'Angelo?"

The hostess blinked, and said, "I have a d'Angelo for three, looks like it was just updated a little bit ago. I can take you right there. The show is about to start."

Did Dom come?

"Still time to get a drink, right?"

She took him to the second floor, a little corner booth that could just barely see the main stage where the workers would kick off the game. Half a dozen players–he assumed, based on the flamboyant outfits from the 1920's–stood milling about with cocktails. While he was distracted thinking about what he wanted to drink himself, she pointed him to the table and Elliot saw who the third person was.

Officer E55146 "Lizard" Wyatt sat next to Mikey, a pint of beer in one hand and a plate of chips and salsa between them. "Elliot! Good to see you. Did you catch up on your sleep?"

He slid into the booth and hid as much of his shock as he could. "Not as much as I would have liked. You're not on QRS tonight?"

Wyatt shook his head as Elliot ordered a Moscow Mule. "Nah, you won't see me on that as much as I used to. I finally managed to pay off the debts, so I don't need the overtime anymore."

"Well, that's good."

What is that, two years then? Two years to pay off the California trip? His daughter's medical bills the year prior? I thought he'd be at that for way longer. Maybe I underestimated how much work he was pulling.

They all had to quiet down as the show began. A narrator came out with a microphone, giving some context to the game. The whole thing was like an improv play. Those that had paid to be background characters had clues for the players to find, but would look no different from the viewers–like Elliot. The head chef of the restaurant had been killed, a closed room murder, and the players had to figure out who did it.

The winning player would get their dinner comped and a ticket to come back at their pleasure to do it again.

"So, your daughter," Mikey said as the waitresses began serving drinks again. "She's all healthy now?"

Wyatt grimaced and swirled his ice. "She's as recovered as can be, but she'll never be the same. You know what's bullshit? They don't even have proper prosthetic feet. They gave her these three toed machines like a damn goat."

Mikey nodded. "Okay, setting aside that goats have two toes, she can walk, right? You know, it's pretty difficult to make a robust piece of machinery as tiny as a human pinky toe. I bet they have good reasons for why they engineered them that way."

Wyatt scowled and drained his drink. One of the players made a cursory pass by their table and chose not to talk to them. "If it was just that, we could live with it. They've got an auxiliary computer now, implanted on her tailbone. It bypasses the damage to work her legs, and you should see this rehab thing they've got her now. It's set up for VR and does variable control of resistance to work her muscles. What it's done for her health you can't even believe it. But the burns..."

"They never got the scars to go away?" Elliot asked.

"No."

Wyatt's daughter had been cityboarding three years ago. Not a recommended hobby, but it was her form of teenage rebellion. By chance, she had landed on top of a commuter train, latched her board right to the roof for a ride. She was only catching her breath and had the misfortune of standing atop a bomb planted by the Centurions, a group of anarchist insurgents. Everyone on the train had been killed in the blast, but she had layers of plastic and aluminum between her and the bomb. It didn't kill her, it just flung her into the air and set her on fire.

She fell two stories and hit a sign with her back, half on fire and missing body parts.

Less than a year later, Wyatt and Elliot had gone to New California, killed the bankers controlling the funds for Centurion, and Elliot had lied to Wyatt about killing Seraphina, who had been there as an informant.

When Elliot came out of his own memories, he realized Mikey was chatting with one of the players, talking fast and slick and messing with them. It was against the rules—the three of them could get kicked out—to give false information about the game, but the player had yet to realize that Mikey wasn't actually saying anything at all. One of the serving staff rescued the player by suggesting the next table over might have a clue and pointing towards an incomplete chess set laid out. The player took the hint and ran over to the puzzle.

"Mikey," Elliot said. "You ever thought about getting into politics?"

"Sorry, wasn't born rich."

"So Elliot," Wyatt said, setting aside his empty drink. "I hear you were the MVP during the raid last week. The way I hear it, Cinder hadn't even gotten off the radio before you put a bullet in the guy. You gonna rethink my offer?"

Elliot opened his mouth to say one thing, then said, "Cinder is actually tossing me from one case to the next. I don't seem to have a choice."

"This have to do with that murder you were looking at this morning?"

"Maybe, maybe not. Would you believe that some whack job threatened the CEO of Heartsteel Corporation?"

Wyatt whistled, and immediately had to wave a curious player off. "So what, they brought you in as the resident expert?"

Elliot rattled his glass, peering at the slick ice. At some point he had finished the drink and yet his mouth felt dry. He looked at Wyatt again, slightly older than him but not by much. They were both the same rank, both busted down after the trip to New California. Wyatt had changed since then. Deeper wrinkles in the face, a gaunt look to his eyes, and thicker through his frame despite the excess years. Wyatt carried the killings around with him and it made Elliot wonder if he was doing the same.

Elliot asked, "Are you upset they didn't bring you in, instead?"

Mikey glanced between the two of them. "What's this about?"

Wyatt smiled like they were talking about nothing more than a game. "Sorry, don't worry about it Mikey. Hey, how's your kid doing? Getting in shape for the draft?"

Mikey sighed and grinned back. "You know, it's actually the damnedest thing. He's got real natural talent for fitness, but no motivation for it. He pulled up the minimum requirements and he does those regularly. It's part of his gym class, you know. He says as long as he can do the minimum, he doesn't care. I can't say he's wrong. Unless he's going to join the MPs, physical fitness really won't help after his service period."

Wyatt said, "Oh, that's not true at all. The benefits of exercise really can't be understated. I've done a lot of research on this trying to help my daughter. The fact that he's on a regular schedule is already a huge benefit." He pulled closer to Mikey as he went on.

Elliot could have kept up with their conversation, even if he knew he would get badgered about his own gym attendance, it's lack thereof, and part of him felt he should do just that. He didn't feel like talking much, and ordered more drinks for himself. Eventually the conversation wheeled around to his situation with Amara and Nelson, but neither of them had any suggestions for the current night. All three of them agreed that Amara had to be the one to negotiate it and pull the appropriate trigger.

I just hope she does. How many years did she hide the fact that I was her husband?

His phone vibrated during the murder mystery's final accusations. The timeslot was a mere two hours, and guesses had to be made. The staff drummed up everyone's attention and called on the players to answer questions. Elliot vaguely understood the plot the staff had contrived, but when he read the message on his phone, he completely forgot the game.

"Shit, there's been another killing. What kind of serial killer works each night? That's like asking to be caught," he said, shaking his head as he read the contents of the message again.

"The Heartsteel guy?" Wyatt asked.

"Yeah, he's going after middle management first," Elliot said, just before his phone buzzed again. This time it was an incoming call message. Caller ID said it was Seraphina. He snarled and almost hit ignore. His thumb itched to kill the connection. He knew she would just call Wyatt if he did that though. "One sec."

The moment he stepped away from the table and put the phone to his ear, Seraphina said, "Sounds like you're having a rough go of it, Thomas. Would seeing a corpse cheer you up?"

Thomas?

"Give the job to someone else. Do I look like a fucking errand boy to you? This isn't exactly a complicated investigation. EVE will sort him out quick enough."

"Yes, you do look like an errand boy to me, Blackstone. This isn't the kind of investigation you can just brush off, you know? We're not waiting for a pill smuggler to slip up so we can have QRS pick him up, this is a planned operation. Maybe even multiple people. EVE hasn't turned up shit. She scanned all four of the killings and doesn't have even one person at both of them because the cameras keep blacking out. I don't know if you know this, Blackstone, but she doesn't exactly take long to check who's at a crime scene. Go use some of your old-fashioned training or something. Pay Heartsteel a visit. It's not like you're allowed back in at the party pad, now are you?"

11

The Neurist

2140/07/01

Clyde woke before his alarm went off. He was blinking his eyes, try-ing to figure out what color the ceiling had turned–indigo warm-ing to maroon–when his wall began a chime. He rolled to turn it off and almost smacked his face into it. In a bleary haze, he fought with his sheets and groped about, eventually getting a hand to the touchscreen and killing the noise. The light grew stronger, but stayed in a cool blue as a computer voice said, "Good morning Mr Bondsman. The time is currently oh-six-hundred. Please report to the training grounds at oh-six-thirty to begin your preliminary shift. May I recommend a Heart-steel Protein Blend to break your fast?"

"Just shut up," he grunted, and rubbed his face. His head was pounding. When the computer tried to advise him to hydrate, he slapped the control screen again and silenced it. He was used to getting up early in boot camp, he just wasn't used to being able to drink the night before. The hangover distorted his perception of his new apart-ment, making the little cubby in the tower squeeze around him. The fact that he had his back to one wall and his foot on the other didn't help.

But, it was his apartment.

He folded the bed back into the wall, dropping his night clothes and sheets into a laundry bag and then down a chute. The noise of minimum wage hospitality workers shuttling carts around echoed until he shut the chute. His bathroom had the toilet in the shower to save room, but his shoulders rubbed against the plastic walls as he tried to clean himself. At least the towel was soft.

The same could not be said for his uniform. It was anti-bacterial, stain-proof, unisex, slash-resistant, and a half dozen other things but none of them comfortable. For the amount they were paying him, he could deal with an uncomfortable jumpsuit. When he stepped out of his apartment, he saw everyone else bearing with it too. With flashbacks to boot camp running through his mind, he fell in with the flow of the crowd, climbing the stairs up to the recreational floor of the Heartsteel Business Complex. Most people queued up for the vending machines spitting out the protein blends and Clyde joined the line. They looked as thick as cream and smelled like chocolate, but the machine threw an error when he tried to get one.

"This machine is for Heartsteel employees only."

The ten people in line behind him all looked at him. The hair across his neck prickled as he tried to find an option to manually input his identification number. Someone else reached in and jabbed the corner of the screen, pressing an unmarked button. They inputted a code when prompted and the override cleared. A protein shake popped out for him as the new arrival clapped him on the shoulder. "Sorry I was late," the man said.

"I'm sorry, who are you?"

The man was swarthy and broad through the shoulders. As he pulled Clyde away, he said, "The name's Mohamed, but you should know that we don't really use our names while on the clock. You can call me 335-362."

The protein blend tasted sweet, like an enriched milk substitute. "Seems a bit difficult to remember."

Mohamed chuckled. "Thankfully, we don't have to remember it. It gets fed automatically through our neurals. That's your problem back there. You're not in the system yet, so the vending machine didn't recognize you. Now, I know your ID is 325-930, but that's because I'm your buddy. Once you get the company software though, everything will work just fine."

Clyde was used to company software. Ajitatsu had used their own to coordinate deliveries. It took the planning out of the hands of the workers and optimized it. Half the time the package had to be handed from one person to the next to get from factory to customer. The traveling salesman problem had crumbled in the face of modern computing power, to the chagrin of mathematicians. "So when do I get that? Before or after training?"

"Before," Mohamed said, and waved a hand at the ranks of jumpsuited employees going through a stretching routine on plastic turf.

The two of them rode an elevator up the tower, way up. They didn't stop until the sixtieth floor and emerged to a room with no windows. "Shame," Clyde said.

"What is?"

"Sorry, forget that," Clyde said and followed Mohamed through the corporate clinic. There were wings of patient rooms and nursing stations. He could hear people sneezing and coughing and he saw more than a few people nursing broken bones. It all seemed like even more reason to have windows. Sunlight did the sick good, everyone knew that.

Mohamed took him into a locked corner of the tower. "Barber first."

"I'm sorry?"

"Need it for access to your implant," Mohamed said, tapping his own skull. He led Clyde to a prep room. In addition to plenty of sinks and unmarked drawers, there was a standard barber seat; but no mirror. A bored looking, thirty-something woman walked over. She had half her own head shaved clean, leaving a patch down the middle tied into dreads.

"Come on, newbie. Don't waste my time," the woman said, rolling a piece of gum around her mouth. She had a buzzer in her hand.

Clyde glared at Mohamed. "No one told me I would have to cut my hair."

The other man shrugged. "We don't have hair regulations, but it's required for the procedure. If you want, she can just take a patch off the back, but you'd look weird."

Clyde consoled himself with the thought that he would be paid eighty thousand credits per year and sat down. "Just give me a high and tight."

The barber scoffed. "Okay, G.I. Joe." She at least did a good job at butchering two years of hair growth. A few minutes later, he and Mohamed were on the floor above the clinic. Less medical, more computer.

"Just wait here," Mohamed said, gesturing to a one person waiting room.

"For how long?"

"Until the neurist gets you. Just hang tight. Browse the internet or something. I'm going to go get a smoke," he said, and left Clyde to his own devices. The man vanished out an emergency exit and left it propped open with a cardboard box. No sooner was he out of sight, then a cloud of vape smoke puffed out.

Clyde sat in the only available chair. His mother had been messaging him. Inane things far outnumbered questions about the job. He spent the time sorting through them and writing up a response that would both satisfy her and keep her from prying too deeply. He was just about to hit send when the door opened.

"325-930?" The assistant neurist was as pudgy as a restaurant cat and looked at him with dull, almond eyes.

His first thought was that she might be from UAAF, but he didn't voice that. "That's me."

"Come on, let's get you rebooted."

Clyde frowned and followed her in. The doctor didn't introduce himself, but had on a name badge reading Dr Forez. They sat him down on a face down bed like they were about to give him a massage. Instead, they rubbed anesthetic into the back of his scalp. He squeezed his hands into fists and gritted his teeth as they dug the scalpel in. They almost didn't need the anesthetic: the nerves had never regrown. He could feel them sawing at the flesh, almost more scar tissue than skin. They sliced a flap open and peeled it off the back of his skull, revealing the circuitry that had replaced the bone.

"Now, you might hallucinate a bit," the neurist said, looming over Clyde with his tools.

It losing power wasn't the issue. The implant had been designed to cut itself off safely. The reboot was what threw him. It had to cycle through every sensation after they got it up and running again. While they were gluing his skin back on, he had to listen to an orchestra of tunes and tones. His vision went through a rainbow kaleidoscope of calibration and when the room came into view again, it was spinning. His skin prickled with imaginary sensation till he nearly wanted to vomit, but then it was over.

The implant said as much. "Heartsteel integration is now fully operational!" Silver declared. Not the standard replica voice of EVE which his implant had installed with, but Heartsteel's mascot. Running an app was one thing, but they had changed the operating system files.

Clyde lurched off the desk, knocking the fat assistant out of his way. They shouted at him as he scrambled to his feet. "What the fuck did you just do?"

The neurist's face flushed red and a vein nearly burst from his head. "What the fuck do you think you're doing? You think you're special 'cause you're new or something? You think you can just jump around an operating room you fucking idiot! Somebody get him the fuck out of here!"

The door flew open before Clyde could even get his feet beneath him. Mohamed stormed in, nicotine pen still in his grip. His expression had changed. It had set like stone, like the edge of life had filed off. The man clocked him in the jaw, knocking Clyde back into the wall. Drawers rattled. Clyde threw up his hands, not in surrender but ready for a fight.

Then his implant pinged and updated. Instead of the man's face, his ID was superimposed in front of it, 335-362, in bright green letters. When Silver spoke both, he assumed, of them heard her. "Stand down and vacate the premises," the artificial girl ordered, and the tension through Mohamed's arms waned.

Rather than punch him again–Clyde would have countered and decked him back–Mohamed grabbed him by the sleeve and dragged him out of the operating room. The other man threw him against the wall in the waiting room. "What the fuck did you do, new guy?"

Clyde's heart was racing. It put dull anger behind his eyes, in his breath, in the squeeze of his fists. He needed the paycheck though. His family needed it. "No one told me you were changing my implant... like that."

"It was in your damn contract. Can't you read?"

"The contract said you needed to load proprietary software. It didn't say that software was fucking with my OS. How the hell do I even turn this program off?"

Mohamed shook his head and folded his arms. "It's a safety program you idiot. For as long as you're on company property, doing a company job, or anything like that you can't shut it off. It will monitor you for your own damn protection."

"Protection? From what?"

"From yourself, apparently. Go back to your room. You're done for today. Sleep it off and take your orders in the morning," Mohamed said, throwing a hand into the air as he stormed out of the waiting room.

Clyde straightened up and spent a moment relaxing his muscles. When he could walk without looking like a prowling animal, like he was going to rip somebody's throat out, he left the waiting room and headed back to the recreational area. Halfway there, his implant provided him directions back to his apartment, which he quietly followed while wondering how he would describe the day's work to his mother and hoping he wouldn't have to.

The back of his head started to itch.

Crematorium

The walls of the crematorium were black ash cast in the undulating neon glow of a lava lamp. Fans spun up as the worker tugged the furnace door open. They slid the corpse tray in, disposing of the wrinkled body, and slammed the door shut once more. The gasp of heat from the furnace made sweat break out across their brow, which they quickly dabbed off. They hadn't disposed of the entire corpse, not as it had been delivered. In a jar on their work table was the bloody mass of silicon and gold that had been threaded through the brain, percolating in a light acid to dissolve the organic material.

"Sorry for the delay," the worker said, giving the jar a shake to see how much blood was ready to wash off. "Burner Six is down, so they've been sending me double duty. I swear, Seven here is a hungry beast but this has gotten ridiculous."

"I won't take much of your time. I just need to see the train car victim."

"R12-10-02? I put the magnet on his slide," the worker said, gesturing at the wall. Like a mausoleum, it was lined with metal coffins and labeled Death Row. These were refrigerated to keep them from rotting before their time in the oven. The magnet in question was a caricature of Auroary, the ink rubbed off at the edges.

"Gloves?"

The worker tossed him a box of latex gloves as he walked by, wheeling the stretcher cart to the other side of the room. Some other elderly corpse had to be pulled out and prepped.

Elliot put the gloves on and focused on R12-10-02, real name Mohamed Azir. The rack rattled as he pulled it out and cold air sluiced off the sides. The body had been washed and the wound stapled shut. The metal prongs were sunk deep into the corpse's sternum. Anything less and the ribs would have splayed open. The color of the skin seemed wrong, but Elliot couldn't tell if it was merely an ethnic complexion, too many trips to a sun tanning booth, or the lava lamp.

Probably all three.

"How did you get that, anyway?" he asked with a gesture towards the lamp.

The worker glanced up from digging a cochlear implant out of the corpse's skull. "The light? Pretty nifty, ain't it? Do you know how hard it is to get one of these? That's real paraffin in there."

"Is it an heirloom or something?" Elliot asked as he unlocked his phone and tunneled into the police database. The killing–when Mohamed had been sliced open from hip to eye–had been recorded by the train itself, for all the good it was to the investigation. It had happened when the train came into a station. Busy place, packed full of people flowing between bars and entertainment venues. Enough that a few dozen people were trying to squeeze through the doors at the same time as Mohamed.

EVE had added a tracker to the video, highlighting his head as he tried to squeeze out. The video offered to pause the moment he stopped moving forward, but Elliot let it play. A moment later, the crowd around him suddenly parted. People leapt away as his intestines spilled onto the floor. The loss of blood pressure hit his brain a breath later and he collapsed backwards. Unconscious before he hit the floor and dead when EMT arrived fifteen minutes later.

The crematorium worker shrugged and washed his hands. When he killed the faucet, he said, "No idea, but you can tell it's real wax because of how it flows. Probably from before the apocalypse. All the circuitry had to be replaced. That's a heating pad now, with a secondary LED for illumination. That's basic stuff though. I don't know where that guy got it from, but I've had it ever since."

Elliot stuck his fingers in the edge of the wound. He peeled it open, parting skin and fat. There should have been muscle too, but that was already contracted into rippling knots. It had definitely been a micro-blade. He rewound the video to the exact instant and frowned. "You sound like you stole it," he said, zooming in on the dozens of heads sur-rounding Mohamed in the video.

"Didn't steal it," the worker said. He was setting some kind of con-trol on the incinerator. "The guy was a PSB–public service burning. Didn't have any family to give his belongings to, so now I have it. Perk of the job. Your R12 there is a PSB too."

Elliot stopped and looked at the lava lamp as the worker shoved the next corpse into the incinerator. The flames blazed hotter than the last time, some black machinery within grinding.

No kids? Not even siblings? At least I have… I hope Amara will be there when I bite it.

"Can you postpone this one?" Elliot asked as he traced the length of the cut with his finger, about a meter long.

"No can do," the worker said. "Already said, we're overbooked and overflooded. I have to get all these bodies incinerated before they pu-trefy."

"They're refrigerated though, aren't they? And this is for an ongoing investigation."

The worker laughed. "Half the bodies in here are for ongoing inves-tigations!"

Elliot scanned the room and did some mental math on population size. "I work for the Southern Missou Police Department, not a corpo-rate security team. I'm an MP."

The crematorium worker paused sheepishly and looked at his feet. He mumbled an apology as something in the wall behind him grinded.

It sounded like a coffee grinder, turning bits into powder and pouring them into a canister. "I'm sorry officer, I really don't have the free space. If it's that important, you'll need to find somewhere else to store it. A hospital clinic maybe? The other one who came here, she didn't seem to think it was a big deal."

Elliot scowled. "She doesn't think anything is a big deal."

"How's that body supposed to help you, anyway?"

"I don't know," he said, and started checking the rest of the body. There were tattoos of a few game logos. Metal reinforcement through his left hand; medical record showed he had been left handed and after breaking the bones in fights too many times opted for metal replacements. His teeth had advanced cavities, Elliot could smell the rot just from opening his mouth. Scars across his lips, eyebrow, forearms, and an old stab wound to his kidney. All that told him was the man had led a rough life, most of which hadn't been logged by EVE.

"On the upside, if I do burn the body," the worker said as he carried the canister over to his label printer. The name had already printed and he stuck it on. It wasn't coffee that had come out, obviously. "You'll get the implant."

Elliot checked the database and confirmed the body was approved for destruction. "When will that be?"

The worker pulled a knife out of his pocket and flipped it open.

Ten minutes later, Elliot had a jar of bloody chemicals and Mohamed Azir's neural implant rattling within. He held it at arm's length in the hall, turning it over and checking for any liquid filth on the outside. No matter how he turned it, the bits inside rolled about like an archaic specimen captured by a zoologist. When he was finally satisfied he wouldn't have to wash his clothes for touching it, he tucked it under his arm and placed a call to EVE.

"Hello, Mr Blackstone, how can I help?" The AI's voice was cool and smooth, too smooth.

Elliot started walking through the winding hall, passing by dozens of offices both named and unlabelled. He was in the guts of a tower and half the walls hid structure or utilities, the capillaries of life that supported the upper floors. The air swung between humid and dry, hot and cold. Pipes vibrated and unknown machinery grinded to form the city equivalent of a rainforest chorus. The only upside of the location was the bitrate of his internet connection. "I need to get a neural implant cracked and examined."

"Do you have just cause?"

"The owner is dead, I'm trying to find his killer."

"Are you referring to Mr Azir's implant?"

Elliot shouldered through a door and into a stairwell. The nearest train station was four stories straight up. He sighed and started up the flights. "Yeah."

"Decrypting that will have to go to a judge for review."

That stopped Elliot in his tracks. "Why?"

"The Heartsteel Corporation has a privacy flag set on all neural implants of their employees. Their proprietary software is protected from unwarranted search."

Elliot stood there with a phone to his ear so long someone actually walked down the hall and had to squeeze by him. "What? They can do that? It's on his implant. He died. This is part of an active investigation."

"Technically he didn't own that implant. I am actually obligated to inform you that it should be returned to the Heartsteel Corporation."

Elliot hung up on her and looked at the bloody jar again. Before he could think of a less-than-legal option to crack it open, his phone vibrated in his hand. His wife's name popped up on it. He winced and accepted the call. "Hi, Amara."

"So, it's been a day." She sounded like she hadn't slept all night. Given it was only eight in the morning, that was a reasonable guess.

"My boss didn't waste any time in putting me back to use. You don't want to see what I'm holding right now."

"That's probably good. Things are tense here, to say the least. We don't really know what Nelson is going to do right now. We're rescheduling events and trying to practice without him. I don't know who everyone is going to side with here. It's a mess."

"I didn't think me showing up to cook and clean would make this kind of mess."

"It's my fault. I should have let people know from the beginning but now it's gone so long the blowback might be really bad. There's no avoiding it now. I just hope my career isn't destroyed by it."

"Well, if there's anything I can do... until then, there's a serial killer for me to track down."

She didn't respond. When he finally made it to the top of the steps and out to the train station, he could hear voices in the background, some of the other content creators she was collaborating with. She said, "I have to go. Text me or something."

The line went dead as Elliot stepped onto the train. Everyone aboard took one look at his uniform and shifted away from him. They all left him completely alone as he stared at his phone and rode the train back to HQ.

Medical Prohibition

2140/07/15

Clyde's first real assignment came after two weeks of training, and seemed to be nothing more than a bullshit job. He was given a partner and the two of them were left overnight next to a piece of factory machinery that had sheared a man's arm off the day before. The whole thing was decommissioned temporarily, and no threat to anything but Clyde's sense of smell. He didn't really understand what the machine was; some kind of die press but with heating and cooling and signs warning about electromagnetic hazards. The plant foreman told him what the material was, but the name went in one ear and out the other.

All that mattered was an accident had occurred and no one was to touch the thing until an insurance-authorized inspector showed up the next day. The fact that blood was congealing on lubricated surfaces and the whole device would need a refit because of the delay meant nothing to anybody, least of all to Clyde's paycheck.

His partner, the man showing him the ropes, had his feet kicked up on a commandeered table. He hadn't introduced himself by a name but rather by his number: 336-730. The braided beard and neck tattoos were more memorable to Clyde's mind, if not for his neural implant superimposing the ID across the man's face. "Normally we can smoke," 336-730 said.

"Let me guess, company-provided smoke sticks?" Clyde responded.

"Of course, to go with your company breakfast and your company energy drink," 336-730 said.

"The breakfast ain't bad, but their energy drinks have started tasting sour or something. It burns my tongue."

His partner laughed. "That's the pineapple juice. Tastes good at first, but they don't want you drinking too much in case you have an energy crash on the job. They've got stim-patches if you really need a pick-me-up."

"Oh, because it would be so horrible if I were to fall asleep right now," Clyde said, gesturing to the empty factory floor. With the line shut down, all the workers were on unpaid leave. All the other machines were idle too. It was the two of them and nothing else until their proximity alarm went off.

The system flashed light into their vision and beeped, pointing them directly at the intruder. Both of them leapt to their feet, hands going to the non-lethal weapons at their hips as they prowled over, confused. They had a dozen sensors spread out, far more reliable than their own ears, but the one that had gone off wasn't hidden in the least. It wasn't a crawl space where a camera drone might sneak in, and it wasn't a fire-escape hatch, it was just the hall to the bathroom and they could see it from their seats. Nobody was there.

No human rather.

A black and white calico cat stared at them with a rat dangling from its maw. For a moment, the predator appraised them with gleaming eyes, then darted off and through another motion sensor. Both of them laughed as the semi-feral thing scampered off.

"You know, I used to have a cat," 336-730 said as they walked back to their chairs.

Clyde asked, "You had one? Or it lived near you and took your food?"

"It used to sleep in my lap while I was in VR."

Clyde tried to settle into his chair, but the rasp of ventilation pipes had taken on an eerie tone in his mind. "What happened to it?"

336-730 shrugged. "One day, I was gunna ask my girl for monogamy. I spent two hundred credits on lobster for us. Real, genuine crustacean, not the genetic freaks you can find for cheap. I had just taken it out of the oven and the damn thing stole both tails and ate them."

Clyde shook his head. "Expensive taste for a cat."

"So, I killed the cat."

Clyde sat there, his head pivoting back over to look at his partner. The two of them were alone in the factory and had only met earlier that day. They were coworkers, so he wanted to get along with the man, but he had to clarify. "I'm sorry, you did what?"

Before 336-730 could answer, the proximity sensors went off again. Both of them turned, but did not leap up again. They leisurely checked which sensor was the one that had gone off and tried to check it without standing up. There wasn't supposed to be any danger of people showing up, at least not intentionally, but when they couldn't see the sensor from their seats, they wandered over.

The way the assembly line was laid out, every machine station had a drop loader with an access hall for the autonomous carts. The only way for a human to get into there–where drones and heavy boxes could come flying in at any time–was through one of several locked gates. 336-730 had the master key and jammed it into the lock so they could go check out the sensor that had gone off. "I bet a box fell," he said.

"Wouldn't we have heard a box fall?" Clyde asked, ducking around some of the moveable shelves and picking his way to the backside of the improvised amputation device. 336-730 took the direct path and his shoulders were brushing either side of the fenced hall, so Clyde squeezed around a storage cart. His own boot tripped another motion detector. He was in the process of trying to flag it as a false alarm when he heard shuffling of cloth.

Clyde looked down and saw a shadow that moved. "What the fuck?"

Then it bolted. Whatever it was scrambled. Hands and feet started kicking and grabbing at anything to pull itself away. Clyde had only seen it to be a person by the time 336-730 vaulted a stack of plastic sheets and landed on the far side, cutting off their escape. The person yelped, getting up to their feet and bolting the other way–right into Clyde.

Clyde threw open a gate–not locked on the backside–and slammed it into the interloper hard enough to knock them on their ass. Only then did he see it was a scrawny teenager dressed in black like a mall ninja. The getup made his face look like a full moon in the night, except for the shiny green camera he had for an eye. Clyde's neural implant spotted it as fast as he did, immediately commanding him to bag the kid with a wi-fi blocker.

The spy, journalist, thief, the whatever-he-was kid scrambled away until his back hit a storage crate and he gave up. "Alright, alright, I give up," the kid said.

Clyde shook his head. "You fucked up, is what you did," he said as he pulled the metal-laced bag out of his pocket, just big enough to go around a head.

"It's the only way Callum is going to get justice!" the kid shouted as he put his hands up. "The safety bars had rusted, they broke when he leaned on them and the press didn't stop. That's the company's fault. They have to compensate him but they're going to just bury it and throw him out on the street."

"Not my problem, kid," Clyde said and shoved the bag over his head. It was perfectly breathable, but he wouldn't be able to call for help with his neural implant. If the kid was livestreaming out of his eye, that would die too.

"You're a tool of the corporations, don't you see that? I hope they're paying you enough for this, to be their nameless muscle they use to crack down on people trying to get justice. Heartsteel, right? Everyone knows you thugs are the worst of the bunch. I've seen gangs be more lenient!"

Clyde considered several responses in his head. Heartsteel was playing him plenty, they were also protecting the standard judicial process of getting justice, and plenty of gangs were more poser than killer. One by one he discarded them as pointless, and fished out a pair of handcuffs to restrain the kid with. The metal felt cold and strange in his fingers because he had always figured the only time he'd touch a pair would be on the receiving end.

Now, he had the power, but Heartsteel hadn't actually taught him how to properly use the little manacles. Cuffing the kid to a shelf seemed like a bad idea. His gut said he should put the kid's hands behind his back so he couldn't grab anything, but one of his memories said it was better to cuff in front so the hands could be seen.

336-730 stepped around the corner as Clyde was thinking about it, and moved up without a word. The way the self-appointed journalist was sitting, his back to a crate and hands up, his right arm was beyond the edge of the crate. 336-730 kicked him in the elbow and snapped his humerus in half. One of the broken edges ripped through his skin as the kid fell over screaming. Blood squirted across them as the kid's arm flopped.

"There," 336-730 said, standing over the kid with his hands in his pockets. "Now the meat wagon will deal with him and we don't have to."

Clyde dropped the handcuffs and stepped back. "What the fuck man? You're gonna get fired for that."

"Nah, it's fine. I only did it after you had the bag on. Easy-peasy, no records. No way he can afford a lawyer, so what's he going to do?"

Clyde stood there, staring at his senior coworker who had killed a cat out of spite and was walking back to his chair to wait for a private ambulance team to deal with the problem he had created. Then the screaming of the injured kid muted. The whole world went muffled as his neural implant's new program took hold of his attention. "Thank you for your hard work tonight, 325-930," the program said, its smiling face blotting out his sight. "Once you are off-shift, please enjoy eight hours of rest.

Your training schedule for tomorrow has been eliminated. Instead, we invite you to a health and wellness session with our onstaff professionals who will guide you through a number of exercises and routines to boost your wellbeing. We know that work can be difficult and the last thing we would want would be for our valued employees to be negatively affected by the duties required of them. If you would like to opt out of this program, you may manually reschedule your training classes."

The next day, the psych screening after 336-730 broke the guy's arm was a joke. Doctor outright said just about everything had already been checked through his neural implant. Pulse, anxiety, sleep patterns. Clyde was all smiles and thumbs up. The checkup was more like a routine physical, checking his blood work for stress indicators and such. They still gave him the day off to relax.

His brother was busy studying for exams, so he didn't want to interrupt Johnny, and his mother couldn't get her shift off from the mailroom. That left him alone at the company cantina. The bartenders surprised him. Well curved and barely dressed, the only issue with them was the censor bars over half their faces whenever he looked at them. He was trying to disable his neural implant, to kill the program or do anything so he could actually see the people he was looking at, but Heartsteel's proprietary program ignored him.

The bar Heartsteel operated somehow felt oppressively open. There was only one wall, the counter shaped like a big U, and open park space surrounded it with plastic turf and no tables. Anyone could have drifted away, but a soft focus of light kept everyone glued to the stools and the counters. They all leaned towards the beer taps and watched the myriad of televisions with Arena fights, War Game footage, reports of gang shootings, and Heartsteel's internal news program rambling about employee satisfaction and new work contracts. None of the televisions kept Clyde's attention.

He was halfway through a beer and almost to the point of peeling his skin patch off to manually disable his neural implant when he finally saw a woman's face. She was young, dressed cute, and not censored.

In fact, her entire presence seemed to be ignored by the machine in his head. No ID, no organization charts popping up, nothing. Clyde flagged the bartender down and ordered an Invite. A few minutes later, to obscure whose it was, the bikini wearing bartender strolled over to the girl with a basic mix drink and offered it.

The girl shrugged and took it.

Clyde got up from his side of the bar and walked over before anyone else got ideas. He couldn't tell if anyone else was looking at her because the other men at the bar had their eyes covered by User IDs, but he didn't want to take chances. Going with the first thing to come to mind, he sat down next to her and said, "You've got more fashion than the rest of the cantina combined."

The girl turned and put an elbow on the counter as she looked him over. While he was in company fatigues, she had on shorts that exposed plenty of her slender legs, along with a faux denim jacket that matched the bucket cap hat perched atop her head. She almost looked like she had stepped out of an advertisement, but the augmented cattail hanging between jacket and shorts was perfectly unique. "It helps that I'm not contractually obligated to look like a prisoner."

"Most people say a uniform looks good on a man."

"Only when the uniform is a respectable one. Uniforms don't do anything for trash men."

He smirked. "That's because you don't know how much money a trash man gets paid. Not just anybody can go in the nastiest corners of the ghetto to plunge out burst bags of bloated bile. It's just too bad they don't let them bring flamethrowers to make the work easier."

After a moment she smirked back at him. "Burst bags of bloated bile? Where'd you get that line?"

"From my sister actually. She's doing her service now, but she had a big poetry phase back in school. Some of her lines stuck with me."

Something in her smile changed from flirty to surprised. "Not the answer I was expecting."

"I'm just glad a few good things stuck with me for all the trash I had to wade through when she was learning, you know? She spent an entire month obsessed with limericks and let me tell you; there ain't no fucking men from Nantucket anymore."

The girl with the cat tail laughed and sipped her Invite–rum and cola by the smell of it– before she said, "What's your name?"

"Clyde. Can I get yours?" he asked, signaling the bartender for a fresh beer. The imposition of censorship on the bartender's face made her seem like an NPC out of a simulation, like someone he shouldn't be talking to.

"Clyde, huh? You must be new here."

"Just started a few days ago. This is my first drink at the cantina actually."

She held her drink up for a toast. "Congratulations. You're the first person to actually give me a name instead of a number when I ask. My name's Claire."

"Are you new here too?"

"Oh, I don't work here."

Clyde frowned and sipped his drink. The two of them were sitting in a corporate cantina, inside a tower almost entirely owned by Heartsteel or at least other similarly locked-down companies. Just to get inside required three security checks by a security company no less. And to top it off, his hiring contract had been very specific that visitors were not allowed, due to the thin walls, the small rooms, and so on. It was bad for morale, they said. Go outside to visit with people they said.

"So, how did you get in here?" he asked.

Claire giggled and drained her drink. "Clyde, I'm your client. I'm the one paying your bills, don't you know? Well, one of your clients anyway. The people I represent won't be using every single one of you foot soldiers."

"And you're spending your time... between meetings? Getting a drink?"

Claire twisted in her seat and crossed one leg over the other. Something had changed in her demeanor and become as catlike as her tail. "Do you know why I like Heartsteel?" she asked, and continued without letting him answer. "It's the privacy. It's a real selling point. See? Watch this." She did something with her neural implant.

Between one blink and the next, Clyde lost sight of her. She didn't vanish from his sight, but she was occluded completely, like a sheet of darkness had been slammed between the two of them. Green text appeared on it along with a rough outline. "VIP," it said. Then it vanished again.

Claire grinned. "I can have as much privacy as I want when I come and go from here. Free drinks too. It was nice to meet you, Clyde."

He frowned and thought about asking for her number, but he could already hear Mohamed yelling at him for harassing their employer. He stayed at the bar and tried to clear his tab. He was thinking about movies to watch or games to play, not quite feeling like socializing anymore, when the bartender came back. He couldn't see her eyes, but he could see the confused frown on her face.

"Your account was denied, 325-930. Says you have a medical prohibition?" she said.

"No I don't. Did you get the wrong number or something?"

She scoffed. "Babe, I'm not the one who puts IDs in. The machine knew it was you and the machine says that you're not allowed to drink. Doctor's orders."

Clyde frowned. The doctor hadn't told him he was sick. "Well, how am I supposed to pay then?"

The bartender shrugged. "I'll have to just comp them. A medical alert should have come up in the first place. Lucky you, I guess. Sort of. Silver lining at least."

Clyde stood up from the counter and walked to one of the darker corners of the indoor park as he checked his message inbox. Sure enough, there was a high priority alert from the medical doctor–not the neurist–telling him to report for additional testing first thing in the morning. The screening tests had come back with positive indicators of stage 1 cancer and they had to do a full body scan to find the tumors.

The world fell out from him. The knowledge itself was like a cancer that ate away his insides and immediately left him hollow and cold. The message hadn't introduced the idea gently. He could barely grapple with it. Clyde shuffled back to his apartment but he didn't sleep. He pulled his bed down and laid down across it, but he couldn't even close his eyes. He had cancer, the same thing that killed his father.

He told himself that there was a big difference between him and his late father. He had insurance; corporate insurance. He could get it treated so long as he kept the job. Maybe even get a new organ to replace the cancerous one. They had the technology. It was just a matter of money, and that was what insurance was for.

Most of all, as he laid in the darkness feeling the hours crawl by, he knew that he could not tell his mother. The worry would kill her.

14 |

The CEO

2140/10/19

Elliot woke to two messages, one from Amara asking if he could come back to the party pad, and another from Cinder telling him he had to show up to Heartsteel's headquarters to meet with CEO Robert Dixie, head of Heartsteel. Vice-commander Chase had been copied on the second email.

When he arrived at Heartsteel's HQ, he was in full winter uniform. Late fall winds whipped hard and cold between the thin peaks of Alpha, but broke against the heavy wool of his police cloak. At times, the winter adornment made him feel like a child playing pretend, like a caped crusader; but, wool was as warm as it was rare. What was more, he hoped it would make him forgettable, because he wasn't the only person meeting with the CEO.

Seraphina dressed in what technically fit Californian augment-inclusive code. To make room for her tail, she was allowed to wear a pleated skirt along with thermal leggings, not much different from what she had shown up to the homestead in. Between that, the tight jacket and leather boots, she was like holding a floodlight next to a matchstick.

"Good to see you again, Blackstone," she said as they met in the rooftop garden that Heartsteel used as an entry plaza. Below them, the city was still waking up and moving, each layer energizing at a different rate. Life itself seemed rarified on the eightieth floor.

I wonder what Cinder would look like in a uniform like that? Amara used to pull the look off well. Too bad it's this bitch.

"You look like you're shooting a commercial. If you unbuttoned a bit more, you'd look like you were shooting a porno," he said, and marched to the door.

"If I unbuttoned, I'd fit right in with their mascot," she said as the welcoming computer booted up.

Elliot stopped in his tracks when the virtual girl popped up to welcome them. What a twenty-something girl with a hoodie zipped to right beneath her breasts had to do with a security company was beyond his imagination. "CEO Dixie can meet with you in just a moment, please enjoy a cup of coffee and some pastries while you wait," the mascot said as the deadbolts popped open.

Seraphina snickered at his reaction. "You're a fucking prude, you know that?" she asked as he pushed through the door.

"You don't know anything about me," he said, scanning the waiting room. Elevators lined one wall. Bathrooms and halls were on the other, while a grand mahogany double door stood between him and the CEO's office. There were cameras and access panels which he knew concealed defense turrets. He also spotted the refreshment table. The smell of fresh donuts registered in his brain before the auto-cooker did.

Seraphina swept forward and cut him off to punch in an order for a double-glazed bear claw. "I know," she said as the machine pissed coffee into a mug for her. "That you're a liar. You're a killer pretending to be a softie, or maybe you're a softie pretending to be a killer. Actually, what I think is you were one and now you're the other. You don't know yourself and you're rather scared your coworkers will figure it out before you do."

Elliot glared at her as she gingerly picked up her steaming pastry, fresh frosting dripping to the floor as she took a bite out of it. "Did you ever hear the saying that everyone projects? Or do you not actually listen to people? I swear you just wait to hear yourself talk," he said as he ordered a basic glazed donut. "You don't even feel guilt, do you? Culpability? Anything like that at all?"

"They wouldn't have me working undercover if I did." She licked her lips clean and smiled.

Wyatt and I wouldn't have gone to Cali if you had acted on the info you were sitting on.

Heartsteel's mascot interrupted them before Elliot said anything further, letting them know that the CEO could meet with them. Both of them devoured their donuts and wiped their faces off before the door swung open. They each had an obnoxious moment of gesturing for the other to head in first. Eventually, Elliot gave her the pointless satisfaction and moved in to meet the man a serial killer had declared to be doomed.

The blood hadn't been wiped off the window. The flaking streaks of maroon still marred the floor-to-ceiling panel behind Dixie's desk. For his part, the CEO didn't seem to mind. "Officers, welcome, have a seat." Then he looked at Seraphina and grimaced in a way that left his eyes cold and calculating.

Seraphina returned his stare with a carefree smile.

"A pleasure, Mr Dixie. Would you mind?" Elliot asked, gesturing to the macabre mess.

"Go right ahead. That madman hit my window with a severed hand. Can you believe it?"

I saw the note in the report, but not the pictures. This is too much blood for just a hand.

"Doesn't this concern you?" Elliot asked, strolling over to the window and looking it over.

Dixie spun his chair about to face him and shook his head. "Not in the least. That's two inches of reinforced polycarbonate. You'd need a rail gun to go through it and I have it on good authority that EVE can lock the firing mechanisms on those."

If she knows about it.

Elliot turned away from the window and saw Seraphina already seated, legs crossed and cat tail flicking over one of the chair's arms. She had left him the chair closer to Dixie. "Do you have any idea who this man is, Mr Dixie?"

The CEO folded his hands together and smirked as Elliot sat down. "Officer, I'm not only the face–well, the human face–of this corporation, but a prominent figure in the Buffalo Party. It's not like I have specific legislation in my name, but there are always extremists who need a target. I want you to realize that I am in charge of a private security operation. I am well aware of how to protect myself, the ways bad actors could target me, and so on. To answer your question, the list of people who would enjoy seeing me dead would take us all day just to recite."

Seraphina laughed. "How about we cut to the chase then. Rather than us playing twenty questions, how about you just tell us what you need us to do?"

Elliot's skin prickled. The cloak hid the tensing of his muscles as he kept himself still and quiet.

Dixie nodded. "You're here for the same reason I still have that blood on the window. I need to look persecuted by this. I need to come across as a martyr. Not just me, but my company. I don't mean to imply that it's a good thing my employees are being hunted down, but it's my fiduciary responsibility to make the absolute best of it that I can. I want to rewrite the narrative about Heartsteel and gain a sympathetic ear."

With the judicial system maybe.

Elliot asked, "Could you tell us how you think Hearsteel is currently perceived? I'm not exactly clear what you think we can do for you. We're officers of the military police. Our responsibility is the administration of justice, not media relations."

"Don't worry. I understand. I don't actually want to interfere with your work at all. I'd just like to collect some material from your work."

"What kind of material?" Elliot asked.

"Video and audio," the CEO responded, and pushed a small box across his desk. Elliot recognized the packaging immediately–a standard recording drone. The only thing special about it was that it was marked as having an extended battery and the factory sealing tape had been broken. "When you're at the various crime scenes, I want that following you and recording. The data will be sent to my media relations specialists. We'll chop it up, put on some narration, some sad music, the whole works. I'll even make sure they censor your faces from it. Don't need to tangle your personal lives up with this little stunt."

What a load of fucking bullshit.

"I don't think we–"

Seraphina cut Elliot off. "Understood. But, you'll understand that this has to be approved by our superiors, right?"

Dixie turned on her and bowed his head. "Of course, of course. You're working with Ford right now?"

She smiled. "Ford is in charge of the GLR. We're reporting to Vice-commander Chase."

Dixie's face wrinkled. "Chase? The one who... Right. How about I get him on the phone?" he said, and typed in the command to his desk computer. Elliot barely had time to straighten up and look at the video camera before the call connected. Thankfully, it was voice only. "Good morning, this is Rob Dixie."

"Mr Dixie," Vice-commander Chase said. His voice was firm and tired, unmistakable to Elliot. "What do you need?"

The CEO lounged in his chair and twiddled his thumbs. "I'm seated across from two of your officers. Badge numbers... E11107 and–"

"You can call me Sera," she said.

"Right," Dixie said. "You're on speaker phone with them by the way. I understand these are the two that have been assigned to track down this serial killer I've got after me."

Not by choice.

"That's right," Chase said.

"I want to give them a recording drone for my own records, both legal and PR. You know, it's possible that our internal analysis will turn up something useful to bringing this madman to justice–getting him off the streets."

Vice-commander Chase hesitated, and Elliot hoped the man was as disgusted by the lies as he was. Then his boss said, "Officers, please co-operate with Mr Dixie. It's a reasonable request."

The CEO grinned at them. "Wonderful. That's all, Mr Chase. See you at the dinner, yes?"

"See you there," Chase said, and hung up the phone.

With glances all around, the two officers quietly took their dismissal as well as the drone. Elliot tucked it under his arm and ignored the computer mascot as he walked back to the garden. Seraphina pitched her coffee cup and stretched her arms over her head the moment she got out. "Well then," the feline-wannabe said. "Are you excited to get to work on a high profile case like this? You might get promoted again and you'll stop being an E rank."

Elliot could have continued on to the trains and gotten away from her, but he stopped and looked at her. "I don't want to be promoted. Why is that so hard for you to understand? I'm just like ninety percent of people in this city."

She put a hand on her hip and shook her head. "For the man who saved my life, this is very disappointing talk coming out of you, Thomas." She enunciated his name hard, like she was speaking a magic password.

Probably because I have my first name hidden everywhere.

"I like working in a level where I can make a difference. This? This doesn't matter. Paying back political favors is all it is. This is worse than nothing in my opinion."

Seraphina rolled her eyes. "I forgot, you like making house calls, don't you? Going around for domestic disputes, picking up drunks from bars, that sort of thing?"

"The kind of work where I get a thank you at the end. Where maybe someone will think better of the world because of it."

"California broke you, didn't it?"

Elliot stared down at his boots. "A lot of things broke me."

"I guess reporting you and getting you demoted two ranks didn't help, did it?"

He glared at her and walked off.

15

Riot At The Chemical Plant

2140/09/15

Clyde's work for Heartsteel became haunted by his visits to the doctors. More often than not, he didn't even see a person. They sent him to rooms where machines told him how to strip, where to put sensors and when to stand up or sit down. They blasted him with x-rays, with MRIs, with infra-red pulses, and more he didn't recognize. Every time he left the automated office he left with the same bottle of pills. Two little blue balls he had to take with his next meal.

The reports to him came weekly, and never improved. The numbers weren't running out of control, allegedly because the pills were immune boosters and should facilitate his own body cleaning it up. The cancer wasn't going away though, and they wouldn't give him anything stronger because he was neither dying nor on their premier insurance plan.

Three weeks after the diagnosis he had quit smoking. The nicotine patches weren't digesting in his body the same, leaving him with stomach pain, headaches, and no patience for anyone. When Mohamed offered him a mask to go with his uniform—reinforced with padding and anti-cut wires—he had taken it. The program in his implant didn't mind everyone wearing masks. Their User IDs still appeared where their faces should have been, just as easy to identify as before.

Assignments blurred together. Sitting at a train station that smelled like a gym locker room. Sitting in a factory spitting out socks for the military. Sitting in an evacuated apartment block that still echoed with alarms. When the program told him that a pair of employees were delinquent, he marched over to get them. There was a strike going on. Wage negotiations with the union were predicated on continued productivity. The program told him to get them back to the factory line so he told them to quit smoking and get back to work.

One of the two got in his face and gestured with the cigarette. He waved it in Clyde's face as he said, "The sealant machine is broken. Delays made it clog. Production... production ain't going to happen today. Tell that to your boss, tough guy."

The program had been set to a heightened sensitivity. Mohamed had explained that too, but Clyde had only absorbed the simplest mechanisms. It flagged people who were violent and dangerous. The gentle green silhouette on the smoker had shifted to yellow as his implant communicated back to Heartsteel. When the cigarette ash landed on Clyde's shirt, a wreath of red flames exploded around the factory worker.

Danger. Legally verifiable and exculpatory danger. Clyde suddenly had the cure for his headache, his irritation, his stress and worry.

He beat the factory worker bloody. Teeth scattered across the floor like spilled beans. The first person to come running over to help was flagged red too and a security woman, 339-184, jabbed a taser into his thigh. They fell to the ground hard, screaming until 339-184 stomped her boot into his gut. He doubled over and coughed without moving much after that. The system downgraded him back to yellow.

In the aftermath, Clyde couldn't tell if he was sweating, bleeding, or maligned with some other kind of liquid filth. It felt to him like his cancer was oozing out through his skin, that he was wearing it on his sleeves.

It wasn't until that night, at some unknown hour beneath an LED sky, that he started to wonder if the guy had been a threat. The doctor's prohibition on drinking had been lifted, in fact the alcohol was treated as a painkiller. He was sort of a dying man, and Heartsteel wanted to be kind to him. So they paid for his drinks and the faceless bartenders poured them double strong. The liquor burned and scratched an itch within him that the cigarettes had left behind.

Drunk and feeling like his insides were nothing but cancerous mush already, he sent Johnny a message. Only after did he see the time on the clock, that the sun was nearly up and his little brother had no business being awake, and then he got a response regardless.

Johnny asked, "You found another job yet?"

Clyde didn't know what that was supposed to mean and told his brother the money was plenty good. The part about needing the medical insurance, that he was sick and dying like their father, he kept to himself. The words he didn't dare let out, he drowned with another mix of vodka and energy drink.

Johnny said, "You need to find a job with a company that ain't evil. The money ain't worth it."

Clyde wanted to smash his glass on the counter, to hear the glass shatter and the tinkle of ice across the floor. He could hear the gasps, the fear, the way people would recoil from him. None of that happened as he kept his actions tame. Johnny didn't know what he was saying, didn't know how much he benefited from Clyde's work. Johnny was just a kid, not yet an adult, and couldn't be expected to know.

"What's got you worked up?" Claire asked as she took the seat next to him holding a fishbowl with a pink swirly straw sticking out of it. There were no fish in the goblet of course, just ice capsules with liquor seeping into the sugary drink. "Is it the cancer?"

Clyde felt the anger flow out of him, his mind shifting gears. "Yeah, pretty much. I fucking miss smoking. It's bad. Real bad. Patches don't do anything for me. I can't sleep—not without this stuff."

She grinned at him. "Is that your way of saying you've got an oral fixation?"

He balked. "Hell no. What are you even doing here right now?" None of his bosses had said anything about him knowing Claire. The absence of response was so stark he wondered if they even knew. Maybe the censorship program had hidden it.

"Here to prep for the big project tomorrow."

Clyde checked the time again. "It is tomorrow."

She shot a finger gun at him. "Sleep is for the weak. And by weak, I mean people who don't have a prescription for sleep spray."

"I ain't ever heard of sleep spray."

"Want some?" She pulled a nasal spray bottle out from her pocket and held it out.

He plucked it from her hand and tried to read the label, but there was no label. He sprayed a blast into his nose and sniffed. "I didn't want to go to bed anyway."

She leaned close enough to him that he could smell her cherry perfume. It brought back memories of deployment, up by the Isles. "Good, because this way you won't miss sign up. The work is juicy today. Heartsteel will be keeping the peace at Sigurd Chemical Plant."

Clyde didn't know if it was the words, or if the drug was already working through his system, but his thoughts cleared. The inside of his nose burned, but there was no buzz in his head. No vague anxiety. His heart didn't race and there was no tension in his eyes. Completely unlike fighting sleep with caffeine, he simply woke up.

And still he couldn't believe that Heartsteel had a defense contract for the primary nitrate producing plant in Bastion. Most of the city's–most of the continent's–gunpowder came out of Sigurd, and rumor claimed a hundred other foul things too. It was directly under the thumb of the military.

"Who did you say you work for?" he asked.

"The people with the big bank accounts. Hope to see you there, Clyde," she said, and planted a kiss on his cheek before vanishing with her drink. He couldn't express what was wrong, but he could tell something would go wrong if he went to Sigurd.

He tried to get up to his feet and chase after her, but the nasal spray had only woken him up. He was still hammered and in nicotine withdrawal. He didn't even remember her taking it back from him.

Hours later, when the security teams were getting lined up and assigned their duties for the day, Clyde tried to tell Mohamed, "I'm not feeling well. I'm sick. Got cancer. I don't think I should go out today."

The older man shook his head, making his braided beard waggle. "Cancer ain't contagious and your vitals are fine. If you don't want to be fired, get in line."

He filed onto the transport train and suited up with more armor than the military had given him. He had enough polycarbonate hidden in his clothes to feel like a medieval knight. While everyone else slapped their helmets on and became nothing more than numbers, Clyde left his off. The ride was halfway across Bastion and his mind elsewhere.

He searched the internet for news on the Sigurd Chemical Plant. No state affiliated news site had a headline. No independent news site did either, until he searched for protests. Then he found pictures that he recognized as outside the plant but without the text ever mentioning it. His stomach twisted, the night's drinking turning into a hangover instantly.

EVE was purging the internet of whatever was going on at Sigurd Chemical Plant, and it was so bad they wanted a private company to take the bad press. He couldn't even find what they were protesting over.

When the train arrived at one of the massive commuter stations for the chemical plant, his neural implant cut out. It gave him an alert that due to heightened security, all non-essential data traffic was suspended. Step by step, he marched out in line with all the other people Heartsteel had scalped from other companies and corporations because they had violent tendencies. His implant told him exactly where to stand and how to square off with a jeering crowd.

He couldn't see any of their faces. The implant kept throwing popups and notifications. It leapt at every raised fist, at every bottle of beer and sign handle. It flagged every possible weapon and tracked hundreds of thrown pieces of trash. It labeled eggs, milkshakes, and empty cans. The complete flood of information blinded him as silhouettes danced from green to yellow.

The voice of Heartsteel's mascot spoke in his mind, cutting through the noise of anger before him. "The VIPs will be arriving momentarily. Ensure their safety."

A waypoint indicator appeared in his vision, and for a moment, Clyde looked away. Another train had arrived and men in prison jumpsuits began to file off. They sneered back at the crowd, shaking their cuffs at them and sticking their middle fingers up. Clyde understood what the chemical plant was doing to keep up production through a labor strike just as something struck him in the head. It was hard and heavy, enough to smack his head aside and ring his senses.

When he looked back at the crowd, the yellow silhouettes began to turn red in his vision and everyone else's.

16

What Happened In Cali

2140/10/18

Elliot took the drone back to headquarters, fully intent on activating it, as he had been instructed, and then putting it to sleep permanently. Like the standard police models, it had tracking software along with its array of cameras. The onboard computer managed collision avoidance while WPS tracking kept it close to him. Specifically, the drone kept close to his phone, because he didn't have a neural implant. No sooner did he try to lock it in a drawer for the night than his phone told him that if it strayed too far from him it would automatically signal distress back to Heartsteel.

He was sneering at it when Ram walked by with a tablet under her arm. She stopped to ask, "You got stuck on the murder case, didn't you?"

He didn't need to respond to that. He just pursed his lips and hung his head. There was another thing besides the drone on his desk that was less than pleasant: Azir's extracted neural implant. "I have to find a cryptologist of some sort."

Ram followed his gaze, saw the bloody jar, and winced. "Is that what I think that is?"

"It's evidence in the murder case I'm stuck on."

"Well, that's disgusting."

"It's also our best crack at direct identification right now. The one who was beheaded, his implant was fried according to the coroner. Not sure how that happened. Gotta investigate that too, but frankly I just want a picture of the guy's face and I hope he wasn't wearing one of those masks. Knowing my luck..."

Ram's eyes searched the ceiling. "Uh, I might know somebody who can help."

Is that a risk I gamble on? I think that's a risk I gamble on.

He handed her the jar and said, "Expense the bill as miscellaneous and make sure they understand not to talk about what's on it."

Ram gingerly took the jar with two fingers, holding it at arm's length. She set it down on her own desk and fetched some napkins to clean the outside. Elliot checked the tacky feeling on his fingertips and sniffed the preservative. Before he could walk to the bathroom and clean up, Cinder strolled by.

"Blackstone, my office, now."

Cinder's office was the largest in the building and not just because she was in charge. The room had enough space for a hologram projector in the rare event that one of the Tribunal, or someone like Vice-commander Chase, wanted to speak with her 'in-presence' without leaving their own offices. For once, the projectors were all cleared off and booted on.

She must have been speaking with Chase. I can't believe how much attention he's giving this.

After he shut the door and the noise cancellers kicked in to isolate their conversation, Cinder said, "I think it's time we had a proper talk about what happened in California."

That's not good.

Elliot sat down across from her, glanced at the hologram projector, and asked, "What about it?"

"That's how you met Sera, isn't it? I need to know what your issue with her is. I don't even know who that girl is, but she's got more pull than I do."

Elliot sneered. "Woman, not girl. She's in her forties. The reason she looks so young is because she's gene-modded. Partial neoteny, extended telomeres, a dozen other tweaks as the geneticists try to brew up an immortal human. And before you ask, no, she's not immortal. Doctors think she'll die of compounded cancer in less than a decade. She was working in New California, under Vice-Commander Chan, when I went over there. I found her shot and took her to a hospital."

Cinder's stern expression softened as she leaned back in her chair and listened. "So, she lost half her life span to look young? Rough trade for a newborn but I know plenty of hags who'd jump for it."

Elliot shrugged. "Depends on how good we get at curing cancer, doesn't it? For her, it won't be as easy as just cutting out tumors and replacing organs. Or so she told me."

"That's a lot to confess to someone with so much animosity..."

He folded his arms and leaned back in his chair as well. "There wasn't animosity while I was in the ICU with her. That came later."

Cinder stared back at him, her eyebrows raising up her face until she said, "Ah."

"Yeah, ah."

Almost every single report for police activity in North America was recorded and produced automatically based on surveillance footage, the comments of the officers, and scraped data from computer systems. It was the main perk of having a camera drone in his pocket. Sometimes a human still filled their report out manually and the difference in details was always immediately obvious. Namely that there weren't any.

Seraphina's report read along the lines of, "Officers Wyatt and Blackstone arrived at 52242 Unity Drive, District 1 at sunset, pursuant to an active criminal investigation. Upon hearing gunshots, they forced entry to the residence. Internal security measures activated automatically and the officers engaged with lethal force. The homeowner was killed in the exchange. Due to irrecoverable damage to their computer systems, all other investigations into Theodore Bellman have been deemed impossible to pursue and terminated. Proper disciplinary action suggested for officers Wyatt and Blackstone." Vice-Commander Chan had appended a demand that he and Lizard be expelled.

They were only demoted.

Cinder put her arms up behind her head and said, "Well, I guess there are limits to what you know and don't know, Eve."

Elliot's head snapped up, and over to the hologram projector as it came to life. Eve's avatar appeared as though she were leaning against Cinder's desk. Her hair was darker than usual and done up in loops. Part of Elliot wondered if she was taking cues from Fumi Sokolov's fashion, but the concern on her face made him sink even further into his chair. He said, "So you've been watching me."

She frowned and crossed her arms. "I mean, mostly I've been trying to cross reference a total suspect pool of about ten thousand people to find one human that matches three murder scenes. The department is literally paying to rent excess server space from Mercurial because I have to analyze twenty-four hours of footage from seventy different cameras. But when I'm not wanting to scream at the universe for making human beings too similar to each other, yes. I've been watching you, Blackstone. By the way, why does she keep calling you Thomas?"

Elliot smirked. "She thinks it's my first name."

Cinder wrinkled her nose. "Blackstone, are you going to be able to work with her, or not?"

"If I don't," he said, "she'll track down Wyatt and we'll have a whole new kind of problem, because Wyatt's the one who shot her. He doesn't know I took her to a hospital... I never told him."

She pinched the bridge of her nose. "Alright, clearly, my office was the wrong place to have this conversation. I'm putting a pin in this. That alright with you, Eve?"

The AI sighed. "May as well. Officer Seraphina Roy has been recalled to MPHQ for the next two days on a black project of some kind. She won't be in attendance tomorrow."

"What's tomorrow?" Elliot asked.

"If I can keep you on the case," Cinder said, "tomorrow you'll be going to Heartsteel's training facility and having a look around. Chase got the warrant signed half an hour ago. This killer isn't just going after the CEO. His grudge is with the entire corporation. Which–"

"I don't have access to," Eve said.

Elliot closed his eyes. "So, time for some boots on the ground work."

Cinder said, "You know the drill. I can't spare Ram though. She's on a learning project right now, so you'll have to go by yourself. When I get off shift though, I'm calling you up and we're going somewhere private so you can actually tell me what happened in California. I've let it slide as long as I could, but now I need to know."

"I'm free tonight," Elliot said.

"No, you're not," Eve said. She tilted her head and smirked. "You're already spoken for tonight."

"I am?" he responded, and his phone buzzed.

Amara messaged him asking if he could come back to the streaming pad.

The place was quiet when Elliot arrived. It stank too–no one was taking the trash out. He still had the key to the apartment, so he let himself in, finding it as desolate as a crime scene. He couldn't hear people chatting into headsets, but they might have just been in simulation and doing it there. He walked down the hall, avoided the kitchen, and checked one room after the next. Nico the Giant was asleep in one room, but most were empty.

He found Amara in their assigned bedroom and knocked on the door.

She turned and looked him over. Her hair was a mess that didn't fit with the hyper-vibrant [Zom-Fortress] tank top she had on. She sighed. "You're in uniform."

"Underclothes don't count, do they?" He had on his typical pants, but not the buttoned shirt nor his badge. The only thing that would stand out about his white t-shirt was the quality of the material.

She shrugged. "They would to Nelson, but he's gone, which means we're down a player for the tournament."

"I hope you weren't thinking to swap me in as a replacement."

She laughed and wiped a tear from her eye. She hadn't laughed hard enough to cry, so it must have been stress. "No, actually I think we have that under control. There's a good PR move to be made with this other woman who was late to the party. She's good at the game. Maybe not as good as Nelson, but she's better at defense building than any of us. I figure it's a good trade and the narrative is great. We kicked out a creep who picked through my stuff and brought in a woman who keeps her nose clean."

"That's a good thing, right?"

"If he doesn't find a way to retaliate or something, but it could be good, yeah. I've increased my subscriber count by almost a thousand today alone, so that's good. Everyone else is on my side, your cooking helped."

Elliot laughed. "That's surprising. I'm a terrible cook."

She smirked and stood up. "Their standards are low," she said, and walked over to embrace him. The moment fractured almost as soon as it started. She pulled away from him with a quizzical look. "What's wrong with you? You're tense."

His fingers trailed across her arms and fell to his sides. "I'm being asked to cut my vacation short, by top brass."

She crossed her arms and stood there, the only noise was some machinery from the kitchen. "Well, on the bright side you could get your old rank back."

If only she knew. If only I could explain this mess.

"It's not a good thing. Hell, it's dangerous work. They've got me on... They're asking me to track down a spree killer. Three kills so far that we know of. I have to make a trip and go to the company he's targeting tomorrow."

She frowned and closed the door behind him. The bedroom was small, but it had good chairs set up for VR. She took one and gestured at the other. "If this were something to brag about, you'd have said so by now."

He sat and hung his head. "They want me protecting a pretty bad guy."

"How bad? As bad as the thing with the kids?"

"Not that bad."

She crossed her legs and chewed her knuckle. "Are you comfortable helping this guy?"

It's kind of my job to help him. He's part of the system and I protect the system. The only reason we got away with California was because that banker was obsolete. He was part of the old shell, molted and cast off by the society he created. The ones with power didn't mind him being gone. Dixie is in the here and now.

"I don't know," he said. "I'm going to go figure out a motive tomorrow. I'm hoping that there's no correlation between effectiveness and justification."

"Maybe... We keep this under wraps."

Elliot looked up at her and felt his face set. Extraneous thoughts dwindled and he looked at his wife–how she was tapping her foot and chewing her nail and not looking at him. "You're worried about blowback still?"

"I mean, yeah. It's one thing if you were on vacation and we could control perception, you know? But, if people are going to jump to dig up dirt on you–people do that kind of thing for fun–then it's a bad idea for an active investigation to be going on, right? People will believe whatever they want to believe."

"I took this time off to be here and with you."

She stood up and turned away so she could pace the room, still not looking at him. "Two controversies back to back could get us disqualified. All these expenses would be for nothing. Hell, they'd hold me responsible for the costs. My entire war chest would be empty. I'd have to cancel the merch. Shit, I just pre-ordered a resistance rig. Oh, by the way,

I need to take over the guest bedroom. I think it's time that I just need the whole space as studio space. Nobody ever comes over."

Nobody comes over because you've already destroyed the entire house with your leftover junk. With outfits and obsolete equipment. You've made a trash heap out of our apartment and you barely break even.

Amara didn't care that he didn't respond. She just went on. "This thing's really cool actually. I should show it to you. You'll love it. The whole thing is rigged up to allow body use while in simulation. Not only does it prevent atrophy but it's better than the gym because your implant can numb your physical body. There's maybe some soreness risks but I'd be able to reclaim hours in the day to get back in shape and I'd be so much more confident doing in person events and recordings afterwards. I know you've been watching my waistline plump up and my skin sag and I know it's gross. I see it in the mirror every time I put on makeup and I do appreciate that you haven't made a big deal out of it. I want to change that and I can, if I can just buy this piece of equipment. I can't afford it if this whole team falls apart though. You understand, don't you?"

Money. Right back to money. It's always money. I thought she said she didn't care about the pay cut. So much for that. So she's been lying for the past three years? Ain't that great.

"Well," he said and stood up. "I guess I don't know why I came here."

Amara froze with her back to the wall. Her mouth hung open for a moment. "Well, I didn't know what kind of work you were doing. This is new info, you know? It got dropped in your lap by the sound of it."

"Right, so, if this had been there before I showed up, you would have told me to stay home in the first place, right? That just brings us back to square one, doesn't it? Back to you doing your thing and me doing my thing."

"Honey..."

He put up his hands. "I'm sorry I told you to do something about Nelson. Clearly that was a mistake. I guess I'm just a big fucking problem for you right now, so I'm going to get out of here. I'm not on a proper sleep cycle anyway. Maybe I'll finally listen to Wyatt and hit the gym. That'll be great, won't it?"

"Babe, you can't take it that way."

His hand was nearly to the door handle when his body stopped. He turned on her, nostrils flaring. "Don't! Call me Babe. Bastard's blood, woman, you had an entire fucking mood where you wanted me using your fucking screenname. Don't 'babe' me."

She sneered back at him. "Would you rather I call you Elliot?"

He threw the door open and slammed it shut behind him.

One of Amara's teammates, Chrissie, froze like a spooked deer with a beer in one hand and a cookie stuffed in her mouth. They stared at each other as Elliot grimaced. Chrissie was head and shoulders the most popular and profitable of anyone in their team. "Sorry, didn't mean to be eavesdropping."

Elliot shook his head. "Thin doors."

"Yeah," Chrissie said, putting her free hand on her hip and nodding. "On the bright side though, I guess there's no more doubt about the two of you being married. If the two of you were able to act out a fight like that, you'd be in the movies or something."

Or grifters.

"I'll be out of your hair in a moment."

Chrissie shrugged. "Give it a bit of time but don't make yourself a stranger. Want me to shoot you a text if we need a beer delivery or something? We'll be getting carryout while you're gone and full stomachs are hard to argue over."

What the hell does she know about us? Don't offer me your pity just because you spend more time with my wife than I do.

"I've got work to do. They canceled my vacation."

"Right, right, go save the day or whatever. Protect some lives and all that. Just, do us a favor? If they put you in one of those killer suits, don't take your mask off. PR can rehab a detective, not a thug."

Elliot shook his head and headed to the door. "I'll keep that in mind."

Chrissie cupped her hand around her mouth and hollered down the hall, "And you really should get excited for that resistance rig! It's a miracle worker, you know?"

Elliot went back to his house and got dressed in his uniform once more. As he headed out to stroll through the killer's hunting ground, EVE messaged him her condolences.

17

Hide The Problem

2140/09/17

Clyde had something of a fever. He was burning up inside and belonged in a clinic, a hospital maybe, at least with his family laying around and eating soup. His body ached and he didn't know if it was from the melee, the fever, or the cancer. Pain suffused his arms and his hips. It put blinders on him and soaked his brain with the minuteness of the moment. It made him remarkably easy to command, to order around. The act of dressing, even in combat armor, was a dull routine resurrected in his mind from years back in military training.

The bump and jostle of dirt and the rumble of a diesel engine didn't seem out of place till he had fully roused himself. He and two dozen other Heartsteel employees–they still had their User IDs–had been packed into an LAPV. They were strapped down and buckled in, half-cocooned by their foam seats to dull the stiff suspension. The only road in Bastion was between the wall and the city and too smooth to be what he was feeling.

They had taken him out of the city, in a military convoy no less.

He searched his memory and his implant. A brief overview of the mission had been stored, telling him vaguely that they were being deployed to protect a genetics lab in the Nebraska territory. The ETA was hours out still, with no marker for a food break. Most of his coworkers were asleep, and those awake had their helmets half open so they could eat. He popped his own seal with a cough and wiped his mouth off before stuffing a water bag between his lips and sucking. It stung going down.

Trying to pull up his inbox gave him nothing but buffering delays and junk mail. He watched with his mind as one message after another queued up to offer meaningless trash. New albums from artists he followed. A sale for the sequel to a game he played months ago. An invite to an in-person bar crawl through Neo-Akihabara. Even obvious junk managed to get through the filters. Half a dozen articles about the Sigurd Chemical Plant had been recommended to him–based on the likes of his friends apparently.

The last thing he wanted to think about was what they had done outside the Sigurd Chemical Plant. As he glanced around, the entire truck was nothing but people who had been deployed there, had protected the safe operation of the factory. They were the ones who had flooded the local hospitals with admissions.

Then he saw a message from his mother saying, "COME HOME NOW."

"Shit."

The people across from him looked over and he buried his head, waved them off. He tried to pull up the whole message to see what had happened, but there wasn't enough data connection. The truck was moving too quickly over one of the old freeways. He'd have to wait until they arrived at the genetics lab and connect to their relay.

Sleep overcame him out of habit. Without the energy to play a video or a game through his implant, he had no way to resist it. Someone kicked his legs in their rush out the back to relieve themselves. For his part, he had sweated all of his fluids out, leaving his underlayer heavy and sticky. Once he realized they had arrived, he clipped his respirator back on and unbuckled.

Unabated sun washed across the world. Pale grass stretched in every direction, flowing around creeks and ponds with spots of trees and bushes. The wind blew, twirling turbines across the roof of the laboratory. The building had been planted down in the field, its only companion a barn nearly mile away. Beyond a field of asphalt once painted with parking lines, it was two stories of brick and glass with half a dozen additions slapped onto the sides. The main body was all red brick, but half the wings were cinderblock or poured concrete. One was even modern construction foam. Together, it formed an outpost of civilization in a wilderness shared with geese.

And the blighted, somewhere out there.

"Why aren't the lights on?" 410-289 asked, zipping his trousers up again.

Clyde's question was more to the point. "Why aren't I getting a data signal? There's a comm relay here, isn't there?" His question didn't have an intended recipient, but he had said it loud enough for everyone to hear. When no one answered, he asked, "Who's in charge?"

Again, no one answered.

He hobbled over to the front of the truck because his legs still hadn't woken up from the long ride. He had to grab the handle and hoist himself up on the foot bar to check inside. The windows were tinted as well as bullet-proof, but he could still see through them. Nobody sat at the helm. The entire drive had been autonomous.

Clyde couldn't tell if he had a bad feeling or if he was just going to puke from the fever and the stress. Nobody was taking charge, nobody giving commands. People milled around and scoped out the wilderness. They clustered to little groups and meandered the premises. Nobody from the lab came out to meet them. Clyde couldn't even see any lights on. In fact, the only movement was the twirling wind blades at the roof.

Feeling the aches in his body even more, he put his back to the wheel and slid to the ground. He tried to check the group and find people he knew, but their numbers just blurred in his vision. He couldn't make sense of the images jammed into his sight by the neural implant. All of his coworkers, a security force hired by Claire and sent out to the middle of nowhere Nebraska. He still couldn't believe she was government, but there were dozens, hundreds maybe, of government organizations.

Some had more funding than others. Some had more personnel than others. Someone along the way had mentioned that the CEO of Heartseel was politically connected, and that checked out.

He just didn't understand what they were doing at a genetics lab. There was supposed to be a good reason for private security to go outside the walls.

Evidently, a good amount of his coworkers thought the same. He couldn't read their numbers, but he saw a group of them head over to the front doors of the lab. Clyde watched them rattle the handles and jab the keypad and wave at cameras, all to no avail.

Finally, someone took their respirator off–they weren't really needed unless blighted showed up–and asked, "Are we in the right spot?"

Someone else, another unisex mass of armor, said, "How could we be in the wrong spot? We were driven here, dumbass."

The others started trying to place calls, but nobody jumped up saying they had a line back to headquarters. At the same time as a few people dug out the emergency radio, Clyde pushed back to his feet and headed away from the group. All of North America had satellite service thanks to the military, it was just low bandwidth because nobody was supposed to be anywhere without a relay. If someone did end up without a signal booster, an emergency was assumed and access was never restricted.

So long as he got away from the others, into his own little spot of signal, he could pull up his inbox. He trudged off, confident no one would really care where he was or what he was doing. Soon enough, he was a gray figure amid waist-high grass. He stood at the edge of a pod, like one giant sheet of glass capturing the deepening color of the sky. The wind blew, pushing him towards the water and in his weakened state he almost toppled in to become one with his reflection.

His mother's full message read, "Come home now! Johnny got killed. Quit that fucking company. They killed Johnny. He was at one of those protests. Come home at once. I'm trying to get Rachel too. We need lawyers. We need the press. We need to get justice!"

Clyde fell to his knees, sinking into the mud and straw, vanishing between cattails. All he could do was breathe and sway. He couldn't even process the information, it just soaked through his body like the autumn air. When he pitched forward, his hands splashed into the water, vanishing in swirls of mud. His stomach heaved and he barely ripped his respirator off in time to puke into the lake. The twisting and heaving wrenched against his insides, spiking pain that made him groan and heave again.

When his stomach settled, he rocked back, sitting down on his heels and taking ragged breaths interrupted by coughs and hacks. Cold sweat dripped down his neck and back, mingling with his tears. Those surprised him. He couldn't remember the last time he cried and he wasn't sure he could actually feel the sadness that wracked his body. It was like he had been given a book but had the lights turned out.

Nobody came looking for him, even though a casual glance would have marked him out amid the grass and weed. The computers all knew where everyone was. He would have been a floating number in the field, body or no, as disconnected from him as he was from himself.

The only reason he knew that nobody came looking for him was because he woke up in the field shivering. The sweat seemed to have changed temperature on him, left him clammy and chilled but less sore. The sun had set, revealing the mural of stars overhead, half smeared away by the glow of a brush fire in the parking lot. Smoke plumed up, diffusing to nothingness in the east as his coworkers chatted and complained. He saw them digging through MRE bags as they huddled their heads together.

He wondered how long they would be left at the lab. Obviously, nobody was home. They had been sent out of the way to keep them out of trouble. It was a PR thing and nothing more. They had done their job, made the government happy and gotten their pay–presumably–but now they were a liability until the news cycle rolled over.

He was probably going to miss his brother's cremation because of Heartsteel; because of CEO Dixie.

The geese honked. Some time in his past he had taken a biology course and he tried to remember what he knew about geese. The plains had snow geese mainly, but he wasn't sure if they were supposed to be migrating already. They could have been early, or maybe they were local birds, but it was still late at night and they seemed to be flocking into the air. One black silhouette after the next shot into the sky, flapping wings and honking like a dog had chased through and stirred them up.

There were no dogs in Nebraska though. Some feral wolfhounds, but those wouldn't be stupid enough to storm a flock of geese. In fact, he could only think of one thing in the wilderness that would spook animals out of roost for the night. And that something stood up on the other side of the pond. It stood blind and black against the stars. Lean and haggard, it stared back at him with drooping shoulders and a hunched back, nearly dragging claws against the muddy brush. The flesh of nightmares waded towards him slow and casual, as if it knew he didn't have a gun. The only weapon on his person was a stun prod

"BLIGHTED!"

18

Decline Of A Company

2140/10/19

Heartsteel Corporation owned a full tower near the center of Bastion, all eighty floors with rights to the infrastructure below. For that amount of investment, Elliot had assumed that they would have tens of thousands of employees. He found a ghost town.

A woman who quietly introduced herself as Zoa took him in from the outer doors on the twentieth floor and to the interior parks. The way the tower was structured, most of the weight sat through the exterior walls, leaving the insides as hollow and worthless, fit to gape with plastic parks or rot with unpopulated dormitories. Elliot saw both on his tour through the facilities, though they were all dressed up to seem like advantages. The computer tried to pitch the caverns as room for growth, apartments to house new employees.

It was only when the tour faltered, when he and Zoa stopped at the first working coffee station, that the truth began to trickle out of her wrinkled and beleaguered mouth. "We had a bunch of teams, until about a month ago when most of them died. People don't stick around for a dying company."

She had her coffee, burnt black brew, in a little plastic cup. Elliot took his in an insulated cup, leaning against the opposite wall as her and feeling his intuition forward. "What happened a month ago?"

She looked at him with purple and wrinkled eyes. "They let most of the guards, the security forces... you know, the people who produce the fundamental value... Bastard's blood, I mean I know that the cubicle workers and the accountants and all that, I know they earn their paychecks but at the end of the day, the value this company produces comes from the boots on the ground, you know?"

Elliot said he did know.

"Dixie, that callous ass, he sent them out to secure a piece of shit nothing for the military. Paid well enough, I guess, but the risk. He gambled and he lost. The whole group of them; they died. Place was overrun. Chaos, raiders, blighted, we don't really know. At the end of the day all that matters is that they died. I bet a bunch of them would have survived if the auto-trucks had been freed up, but by the time the signal came in from HQ here, it was too late."

Elliot said, "You're not exactly a spokeswoman from this place, are you?"

She sipped her coffee again and said, "No. Are the military police hiring?"

"Always. Do you have a clean record?"

"Fuck," she said, and sipped her coffee again.

Elliot mirrored the action, and asked, "I've checked a bit of the history. Heartsteel is a contract based company right? Most of their work was from a while ago. Union busting mostly. The government must have been real happy with them. What went wrong?"

Zoa jerked her head and led the way to a bar. There wasn't anyone working the taps, but the atmosphere was unmistakable. The stools were better than standing, and Zoa took one. "The difference was bad PR, and fuck you, Dixie, fire me if you want," she said, reaching over the counter to get a glass and pump it full of beer.

Elliot stuck to the coffee, glancing around at the balconies and walkways, all kept in gloom to give the bar ambiance. "The last big operation I could find record of, as far as the news operations were concerned, was protecting Sigurd."

Zoa scoffed and downed half her beer. The tap refilled her without a question. "They didn't pay nearly enough to cover the damages."

"To people? Or reputation?"

"Reputation," she said. "We've been untouchables ever since. Because people got video of kids dying in the riot–kids who had no business being there!–nobody has been willing to hire Heartsteel."

Elliot frowned. "It's not like you're defaulting on loans, is it?"

She sneered. "Just because the banks are letting us slide doesn't mean there's a future for this company."

"I think that's exactly what it means. If they never call in the loans, then it doesn't matter you're not making money."

Zoa gestured around the empty park, where people should have been chatting and drinking, or at least slacking between work shifts. Nobody was around. The only other people he had even heard distantly were the few people holed up in their micro-apartments and keeping their heads down. "You see this? This is what you get when people are only here to get a paycheck, when we're just here to keep the lights on, our stomachs fed, and our families taken care of. This is a shell of a company... It's like someone froze a balloon that should have been expanding and we're just the plastic shell that remains after someone–the press–jabbed a needle into it. The pressure–the will to grow–is gone."

Elliot nodded. "You say that like I'm wasting my time here."

"Aren't you?"

"It's better than believing the media, isn't it?"

She snorted. "I suppose that's true, but we're a corpse here. The killer? Could be any one of a thousand people with good cause."

He nodded and drained the end of his coffee. "But," he asked, "how many of those people have the training, the skills, to do what's happened so far?"

"Plenty," Zoa said.

How wonderfully useful to my investigation.

"Could you show me around any areas that your boss is likely to enter? Where he would come and go to make appearances? That sort of thing?"

Zoa nodded and took him to the elevators that connected all the way to the top of the tower. She explained that they were currently on the park floor, which he probably wouldn't go to. Family members could come and go there, some of them were allowed to have visitors too. The elevator was secured by cameras and concealed weapon panels. Elliot rode up to the next stop with her and took a look around the meeting rooms that Heartsteel had. All the walls were SMARTglass, which meant their opacity could be changed electronically.

"Not that I need to tell a security company how to protect someone, but I'd suggest that if Mr Dixie ever comes here, you should tint his room and un-tint every other room."

Zoa managed to smile and not roll her eyes. "Of course."

The next stop was more like a traffic mesh. Three different train lines brushed against the tower, forming a triangle across the fortieth floor. Nearly all the floor space was dedicated to walkways, elevators, and staircases to distribute arrivals efficiently. It seemed built to handle hundreds or even thousands of people at peak hours, but the two of them had the place to themselves.

"How many people did you lose?" he asked.

"On Dixie's failed trip? About one hundred," she answered.

That's not enough to do this... well, I guess it depends on who the one hundred were.

"People quit?"

Zoa snorted. "Call it one hundred people dead because of an accident. Half of them had families living here, so that's two hundred people gone on the face of it. The next wave of people to leave were the ones with kids. Parents don't like it if they don't think their children are safe and the protests were pretty bad. Suddenly, half the school system was vacant and they had to shut down to restructure. The adjacent neighborhoods couldn't just absorb the kids, so lots of them were scattered across Bastion to boarding schools. That tipped the scales for more people to find new jobs…"

"Sounds like a cascade failure," Elliot said.

"That was exactly what happened. Think about being a regular employee here and realizing that everyone older than you, the ones with spouses and kids, are running away as fast as they can? If you're smart, you'd leave too."

"Like rats on ships, yeah."

"We lost ten percent of employees."

Elliot frowned as she stared at him. He shrugged. "That's normal turnover, isn't it?"

She smirked. "Per month, for three months now. We were in trouble before Sigurd, you know?"

That would do it.

"I imagine that your workload didn't reduce either, so what? The rest of you are pulling double shifts now?"

Zoa finished her drink and chucked it into a trash bin. "Spot on Mr Law Man."

"Any other floors to show me?" he asked, and turned his attention to his phone. The rest of the trip he half paid attention while he messaged EVE to do a cross reference search of people who had left the company and had close friends and family with damages from Heartsteel, then see if any of them had been at any of the crime scenes.

"What can you tell me about Mohamed Azir?" Elliot asked as the two of them walked through a self-congratulatory museum. It was good for photo ops and not much more. There were portraits of the previous CEOs along with major events, but that alone wouldn't have filled a modest room, let alone a museum floor. To occupy the rest of the space, sculptures and pieces of modern art had been purchased. They must have been for money laundering, because every artwork put together didn't have as much soul as one piece from A-Maze.

"Mohamed Azir?" Zoa responded. "Middle management guy. They put him in charge of new recruits and he did a decent job getting them ready for work. Always skipped practice though. Frankly, the company isn't missing anything for his absence."

"Not one for making friends?"

She laughed. "Funny you say that, most of the people he mentored ended up out in Nebraska and got killed."

Elliot stopped in front of a massive field of yellow paint, stippled and splashed with black. "Is that a coincidence? Do you think these kills–they're targeted, you know–have something to do with the deaths at Nebraska?"

"Officer, I think you're asking the wrong question. The deaths have something to do with the people who defended Sigurd Chemical Plant. Shouldn't you be looking at who has a motive to attack Sigurd? Just because one guy showed up to Mr Dixie's office doesn't mean this isn't an organized terrorist cell."

That would make sense, but if that was the case they wouldn't have brought me on. They would have gone directly to Wyatt's division. Seraphina wouldn't be involved. Maybe there's negative evidence to be had. Maybe someone knows what the active cells are up to? Or someone is just dropping the ball. I should have a sitdown with Wyatt and confirm.

He shook his head. "What about Glenn Clarkson? How would he figure into the scheme here?"

"No idea," Zoa said, her eyes unfocusing as she presumably searched her implant. "He and Mohamed were in different departments. Looks like a recent promotion. was more responsible for body guard duty, sticking himself like glue to high value clients. He was one of the few people that could be trusted to put his body on the line."

"So, he used to work with Azir?"

Zoa scratched her chin and squinted her eyes. "I'd have to check the records. One sec... Ah, looks like Azir mentored him about a year ago, but there's nothing strange about that. He had some red marks though. HR was concerned that he took his job a bit too seriously, if you know what I mean."

"He hurt people?"

"We all hurt people."

"Would you be able to give me your org charts? I want to provide that data to EVE to augment her visual analysis."

"You'll have to make that request to... your request was just approved," she said, rolling her eyes.

Elliot turned to the nearest camera and nodded to it. "Thanks for the tour. I'll let you know if I need to come back, but I've got some leads now."

At least, I hope Wyatt does.

19

Survivor

2140/09/18

Clyde opened his eyes in firelit gloom. Logs crackled and yet his body shivered. A slight move made him groan and convulse. Woolen blankets were draped over him, half as sodden as his body glove. He was wet. That brought back the memories of the river. Of running and running, chased by blighted until they went back for easier prey at the lab. He had gone down the highway, back toward Bastion, as far as he could. He had run until his heart burned and his legs went numb.

That was when one of them had got him. As patient as a landmine, one of the blighted had followed him in the darkness and jumped him. He had been crossing a bridge, using the railing for support and trying to force himself forward. Both he and it had fallen into the river and then...

His vision swam. Lights and colors darted like a school of startled fish within his eyes. An ear-piercing screech blared between his ears as he twisted and gasped in pain. When it subsided, he had fallen off the cot. For a moment, he stayed on all fours panting and took stock of himself.

The metal plating had been removed from his armor, but he had been left in the synthetic sleeve. He couldn't find any bites or tears in it, but it squelched with water. It was a miracle he had resisted hypothermia. Or it was due to whoever had fished him out and brought him to their cabin. Touching the numb part of his face, he found cloth bandages wrapped around his head. Blood caked the back of his skull.

He had been bitten. He couldn't imagine how, not through his helmet, but a blighted had got him. He had to get back to Bastion, had to get scoured. That or eat a bullet.

"You're not infected," a man said, his heavy boots thumping the floor boards. He came in from another room with a cast iron pan in one hand and a slab of dripping meat in the other. He was swaddled in layers and coats, both wool and leather and everything tattered around the edges. Some seams had been repaired by hand, marking him as a survivor, but there weren't supposed to be any survivors this far west.

Clyde asked, "Who the hell are you?"

The man scooped out a wad of something white from a can and slapped it into the pan. When the flames licked it, the rendered fat sizzled, then the man looked at him with one eye, for he lacked the other. A black eyepatch covered the disfigurement and was nearly mirrored by the onyx pupil that remained to him. "I'm your savior. You may bow and scrape at my feet if you wish. By rights, you should call me Lord and master."

"Ain't nobody my Lord."

The man grinned. "You think you're alone, do you?" The bloody steak splattered the lard, juices boiling and burning as the rich scent enveloped the room. Clyde's attention wasn't the only one to get sucked in by the food, seemingly. A dozen paintings covered the walls, dangling from nails and hooks, resting against exposed support beams. Immortalized visages of people past, cast in oil upon the canvas, looked upon the man cooking, enraptured by the simple act.

Clyde's stomach demanded the fixation more than his mind did. His mind wanted to flee, and secretly he tried to place a call. Touching upon his implant, even in such a ginger manner, caused the flood of noise again. He fell to the ground, digging at his temples and crushing his eyelids shut until the spasm of thought subsided.

The man chuckled. "Not very bright, are you? But, God makes men in all forms, now doesn't he? It's your government that wants to smash you all into the same mold. I don't know how it happened, because I only found your body later, but you can't use your brain computer anymore. When you fell in the river, or perhaps a little bit before, you hit your head. Crushed your helmet and cracked your skull. It's a little miracle that you didn't snap your neck."

Clyde rubbed the back of his neck and felt the stiff muscles and inflammation of bruising. If his neural implant was broken, he couldn't call for pickup. It also meant the program wasn't thrusting itself into his vision anymore. He could look at his savior and see the man's face, not a number. He could see the streaks of dirt, the square jaw, but also the softness of youth. Not a child, but not as old as he himself was either. All the survivors he had ever seen had been gaunt and hardened, their eyes like flint in sunken sockets. Suffering had colored their features, but this man seemed impervious to it.

"You saved my life then. Thank you."

The man grinned. "Ah, so you can be thankful. Color me surprised. Maybe I will share some of my bounty with you." Out came a knife as long as his hand. The man jabbed it into the steak to flip it over, then sawed the steak in half, separating the two pieces to expose the tender red within.

Clyde's stomach growled and he took a seat on the floor next to the hearth. There were no other seats, hardly any furnishings at all besides the paintings. Dirt caked the floorboards and sullied the golden frames, but the fire was warm and his body was shivering. "Are you with the Isles?"

The man stirred the meat with the tip of his knife. "I used to be."

"Long ways away."

"I travel."

"Long way back to Bastion."

The man laughed. "It's a long way to the bottom of a cliff too. Doesn't mean you can't get there quickly."

"It must have been an eight hour drive to get here, and the auto-trucks are crawling with blighted. I'd have to call in a helicopter or something. Except I can't, because my implant is busted and I don't have a phone. I don't even have a gun to go back to the lab and get one of the radios. Unless you've got a radio."

"What would I need a radio for?" the man asked. "If I want somebody to talk to, I can just fish one out of the river and when you're good and ready to go back, I'll toss you in the river again. Now, until such a time, as is ancient tradition of travelers receiving hospitality, I expect to be told your story. I would like to know what it's like in your glorious prison." He flipped half of the meat onto a ceramic plate and held it in front of Clyde, the seared flesh still oozing life and flavor.

The aroma made his mouth water, but fear held him back. "Where'd you get the meat?"

"Deer herd."

"But the deer are infected, aren't they? They're a reservoir population."

The man rolled his eye. "That's why I cooked it. Humanity has dealt with parasites since before we crawled out of the oceans. Our greatest weapon against them was developed two hundred thousand years ago and we use it to this day. I can keep it to myself if you'd like. It's not going to do anything to me."

The steak had turned pink throughout. Clyde took the plate and hunched over it, using his fingers to get it into his mouth bite by bite. Once it hit his stomach, he began to talk. The man asked questions about strange things. He showed no interest at all in neural implants but asked repeatedly about the quality of the water and the various news outlets. He asked about the void masks and the criminal organizations, but not about EVE.

He said, "I'm not interested in the machines, boy. I want to know about the state of the human soul."

Clyde looked down and turned the piece of meat over between his fingers. The chill still hadn't left his body, even sitting so close to the fire it seemed that part of his suit would melt. The only improvement in his condition was no coughing and that his broken implant wasn't making him hallucinate. "I don't think I'm the best to tell you anything about a human soul. I'm not sure I have one."

"So, you're an atheist? Or you're just not able to create?"

"What, like art?"

The man gestured to the ancient paintings that surrounded them like an audience. "Wonderful aren't they? Took these out of... I suppose I don't remember the name of it anymore, but there was a museum in Chicago. Nobody was taking care of them, not a very important thing to think about during the end of the world I suppose, so I helped myself. These masterpieces, they took somebody half their life to devout their souls to the art so they could communicate to us with them."

"I can't say I've ever met a painter. A few people who work with computers I guess, but nobody paints anymore."

"Nobody paints," the man repeated. He shook his head. "Music at least? Tell me people still play music. I can't keep a tune or a rhythm to save my life, but I still love music."

"Some people, here and there. I went to a karaoke bar once, but nobody was any good at it."

"Shame, a damn shame."

"You got a radio, mister?"

"Nobody plays music over the radio anymore."

"I meant so I could call for help."

"Ah, no. Can't say that I do. I can get you back to the city though, don't worry about that. So long as you pay your due, I'll keep my end of the hospitality."

Clyde stuffed the last of the food into his mouth and swallowed. "Have I told you enough to use your bed again?"

"So soon?" the man asked, prodding the fire with an iron poker.

"I'm sick."

"I believe your fever already broke."

"No, I mean I have cancer. My lungs are rotting. It's probably going to metastasize or something. They won't give me the expensive treatments. They're just keeping me alive and now I'm out here and I'm gunna die like my little brother died and like my father died and this is probably the end for me."

The man sat back in his chair and looked down at him. After a time, he said, "Take your rest. I'm going to go have a look at that lab you came from."

Clyde considered warning him not to, but the man obviously knew about the blighted. With a nod, he returned to the small bedroom. He didn't undress, but he did unzip his suit to let the trapped moisture escape as he crawled beneath the blanket once more. He shivered as he slept. He awoke at dawn and the man had returned, but Clyde didn't ask what he had found. He didn't want to hear about all the people killed and the man didn't offer the knowledge.

Dinner came in the form of a vegetable soup. The bottom of the man's pot rattled with cracked bones. The marrow seeped out into a rich oil that coated every piece of potato and carrot and gave Clyde's stomach knots as it experienced the concentrated nutrition. As he ate, he paid for it with answers about movies and video games. He spoke about bars and mixed drinks and how he had met a girl with a cat tail at a bar. Something about her put a grin on the man's face.

After the sun set, Clyde had spoken about 336-730 breaking the guy's arm and about how hardly anyone knew each other's names in Heartsteel.

"That's by design, from what I can tell," the man said. "I hereby say you have paid your dues to me, Mr Bondsman."

Clyde scoffed. "So you think I've told you about the human soul?"

"Not one speck of it, no." The man laughed. "But that's not your fault, from what I can see. You had your soul beaten out of it, or rather your own perception of it. You are a soul, afterall. People tend to forget that. But, this Heartsteel company... I hate to call it a company at all. It might take money and use it to hire employees to do work, but no, companies are voluntary. There's a reason we use the same word as for a company of soldiers, or to have guests over as company. To call it a corporation is closer to the truth, that comes from latin, corporate. This Heartsteel entity however... I'd say it's closer to a plantation, stocked not with employees but with slaves. You weren't even allowed to go see your family as you toiled for them. What's more, the only connection you made with another spirit was because she was the one being in the entire building whose face you could see. Everyone else had a wall in front of them. So, I have a question for you."

"You've been asking me questions all day."

The man grinned and set his bowl aside as he leaned over to Clyde. "Would you like to get justice?"

20

Blood Sample

2140/10/20

Elliot and Ram stood outside the walls of Bastion, squinting their eyes into the rising sun and smelling the river stink of the Mississippi inflow. He sipped his Zeus energy drink and blinked, grappling with the reality of the thing before him. "What?"

Ram lit up a cigarette and shrugged. "I told you."

He spun on her. "I thought you were done smoking?"

"Eh, it's harder than you would think because my boyfriend smokes. I swear, I'm going to stop. I'm halfway through this pack, alright? It was a gift. Real legit tobacco from the Isles. I can't just throw out expensive stuff like this."

She's going to get me smoking again at this rate, but the bigger problem is... how? Where did this come from?

He turned back on the anomaly, the thing that should not have been. A hundred years ago, the river would have swarmed with the things, but a hundred years ago the walls of Bastion hadn't gone up yet. He could only be thankful that the two of them weren't looking at the corpse of a blighted, but that at least he would have understood.

He couldn't fathom a reason for there to be a rowboat pulled into the mud and weeds of the Mississippi. How it hadn't been trampled by the auto-barges baffled him, and the convoy from the Isles had been over a week prior. Then again, the convoy wouldn't have said anything about it.

No, maybe that's exactly what this was. Maybe some deserter floated down to link up with the convoy.

"When did this get here?"

"About two weeks before the convoy."

Damn it.

"The motion detectors didn't clue us in?"

"The motion detectors are exactly why we know this is here." She gestured back to the wall. There was a slightly glossy spot near one of the official doors which they had used to trudge out along the river. "Allegedly, disease control already did a sweep. It wasn't a blighted, so they passed the data over to us and Cinder gave it to me saying it was a milk run but... well, you'll see."

Elliot groaned. "And naturally, we didn't get the alert until days after, did we?"

"Bingo."

He headed over to the boat and looked at it. It was made of aluminum and had been patched half a dozen times. Dirt, crud, and mold had colonized every rivet and seam, giving it an abandoned look. The oar was strangest of all: carved out of wood. A standard issue life boat paddle was rare but easy enough to get. There was a factory somewhere in Arkan that made them for the Atlantic Fleet, and surplus was sold to the Isles.

So who would hand-make an oar? If they did it for fun, you'd think that it would be less crude. Frankly, this is a waste of wood if it came from inside Bastion.

"Did you find any footprints?" he asked.

Ram shook her head. "Rained out. The initial report found some footprints, but they were just standard issue. I have pictures."

He cocked his head and looked at the pictures. "This might be the strangest thing I've seen in months. Do we have a picture of them?"

Ram flicked her cigarette butt into the river. "Yeah, that's the weird part. I kept putting in requests but that Paige Palmer is transferring out and... ugh, Mr Blackstone it's been a mess."

He sighed. "Hold on." He knelt down beside the boat and ran his hand across the seat. The rain had rinsed it relatively clean, but there was a dark ring around the seat screws. He searched his pockets and finally found an evidence bag, a sterile scraper too. Taking that out of the packaging, he dug at the head of the screw and the material flaked off.

Blood.

The bag was technically expired because he had left it from last winter in the inside pocket of his cloak, but he popped it open regardless. He gently brushed the flakes into the bag and sealed the sample. "Got him," he said, holding the bag up for her to see.

Ram blinked. "You have got to be kidding me!"

Elliot snickered. "I do have a few more years experience than you, you know?"

Ram groaned and spun around. She stomped back to the wall, waving for him to follow. She didn't go back to the door they had used, but rather to a rusted spot that had a fresh sheet of steel welded on. The earth was rutted out, washed hard by the rains. Overhead, Elliot could see one of the wind tunnels that ran through the insides of the wall like arteries. He couldn't hear the whine of the turbine, and he guessed from the enormous drip of moss coming out of the hole that it wasn't operational anymore. Poor drainage from storms had washed out the earth and exposed cracks into Epsilon level barely hidden by scrub and weed.

Just like how Kyte snuck out the other week.

With the repairs welded on and half buried by fresh dirt, he doubted it could be used again, but what furrowed his brow was what Ram stared at. "That's a camera," he said.

"That's a useless hunk of silicon, completely fried and shorted," she responded.

Elliot didn't have a neural implant, so he couldn't ping it directly but there were supposed to be power indicators. It was as dull as a rock. "Well, a blighted can't do that. And someone joining the convoy wouldn't bother."

"A blighted isn't going to use a rowboat either. Is this, like, a foreign spy or something?"

Elliot scratched his chin and stared at the camera. He turned the facts over in his mind and shook his head. "Doubtful. Something like ninety-nine percent of foreign spies arrested were Bastion-born. They flip people over the internet with propaganda and money. If they need actual boots on the ground, they can just fly someone in with a false identity working for some corporate subsidiary. Nothing we can do about that if we don't want to torch the Pacific trade routes. This... I don't know. There's hardly any reason to do something like this except–"

"CZAR smuggling, right?"

He pressed his lips into a line and nodded. "Let's go inside. I want to see where this hole is connected to." The perimeter of Bastion was theoretically easy to maintain. It was one of the few walls in the world that had to be maintained and all the power they could need was available. The entire circumference was approximately three hundred miles in length, a tiny fraction of what America had once protected between the United States and Mexico. Still, the determined would find a way.

They entered through the access door after measuring the distance. Just knowing how far they had to go didn't make it easy to find the correct tunnel. Epsilon was riddled with derelict tunnels and pipes like gargantuan termites lived in it. Some could be walked through and others were too small for anything but a recon drone. The report that Disease Control had sent over seemed like it was technically accurate, but being told the breach had into Power Coupling Point 298 meant nothing to either of them.

After half an hour, Ram managed to triangulate the correct passage thanks to her neural implant. They had to go up a floor to what seemed to be a fraction of a general walkway, but cut off by recent concrete walls. Elliot didn't even guess what they were crossing over as they descended to Power Coupling Point 298. Contemplating how close he was to clogged sewage wasn't helpful.

The breach had been patched up with construction foam to reinforce the sheet steel. He could still see where the old concrete had been power washed. He sighed. "There might have been more blood, but not anymore. You'd think that Disease Control would have a bit more forensic care, you know?"

"Footprints and fingerprints were all destroyed too, and once the intruder got in through here... well, we just spent half an hour lost and we have maps."

He frowned and looked around the little room. Overhead were the uplinks to the wind turbines. Years ago, energy would have been pumping down past them, through the transformers and out to the city. Workers would have been regularly checking the computer, the feeds, the energy readings, and so on. Then the turbines broke and Congress had no money to fix them, so they were abandoned like so many pre-apocalypse cities.

"If we're lucky, the blood will just ID the perp, we'll know who they are, and QRS can pick them up for smuggling or whatever they did."

"And if we're not lucky?" Ram asked.

Elliot searched around his pockets and pulled out a pocket knife. Without a second thought, he committed a crime. He wasn't worried about it, because the energy company responsible for the turbines had gone out of business when they got shut down. Every employee with connections escaped to elsewhere and that left nobody with a legal right to press charges as he dismantled the security panel to the wind turbine. Behind the monitor was a cavity that smelled like a swamp. The illumination from his phone showed the copper busbars and wiring had almost completely turned green with oxidation. When he tried to put the panel away, a dozen wires and ribbons held onto it. A moment of fighting it, and he spotted what he was looking for regardless.

The circuit boards covering the back of the panel like a mosaic had flash burns between the pins. There had been an induced surge.

"Well, I imagine this is going to get somebody's attention. I just don't know whose."

21

Nothing Left To Lose

2140/09/19

After weeks of absence, still none of the passcodes had been changed. Clyde figured that it was too much trouble changing locks and updating every man, woman, and child who worked for Zarah's group without having the passwords leaked regardless. He had just tossed his clothes into the wash machine without tags and stolen a new set from an abandoned rack when somebody bumped past him again. "Put your mask on, idiot," they said, flipping him their middle finger before they vanished back into the sinew of the hidden city within Bastion.

Clyde's mask was back at his mother's apartment, and he knew he would need it if he was going to get justice.

The survivor who had saved him had fed him and put him on a boat down to Bastion, had done what he could to prepare Clyde. Two weapons hung at his hip, and he stole a duster jacket long enough to hide the twin blades. One a micro-blade and the other something special, he felt like a Japanese samurai.

The city smelled different to him as he slipped out to the bridges. His neural implant didn't work, so he couldn't take a train. He had no money and no identity, but nothing stopped him from blending into the meandering crowds of drunks and commuters. He passed among the millions of people performing their daily migrations around the city, carrying the other gift the survivor had given him.

The boat hadn't been free. Rather, it had been stolen from the survivor by the half-broken body of a blighted. The very same creature that had nearly killed Clyde days prior clung to the aluminum hull. Gravity and rocks had pulped its wiry body. The flesh had turned oily and blistered. "Can't leave that any longer," the survivor had said, handing Clyde the first of the blades. "Here. This one's for flesh."

Clyde had pulled the sword from the sheathe and stared at it for a moment. The blade was so thin and weightless it vibrated with every pulse of his heart. He had seen a demonstration back in bootcamp of a micro-blade dropped onto a pig carcass. The sergeant had to grab the haunch and peel it open like parting lips because nobody believed anything had happened. The edge had simply passed through the meat and stuck in the table.

When Clyde swung, the blighted's head fell into the river. With his boot, he knocked the corpse out of the boat, but the twisted hand refused to release the edge, so he lopped that off too.

"Good enough," the survivor had said, and pried the severed hand off the boat. From a supply pack in the rowboat, most of which he kept for himself, he produced a jar, which he dropped the hand into. It splashed into a clear fluid. "Bleach. Give it enough hours to pickle and it will be safe enough. Still, it will make a great gift. Very old school. Survivor style," the one-eyed man said with a wicked grin as he screwed the lid shut once more.

Clyde carried the hand of a blighted through Bastion, the largest encampment of humans in the world. A refuge from the disease that had brought the world to its knees so long ago. The weight in his grasp far exceeded the mere mass of chemicals. Sealed shut as it was, not a single sensor from the walls to the heart of the city had noticed what he carried.

Traversing the city without an implant was strange. Not just the lack of Heartsteel's constant monitoring, but the advertisements were different. When he walked by, signs didn't change. Holograms didn't chase him down. No franchise reminded him about outstanding loyalty points or sequels to movies and games he had previously bought. The city stared at him, through him, and past him. He didn't even need a mask; he already was nobody.

The first people to care about him were a pair of middle aged men in anonymous uniforms sitting in the alley park outside his mother's apartment. They stood up and walked over to him. One hooked his thumb at the door and asked, "Are you Mr Bondsman? Ah, Clyde Bondsman that is."

"Who are you?"

The two men shrugged at each other. Neither was in particular shape and it seemed that the most effort they put into their bodies went to shaping their beards, graying already. The other one answered, "Light security for Greytree Apartments." It took Clyde a moment to remember that was the name of the local landlord. "We've been trying to get a hold of you all day, assuming you are Mr Bondsman?"

"Yeah, that's me. What's up?"

The first one cleared his throat and stuffed his hands in his pockets. "We were told that you were out of town, difficult to contact... judging by your attitude, it seems that we're the bearers of bad news. If you could turn on your neural implant, I believe there's a doctor from the local clinic that has left–"

"I can't. It got damaged. What are you talking about?"

The men frowned and shuffled their feet. The talkative man said, "Your mother passed away last night, Mr Bondsman. Her heart stopped working last night and EMTs didn't arrive in time to save her. As per the terms of her lease contract, the property has now transferred to you, as well as responsibility for–"

Clyde exploded. "You think I fucking care about contracts? My mother is fucking dead?"

The man stepped back and put his hands up. "I was just trying to say that you're not going to be pressured or anything for a few weeks. We respect the need for a–"

Clyde shoved past the men and nearly dropped the bleach jar as he ran to the apartment. The door handle was locked, but not the deadbolt. With a bit of force, because the electronic lock couldn't see his neural implant, he wrenched the door open and pushed through. Lights flickered on as he swept into the kitchen and through to the living room. Nobody welcomed him home. The tv was dead and no games idled in Johnny's room. There were echoes and ventilation noises.

One of his mother's shirts was discarded on the ground. It had been sliced open down the front and just left there. He knelt down next to it, sinking to the floor as even more of his insides were reduced to emptiness. If he hadn't moved into Heartsteel's apartments, he would have been there for her. Johnny should have been there, but Johnny had gotten headstrong and done something stupid, something else Clyde could have stopped.

After some time, Zarah walked in. Her running shoes softly padded on the tiles behind him. After a few noises of trepidation, she said, "We heard you were dead."

"Is that what happened to Mom?" He gestured to the recliner, the one she had always sat in. The empty liquor bottle at the side was the only new addition to it.

Zarah wrapped her arms around herself. "Both her sons in the same week, the overwork… I mean, it's not like the doctors did an autopsy and even if they did, I'm not family. I wouldn't get told."

"You're fine," Clyde said. He stared down at his lap. "This has nothing to do with you. It's not your fault. It's mine and it's Heartsteel's."

"Clyde, you didn't do anything wrong. You know that, don't you? You didn't know anything like this would happen. Whatever you do, do not blame yourself."

He sucked in breath, inflating his chest to drag his head up a fraction. Staring at himself in the reflection of the dead tv, he said, "There's a little tiny difference between blaming yourself, and taking responsibility. Half my family is dead, Zarah. I'm going to go take responsibility for it."

Her response surprised him, and came delayed. She asked, "You hit your head, didn't you? That blood—your neural implant is broken? When Heartsteel called up, they said your implant was confirmed disconnected. That was their justification for not going to get your body. Looks like you're here safe and sound though. Got your own ride back... Do you know what happened to your little brother?"

He glanced over his shoulder at her. "Yes."

"Are you going to do something about that? Do you need a lawyer?"

"No."

"I thought you might say that, Clyde. Can I take you to meet someone first?"

"I'm a little..." He sighed. "Who?"

"My boss would like to speak with you. She's somewhat in the business of political philanthropy, you might call it."

"I don't need any charity."

"Clyde, with all due respect, what you need is a fucking therapist, but you're clearly not going to go get one of those. I wouldn't be surprised if you went looking for answers at the bottom of a bottle, but I also think you're not going to do that. Don't you think it would be the smart thing to do if you went and got a little help from a professional?"

Zarah's boss was the one who owned the laundromat, who operated the network of tunnels outside EVE's vision. He couldn't deny it would be helpful, so he stood up and walked to his old bedroom. The few months he had been gone, nothing had changed—not even the sheets. He found what he was looking for: the void mask. He drummed his fingers on it as he walked back out and nodded at Zarah. "Alright, sure. Take me to her. Now, please," he said, and put on the mask.

22

Unlabeled Expense

The results on the blood analysis hadn't come back in yet, which provided a full cover on the stalled investigation. It allowed him to leave his phone at a restaurant along with Heartsteel's spy drone and follow Ram to the guy she knew. He brought Azir's neural implant because he would need to be paid under the table and it turned out that she still didn't have access to department petty cash. He stopped her before they arrived when he realized where they were going.

He cornered her near some vending machines, an out of the way cubby where he could hiss at her. "This is the guy you're dating?"

She didn't meet his gaze, fidgeting her fingers as she said, "I mean, everything was sorted out amicably, wasn't it? Not like he got charged with anything."

He brushed his hand back through his hair and composed himself. They were in Delta, but not a corporate sector. It was the kind of wild west unregulated capitalism that could suck people up from Gamma. More money changed hands, but they had the same climate control, the same food, nearly the same air. The only big difference was in the crime: white collar rather than violent. Elliot and Ram were down the hall from just such a criminal, if only the courts had evidence against him.

Or rather, if he weren't willing to cooperate with police investigations to buy himself temporary amnesty.

"But you're dating him?"

Ram laughed and scratched her cheek. "I mean, yeah. He asked me out during some of the follow up and... look, Mr Blackstone, we were just the other day talking about how hard it is to find a man worth dating! He's smart, he's ambitious but not for power, he's a creative soul and a bit of a gentleman. Sort of. I mean he can be kind of hard but..."

But, he's attractive enough to get away with it? Or do you like a hard headed guy?

"Ram, you shouldn't be mixing work and pleasure."

She stamped a foot. "I'm not! He's not involved in any active investigations. He doesn't work for the police or anything. It's totally legit. You know as well as I do that literally anybody in Bastion could be arrested with enough investigation. So what's the harm?"

Elliot groaned and resigned himself to deal with it later. "Come on. First things first." The vending machines also had a series of old lockboxes. He slotted a credit chip and bought an hour of protection before stashing his phone as well as Heartsteel's spy drone. Hoping that the mechanism hadn't been broken by cityboarders, he shut it, picked a passcode, and left them behind.

The two of them headed down the hall and she knocked on the door. Instead of an answer, the locks sprang open. She stuck her head in and said, "Miccolo, we're here."

For the second time, Elliot stepped into a cybernetic madhouse. What should have been a four bedroom apartment had been excavated into a workshop studio. He couldn't even see the backwalls, just racks and shelves of electronic materials. There were silicon molds, circuit board printers, jars of chemicals for uses he could only guess, and those were the relatively normal things. It was the hands and feet ranging from animatronic to prosthetic that unnerved him. If they were at least still they would seem like doll parts, but most were moving and wiggling. They cycled through flexing and relaxed with computers recording everything.

This was all because Miccolo was ground zero for open source humanoid robots.

"I'm back here," he said as he paced around a naked, female-type robot standing in the one spot of floor that didn't have clutter. The way he had the roof set up imitated the natural sky. Huge panels of LEDs shifted between blue to lavender to red as the primary illumination made a dramatic rendition of a sunset. It warmed the artificial mess and put a depth of color into his hair and clothes that simply didn't exist down in Gamma. He was in business attire with the sleeves rolled up, accented by a slim suit vest. A degree of fashion entirely unnecessary for someone who was their own boss.

So that's what Ram saw the first day, is it?

Elliot had to step over razor blades just to get to him. Miccolo didn't seem to mind what he was stepping on in the least, all of the techie's attention was on the machine: Angela. Miccolo jabbed his finger into the custom-built android, watched her straighten up again. He grabbed her wrist and lifted her arm only to drop it; the machine swayed but stayed upright.

"Having fun?" Elliot asked.

He looked up, glanced between the two of them and grimaced. "Nice to see you again, Detective."

"I imagine it is."

Without Sokolov paying him, I'm about to be his biggest benefactor.

Miccolo stepped behind the machine and said, "I hear you need to see what's on a neural implant? Did you get one installed poorly or something?" Then he grabbed Angela's hair and yanked down on it. Her head snapped back, her knees buckled and arms raised. The machine didn't fall. If there had been a yelp of pain, Elliot wouldn't have known it was a machine.

He glanced over at Ram and saw her blinking, wide-eyed at the school-yard attack. Elliot cleared his throat and held up the jar with

Azir's implant. "This is evidence in an ongoing investigation, but it's encrypted."

Miccolo pivoted away from his robot and frowned. "I thought it would still be in a head. How silly of me."

"Is that a problem?"

"Not at all, this is easier. I have direct access now." Miccolo held out his hand as he walked past. He took it from Elliot and took it over to one of the dozens of tables strewn with electronics. He frowned and gave the jar a shake as he peered at the bloody gel still clinging to the wires. "Angela, put on some music, would you?"

On command, a chorus of string instruments began to play a faintly familiar melody. "A fan of the classics?"

"Sort of," Miccolo said as he unscrewed the evidence jar. He fished out the implant and spread it across a tray like he was dissecting it. "This isn't from a composer or anything. It's just generated. Something composed might actually distract me. Pure noise is better."

Elliot glanced over at Ram, who shrugged. In a half-whisper, she said, "I don't think this will take him long."

Elliot glanced around the room as the din of servos, quiet as it had been, began to vanish. The absence was more notable to his ears than their presence had been. One by one the test apparatuses shut off and the associated computer screens switched to idle. Miccolo had the neural implant pincushioned with probes and clamps, along with a thick plug jammed into the main socket.

Elliot asked, "Now, I don't mean to tell you how to do your own work, but don't you people usually demand payment upfront?"

Ram's face colored. "What do you think you're saying, Mr Blackstone?"

Miccolo shook his head. "Oh, I'll need payment before I unlock it, but the quote depends on who's lock I'm breaking. Associated risk and all that."

"It's Heartsteel's lock."

Miccolo stopped, his fingers hovering over his keyboard. "Heartsteel you say? I saw them in the news."

"Yeah? What for?"

"Killing people," Miccolo said.

"Well, that has nothing to do with us today," Elliot said.

As far as I know. It would be a pretty good motivation if we could just find somebody that went to each of the kills.

Miccolo shook his head. "Are you helping them or hurting them?"

"I'm not at liberty to say, and it of course depends on what data is in that neural implant."

"You'll be paying by credit chip, right? I want one thousand credits for this."

Elliot sighed and ran the numbers in his head. He tried to estimate how much budget Cinder had given him for his department and what else he might need to spend on. There seemed to be some degree of inflation with the prices. "Fine," he said, and took out two credit chips along with an exchanger. Bulky and archaic, but he wasn't going to trust Miccolo's device to not rip every shred of data. He transferred a thousand credits to the disposable one and walked it over to Miccolo's desk.

"This is illegal," the techie said, eyes locked on the flashing code.

Ram laughed. "Are you serious?"

Miccolo shook his head. "No, I don't mean you paying me. I mean this implant's encryption. They changed the BIOS."

Elliot took a moment to process what Miccolo meant, and looked down at the device. He went over his knowledge of neural implants, remembering all the propaganda they had tried to feed him about how safe they were. Power came from the glycolysis engine, the most advanced piece of technology on the planet. It turned blood sugar into electricity, enough to never need charging, never need external access. That was one of the major protections. Hacking into a computer necessarily required access to it. That was part of the logic protecting the Pishon Line particle accelerator and several other military facilities. Neural implants were in fact two computers, a simulator and an interface. The simulator was the portion that communicated with the internet and everything else in the world. That could be hacked by definition. To protect the human, the only thing a hacked simulator could do was assault the interface with the computer equivalent of sensory input. It wasn't feasible to pass code.

The neurists had explained it like if someone replaced the factory foreman with a turncoat, there still was no amount of screaming or lying the new foreman could do to convince the worker to hurt themselves with the machinery. The workers might not be able to operate the factory with lights flashing and noise blaring and the thermostat set to boiling, but nothing could be broken like that.

That assumed that the hackers couldn't change the coding in the interface, because nobody could without surgically accessing buried portions of the implant. It would be very illegal to do so. Not to mention, the only people who were supposed to know the programming language were government owned.

"Are you sure?" Elliot asked.

Miccolo rolled his eyes. "This here is an M-series Type 512. Released in '33. You still see these all the time because they're the oldest implant able to handle de-localized processing... That means the implant can run as a receiver for a computer's output. That way when simulations get more complex and more demanding, you only have to upgrade your computer rather than your brain. No need to update the wetware. They're obsolete now, but obsolete doesn't mean uncommon. I am very, very familiar with the latency response between nodes. It's pretty much the only thing you can do to debug issues."

Ram spoke up. "Miccolo used to help out when thugs got their skulls knocked in and the doctors had to diagnose whether the issue was brain damage or implant damage."

Elliot nodded. "Now I understand why she recommended you."

Miccolo said, "Heartsteel overwrote part of the ocular interface. It would either let them see what this person was seeing, or to change what they saw whether they wanted it to or not. Maybe both."

This is why I don't have a fucking implant.

"And you're sure of this?" Elliot asked.

Miccolo glared at him. "Yes. What do you take me for? What are you paying me for?"

Elliot nodded. "Hey Ram, did Palmer ever get replaced as our sys-admin contact?"

She frowned and tilted her head. After a moment of standing with her arms crossed she said, "I don't think so, and she's listed as Not Available at the moment. I think I heard Mr Wyatt complaining that he couldn't get ahold of her the other day. Does this need to be reported to EVE?"

Elliot paced the room, scratching his chin and thinking it over. "No, EVE can't actually act on something like this. We need a body. Shit, I can't believe they're this bad at hiring... We need somebody else's sys-admin... Bastard's Blood, do I really have to?"

Ram tilted her head the other way. "Really have to what?"

Ask Seraphina for help.

"Hold on," he said. "Miccolo, I still want the actual data from the implant."

The techie shook his head. "Already working on that. Decryption is in progress. I've got more computational power in this room than most corporations. Anything they put on an implant I'll have... alright, I got access to the data drive. Now then, let's see what he took pictures of, shall we?"

Elliot walked over and watched over the techie's shoulder as he started scrolling through an album of pictures. Most of them were receipts. There were banal pictures of meals and drinks, which Elliot made a note to cross reference for social media proliferation. Then Miccolo stopped on a picture of a person with half their face covered by the number 325-930. They were tall and muscular, but half-sprawled against a wall.

"Is that edited?" Elliot asked.

Miccolo pulled up the meta data and shook his head. "That's the raw data. I guess that answers what they hacked the implant to do." Miccolo browsed through, grabbing other pictures of people and finding them with similar numbers stuck across their faces like name tags.

"Why would they use numbers?" Ram asked, peering between their shoulders. "Isn't that dehumanizing?"

Miccolo scoffed and went back to scrolling the album. "That's the point, Ram. Haven't you seen them in the news?"

"Sorry, this isn't my investigation."

"They're thugs. Assuming you got this from a murder victim, I can't imagine anyone other than the MPs would even care. There was one journalist–they snapped his arm in half and hospitalized him because he was trying to take pictures of a crime scene." Miccolo was almost halfway through the reel of pictures when he stopped to check what apps had been installed on Azir's implant. The collection of games seemed innocuous enough. "Is this enough?" Miccolo asked. "Or do you want his bank account too?"

Elliot arched an eyebrow. "You can get that?"

"Not for a thousand credits."

"I'll let you know if it becomes pertinent. Can you transfer this all to a thumbdrive?"

Miccolo slotted a datastick into his computer and went back to tapping away on his programs. "You're going to report this, right?"

Elliot straightened up and put his hands in his pockets. After stepping back, he said, "Through the proper channels."

If they exist.

"This kind of revelation could ruin Heartsteel, you know."

"It could."

"That would be quite the political scandal."

"Yeah, some people in the Buffalo Party will be pretty pissed, I imagine. We have a hierarchy of needs and responsibilities though."

"Okay Maxwell, if I give you this data, is it going to vanish or are heads going to roll?"

"Oh, heads are going to roll. Just behind the scenes, more likely than not."

And probably not heads nearly as important as you would like.

Miccolo handed the credit chip back, along with the data stick. "Then consider this work pro bono," he said as the workshop began coming to life again.

Elliot took the chips back and vanished them into his pockets. He glanced at Ram, who was smiling at him. "Well, I think I might have misjudged you by your prior acquaintances."

Miccolo grimaced. "Yes, it doesn't reflect well on me that I associate with the police, now does it? If you don't mind now, I have some data sharing conferences to host. I'm working with a motion capture team down in Arkan and they want to know how realistic her balance is. They found it very rude that I was cheating with gyroscopes. Very wasteful of energy."

Ram perked up, steepling her fingers together. "Oh, is that with–"

Elliot tuned out their discussion and gave them some space. He slipped across the workshop, pausing only to glance at the sculpture of cybernetics that Miccolo was giving life to. There was an element to it that he couldn't identify, but it was the same element that always caught his eye in A-Maze's graffiti. It wasn't mass produced, procedurally generated, nor factory stamped. It wasn't like the orchestra medley filling the air, it had Miccolo's attention in it.

Elliot signaled to Ram that she could meet him around the corner where he had left his phone, then left to place a phone call to Seraphina. After catching her up on the essential details, she said, "Well, I can pass this along to our sys-admin, but you realize we'll have to arrest their neurist, right?"

"Okay, is that a problem?"

"The problem is that he's missing."

23

Unseen

2140/09/21

Anne Grief did not strike Clyde as the leader of a criminal organization. She was older, with grey in her curly hair and a bend to her back. She didn't meet him in some grand office behind layers of security, but in a chinese-style diner. Her fingers looked like the blood had been sucked out of them, leaving wrinkles of skin and iron bones. She was also better with chopsticks than anyone Clyde had ever seen, snapping up bits and pieces of the sauced stir fry until she looked him over. "Ah, the unfortunate one," she said, wiping her mouth off with a napkin.

There was no other chair at the table, not even for her pair of bodyguards. They seemed young, possibly her grandchildren. Clyde stepped in front of her and took off his void mask. "I suppose I should thank you for the temporary employment."

Anne waved a hand. "Kill the damn music, would you?" she mumbled, and the quiet sitar music stopped. Then she looked back at him. "The work was nothing. You earned your pay plenty, Mr Bondsman. In fact, I think of that as a sort of try out period for you. You passed."

"I'm flattered," he said, his voice flat.

Anne grinned and gestured at a girl not yet old enough to be drafted. "See that?" the old woman asked. "That's called adult behavior. He has emotions, but he's not acting on them. He isn't controlled by his impulses like a child. Though... you can tell by his tone that he's making an effort. Nobody's perfect. You could remember that too. Now then, Mr Bondsman. I think you have an inkling of what my organization is like, but certainly not the whole picture."

"Nor do I want to."

She laughed. "Good answer. The important thing is that our desires..." she gestured with her chopstick, forming a circle between her and him, "They align quite well at the moment. You know? You want justice, I want CEO Dixie dead. You're an able-bodied man with nothing to lose. I have the resources necessary for you to get something in exchange for your life. You do realize that acting on this vengeance is a one-way trip, don't you?"

He couldn't return her grin. The mirth didn't exist inside him. "That's fine. I wouldn't be the first man to do something like this."

"No! Of course you wouldn't be. Men have been doing this for the last three thousand years, maybe longer depending on your antediluvian beliefs. That's what makes you a known quantity. I wouldn't be gambling on you otherwise. However, I do need to know how you made it back. The rumor mill was rather bleak in their whispers."

Clyde's hand went to his side, where the blades still hung from his hip. Rather, the one did. The guards had taken the micro-blade and left him the other with a scoff. "I got help from a very isolated man. That doesn't matter. I was lucky, nothing more to it. Now I'm here. You have Dr Forez, don't you?"

"What kind of man was he? The one outside the walls," Anne asked.

"A one-eyed kook."

She stared at him, hands and face unmoving. "And... is he where you got that sword? Or did you pick that up after getting back to Bastion?"

Clyde shifted on his feet, glancing at the guards. Both of them had tensed, and their hands probably rested on concealed guns. "He gave them to me, yeah. He had plenty of spares. I think he loots bodies, when soldiers get killed out there, you know? The blighted don't scare him in the least. Like I said, a kook."

"Well..." Anne shook her head. "I believe that would be quite the story, if we had the time to tell it. On the bright side, you didn't make a mess getting your weapons, so the police won't be looking for you already. Zarah says your neural implant is broken too, yes? Nothing to track?"

"Nope, I'm a ghost. It's like I died out there."

"Keep that mask on, from now on. I don't want you taking it off for anything. Only eat in safe houses we tell you about, understood? If EVE ever, and I mean ever, sees you with it off, she will be able to identify you with the mask on. What you'll be doing will be way higher profile than the usual punks in masks. They'll bring out all the stops once they realize you're winning, you ghost."

Clyde cocked his head to one side and frowned. The Heartsteel tower was like a fortress. A security company couldn't afford to have a break-in tarnish their reputation. "If you say so," he said.

"I do say so, and if you want to cut off Dixie's head, you'll listen to what an old woman has to say, yes? Now, Carlos, take our ghost to the visitor's room. He has some catching up to do."

Clyde followed the young man she indicated and let his breath out when Anne couldn't see him any longer. They went through the back of the diner and into another series of stairs, tunnels, and passages. Eventually, the two of them passed through door after locked door and stepped into a small, blacked out room. The interstice of structure had excess padding, enough to muffle the world and isolate them the old, mechanical way. No noise-cancellers were needed, just raw material between them and the city so no one could hear what was said, or what was screamed and pleaded.

Dr Forez sat strapped to an old hair salon chair with the headrest ripped off. They had strapped his ankles, waist, and wrists down, leaving him at their mercy, but so far uninjured. The only sign of distress was the lines of sweat and hair dye running out of his scalp. The guide sniffed and shook his head. "You're the one that worked there," the criminal said, looking at Clyde. "Maybe you know the right questions to ask."

Dr Forez looked up, breathing hard and hardly able to focus his eyes. He had to blink a few times to settle his gaze onto Clyde and wrangling his fat lip to speak was a chore, but nevertheless he said, "Aw, fuck."

Clyde took a moment to look at the bloody man. He stared and he thought about the role that Dr Forez had to play in the grand scheme of Heartsteel. The man was a neurist. He hadn't killed anyone, but he was the primary man responsible for installing that program in their heads. He was the reason Heartsteel employees saw colors and danger instead of people–instead of underaged kids in over their heads. Clyde decided that was culpability enough. He knelt down and grinned inside his void mask. "Hello Dr Forez. Nice to see you again."

The neurist looked between him and the others in the room, only to see Anne Grief's people leave. He recoiled against his restraints, only to learn anew how tight they were. "Look, I don't know who you are, but I've already been through this. I've already said what I can say!"

Clyde laughed. It seemed appropriate to drive the fear deeper. Whether that would make Dr Forez tell a deeper truth, he didn't know. He didn't care either. "You're a sinner, you know that, Doctor?"

"I'm an installation tech! Not a programmer. I can't tell you anything about what they did."

Clyde stopped looking at the man's face. He looked at his hands, how they cringed and squeezed, gripping the old chrome armrest. Part of Clyde's mind began thinking about questions, what he could extract from the neurist's mind. Maybe he couldn't find out what Heartsteel had programmed, nothing that would be actionable in a court. He came up with a few ideas that mattered though. The man was repeating himself, stating over and over again why torture wouldn't work or wouldn't help him, or something like that. Clyde slid his hand around Dr Forez's skull, pressing his thumb to the man's forehead and squeezing. "I think you should understand that I'm a very hurt man."

The neurist grew quiet, his head trembling in Clyde's grasp. He tried to stare him in the eyes but only saw the abyss of the mask. "I didn't... Whatever happened to you, there's nothing I can do about it."

Clyde squeezed until it felt like his fingers would rip off patches of skin and his arm trembled and his muscled ached. "No, you can't bring my family back," he agreed, letting go. He huffed and tapped his finger on Dr Forez's wrinkled forehead. "And I have to take care of this, don't I? The things you can do, they're in that brain of yours. I'd love to beat you bloody, but that might hurt your brain and I do concede I need that. On the other hand–"

Dr Forez had never worked a trade job. He had never toiled in construction or stuffing his fingers through soil to farm. There were a thousand things the soft doctor had clearly never done, and the result was a certain softness and looseness in his body. When Clyde took his finger and bent it back , it almost seemed like the bone bent rather than snapped. The flesh resisted as the doctor recoiled, then it twisted. A moment later, Dr Forez threw his head back and howled.

Clyde looked at the bent digit, quickly swelling and bruising. He grinned. "That's not your brain though, is it?"

Dr Forez bottled up his pain and spat it out at Clyde. "You fucking asshole! You're a goddamn amateur at this, aren't you?"

"So what if I am?" Clyde asked, and grabbed another finger.

Before he could snap it, Anne's boy stuck his head back into the interrogation wing and waved him over. Clyde snapped Dr Forez's middle finger before he rose, and left the neurist screaming and swearing. The thug held up a plastic bag with one black pill inside it. It was an unlabelled hexagon about the size of his pinky finger's nail. "You know what this is?" the kid asked.

"Is that CZAR?"

"As far as you're concerned, it's a truth serum," the kid asked, and put the bag into his hand.

Clyde took the bag and stared at it. In his hand, he held one of the most illegal things in all of Bastion. The most common of contraband at least. If a SWATbot were to show up, it could legally paint the walls with his brains for holding it. He laughed.

"What? Afraid of it or something?" the kid asked.

"You have no idea," he said, and turned back to Dr Forez. The neurist was still hissing in pain, trying to pull himself out of his restraints as he glared at Clyde. Force feeding the doctor the pill was a mere matter of grabbing him by the cheap hair plugs, twisting his head back till his mouth opened and dropping the black pill into his mouth. He had heard it tasted bad, so Clyde clamped his hand over the doctor's mouth and held it there as he jerked and struggled. After a few minutes, he let go. Either it had been swallowed, or it had dissolved.

"The fuck was that?" Dr Forez demanded, spitting the filth from his mouth.

Clyde took hold of the doctor's ring finger. "No need to talk yet. Drugs take a while and I don't really care yet. You see, my mother died and I still haven't really processed that. It's just a thing that happened and I want to make other people hurt because of it. You had a role to play in it, so–" He bent the doctor's third finger back.

The wailing of pain went in one ear and out the other. He stared at Dr Forez not like a man, not like an animal, and only somewhat similar to the examination of an insect. He couldn't think of it as looking at trash because the thing of flesh before him moved and spoke, it just didn't think in a way he could respect. He searched inside himself for empathy and came up empty. So he stomped his heel on Dr Forez's foot until he felt the arch break. Feet and fingers weren't needed to answer questions. It was fifteen minutes more of abuse when he figured the drug had taken effect.

The symptoms were curious and obvious both. The screaming of pain stopped, even when Clyde snapped another finger and twisted the bone until it ripped out of the neurist's skin. He had heard that was an effect of CZAR, the ability to make pain a rational thing rather than an emotional impulse.

"Are you ready to talk?" he asked.

"If I talk, will you let me go?" Dr Forez asked, his words dull.

"I don't know, they might. I'll tell you for sure that I'll move on to hurting someone else if you just help me get them."

Dr Forez rolled his head back and heaved a few breaths. He snorted and spat out a wad of blood and phlegm so he could breathe through his nose again. "You worked for Heartsteel, didn't you? Do you still have your User ID?"

"I don't have an implant anymore. I'm dead as far as their system is concerned."

"Then yes," Dr Forez said. He licked the blood off his lips and grimaced. "I can tell you exactly how to be invisible."

24

Illegal Shipments

2140/10/21

Elliot was covering a QRS shift in the morning when the DNA results came in on the blood. The message appeared on his phone a few minutes after eight in the morning, and he wondered if the results had actually come in the night before and the tech had simply waited. Complaining would do him no favors for the future, so he set his can of Zeus down and looked at the profile of Clyde Bondsman, deceased.

The entire QRS squad had nothing particularly important to do, they were sitting in a mail distribution warehouse. Cardboard and plastic boxes surrounded them, echoing their casual conversations as Colt negotiated with one of the local gang lords. Evidently, this one was more cooperative than Sokolov had been, or perhaps just as cooperative but less dangerous. A shooting had occurred in a local neighborhood, EVE knew who it was and where they had gone, but nobody felt like marching into a computer mausoleum.

Something like that might be taken wrong by the locals. On agreement that the perp wasn't one of theirs, they were rounding the shooter up free of charge. Elliot, along with the rest of the officers on QRS duty, was hardly more than a show of force. Half of his colleagues had their helmets off to smoke, their tobacco giving factory packages some personality before their destinations.

He pulled up the dossier on Bondsman. The man was twenty-five and honorably discharged from mandatory service. He had refused an offer to extend his service and a note appended to his file advised not pressing the matter due to behavioral problems. Upon returning to Bastion, he worked in the restaurant industry, bouncing from place to place with no reason given for the changes until he ended up working deliveries for Ajitatsu.

Elliot stopped when he saw that Clyde's most recent job had been for Heartsteel. That arched one of his eyebrows. The man had been reported dead by Heartsteel, cause of death classified.

A dead man has his blood on a ship that was used to smuggle somebody back into Bastion, and Heartsteel didn't report his cause of death? I think Mr Bondsman isn't quite dead.

Elliot glanced around. He knew everyone else on the QRS squad, but none of them were looking to him for any work. In fact, until Colt came back with the shooter, nobody had any work. He stepped over to a corner of the warehouse and called Seraphina.

"Thomas," she said, and he could hear the smile on her lips. "Is this becoming a habit?"

"No," he said. "I need you to append to that sys-admin request a warrant to unseal the cause of death on a civilian, name of Clyde Bondsman."

She hesitated a moment. "Clyde? What did you say the cause of death was?"

"No idea, but it was put in the system just a few weeks ago. I don't even know how Heartsteel authenticated his death. Why? You say that like you know him."

Seraphina sighed. "No, I'm just kicking myself for not wording a question properly earlier. You had EVE cross reference the friends and family of anyone killed at a Heartsteel protest and look for someone that could be our killer? Clyde Bondsman's little brother was one of the victims. I ruled him out because he was dead too. I didn't check how he died."

"No shit," Elliot said. "If he's alive... well, I suppose that would still raise the question of why EVE hasn't spotted him. I need you to put in for the warrant though."

"And you can't do that yourself?"

Elliot turned his head when he heard one of the industrial doors swing open, the hinges squeaking. "I'm double-booked. Talk to you later," he said, and hung up on her. There was half a word of protest from her that stuck in his ear, but he swept back to his chair.

A man like an ox and wearing a void mask dragged in a twig of a man by the scruff of his shirt. Elliot recognized the smaller man as their shooter, face now contorted by anger and panic. Half a dozen officers in the QRS team circled around the two civilians. Apparently, the shooter's arms had been tied behind his back with layers of duct tape–a bit more secure than handcuffs. They hadn't shut his mouth though. "Let me fucking go. Backstabbers! Quazes. Motherfucking betrayers. You're scum, you know that? Scum!"

Colt shook his head and set his suit to broadcast. Amplified, he said, "Mahmud Fletcher, you're under arrest for seven counts of assault with a deadly weapon and one count of murder. I'd suggest that you keep your mouth shut. Miranda rights and all that."

Mahmud spat at Colt's feet as he straightened up. He snarled. Bruises covered his face and the lines in his throat as distinct as a meth-addict's. Then he glared at the thug who had brought him in. The difference in size–the restraints too–were clearly insurmountable. Mahmud didn't have to squirm out of the thug's grasp though. He kicked one of the boxes in the shelf next to them.

Six hands went to their firearms, but Mahmud just stomped again, ripping the cardboard and spilling bags across the floor. The void mask-wearing thug yanked him back, throwing Mahmud against the opposite wall as everyone else stared at what Mahmud had revealed. Bag upon bag of hand-labeled pill bottles had scattered across the tile floor; the guts of the unassuming package. Mahmud laughed.

Colt pressed the radio control on his wrist. "HQ, this is Officer C00173, hereby requesting all available QRS teams to report to–"

The door out of the distribution room banged open as the masked thug ran. The radio channel buzzed with call outs and coordination. Nobody took charge, just a mad scramble. The thug leader who had been cooperating was dubbed Gorilla. When he ran, most of the QRS team gave chase. That left the shooter for Elliot and two others.

Elliot fell in behind officers D41133 "Dale" and E45513 "Easy" chasing Mahmud. They were calling in for confirmation on firearms, pinging requests to EVE about rules of engagement. The thoroughfare halls out from the warehouse were like roads for automated forklifts, complete with bridges to other towers. The mesh down to Epsilon was only here and there, with residential neighborhoods clinging to most of the walls. On the upside, there weren't many doors for Mahmud to dip through.

Easy shouted, "Taser rounds," as they cornered through a row of refrigeration boxes. Forklifts were gliding through the food warehouse, beeping and squealing as they carried around crates of cardboard across a spaghetti mess of colored lines.

Ah, shit.

Elliot's lungs were burning and he could still feel the bruises across his chest where Gaia thugs had pummeled him. The QRS suit dragged him down and his throat was dry already. A moment's hesitation to switch magazines in his pistol was a moment that Mahmud darted into the stream of forklifts. The machines screeched at him, but hardly slowed. When Dale and Easy tried to follow after, the entire dance of machines screeched to a halt.

Colt's voice barked in his ear. "Blackstone, he's coming your way. Split and stop." A red indicator appeared inside across the visor of his helmet. When he looked over, Mahmud was running straight towards him, arms still tied behind his back. His shoulders swung and jerked as he ran, nearly falling over every step. Given the choice, Elliot let out his breath and took aim.

"South Missou PD, freeze," he ordered as his suit synchronized with the sights on his pistol. Mahmud was on a bridge, dead straight and open. The only cover would be forklifts that had stopped moving because of Dale and Easy. The only door was marked in yellow and black, definitely locked.

Mahmud threw his shoulder into the door anyway, bashing it open.

Elliot fired, only squeezing off one round he was so surprised. It caught the perp in the thigh, but Mahmud still tumbled through. Elliot hissed and called out, "He got out a service door." He sucked in breath and ran after. The chatter of radio responses blared in his ear and he barely picked out anything useful. Other QRS teams were on their way and someone was giving him backup but nobody was very concerned about a man half tied up in duct tape getting away.

The door beyond led to an alley for apartments, each with their doors shut. Apartment numbers were damaged and missing, the overhead lights half-functional. Mahmud was shouting for help, that a jannis was there and more. He screamed for someone to save his undeserving ass. Elliot found him crawling across the ground, his right leg not moving properly. The shock would wear off if Elliot let him be, but there was no need for that.

Pointing his gun at the man's chest, Elliot said, "Just settle down before I get the all clear to kill you. You can either let me hobble you or I can give you a heart attack and let the EMTs sort you out."

Mahmud hissed and kicked at Elliot, but all he could do was squirm up against a wall as he glared. "I'll talk. I showed you the drugs, didn't I? I know things. These people are scum. I'll torch them all down. That's what they get for stabbing me in the back. I'll squeal if you let me go right now."

Elliot closed in, not moving the barrel of his gun from Mahmud's chest. "I'll be happy to hear about it at the station."

"They're hiding a killer."

Yeah, you.

"He's killed way more than me. I think he's at five or six now!"

"Feel free to tell us all about it at–"

Mahmud threw himself up at Elliot, jerking on the ground. "I ain't telling you shit if you bring me in. You got that? I'll roll on them right now but you let me go."

He's getting the feeling back in his leg. I should shoot him again.

"That's not a deal I can make, now stop moving or you're getting another shock."

"He's here!" Mahmud shouted, jerking his head down the hall. "They hid him here, thought you wouldn't notice. There's tunnels, you know? Use your head, jannis. I'm offering you a real killer just to let me go. What am I anyway? That bitch got what she deserved. I'm not a lunatic."

Elliot shot him in the chest, the electro-chemical cartridge shattering like a thunder crack. Mahmud convulsed and groaned as Elliot holstered. He rolled over in his own drool and gave Elliot the opportunity to kneel down and snap cuffs onto his ankles. As soon as the man was hobbled, Elliot tapped a button his his radio and said, "EVE, did you–"

Someone cocked a hammer next to his head. The apartment door next to him had quietly opened and a woman in a void mask had a revolver almost touching his helmet. He couldn't see what caliber the pistol had, but at point blank, several could pierce the armor. "Not another word, jannis."

Elliot quietly cinched the cuffs and held up his hands.

They said other QRS teams were en route, right? Right?

A moment later, kneeling with his hands behind his head, the only thing Elliot could think of was how much he hated QRS duty. The operations were by definition unplanned, chaotic, and dangerous. The worst chaos wasn't even the criminals fighting back, but when random, unrelated things flared up: like a neighborhood block slamming security shutters at the sight of them and sealing him inside with a gun-toting woman.

Of course, for an officer in distress, QRS teams had the legal right to enter anywhere. They just had to use the correct override code with EVE and she would let them in, or manually breach the door. Training had been blithely clear that if they did find a room that they couldn't enter to save someone, then EVE wouldn't let them and they were damn well better off not going in. Radiation exposure was the typical example.

The problem, aside from the gun in his face, was that nobody knew he was in distress.

She had stopped him mid-sentence, and that sentence hadn't even been calling for help. The QRS helmet muffled, but didn't mute, his speech. Even if he could open the radio channel, she would shoot him before anyone arrived. Of course, there was one obvious solution to his problem. A solution which everyone else in the department could have made use of and largely told him to do as well. He had been too resistant to the idea his entire life, and especially so in the last year.

If he had a neural implant he wouldn't need to speak to call for help, he could just think of the message like a telepath. Instead, all he had was a phone and he couldn't just take that out to text someone.

Eventually, the other teams would show up to help him, and find that the doors had been locked. Most of them would be concerned with the thug still at large, but some would show up. He could already see their confusion and he wondered how long they would spend trying to make phone calls because they assumed the security shutters were closed accidentally. Nobody on the team that he knew of was so gung ho that they would cut a lock just because it was in their way.

The next best thing he could do was turn on the open channel and ask her, "So, like... is someone else–"

"Shut your mouth, jannis," she said, moving the gun closer to his head. "You think I don't know you've got a radio in there? You think I'm stupid?"

Elliot didn't answer, but Mahmud did. The man had recovered well enough to spit the bloody drool out of his mouth–must have busted his lip falling. "Oh, well then! Aren't things getting spicy now?"

"You shut your mouth too!"

"Why?" Mahmud asked with a grin. "You got two guns on you? Because if you take that gun off Mr Policeman there you're fucked."

A surprisingly good point coming out of him.

The woman took her eyes off Elliot, but not the gun. "Do you want to find out how fast I can gut shot you when the jannis isn't expecting it? Because I can do it pretty quick."

I wonder if the radio is picking any of this up.

Mahmud sneered back with bloody teeth. "Who do you work for anyway? Song? Someone else?"

"This is unclaimed territory. Nobody is going to be pissed off if I kill you here."

"Except the police."

Elliot's radio crackled with a voice he couldn't place. "Blackstone, did you get the guy? What happened?"

Oh please, please, please, realize I'm fucked here.

The stress was starting to get to him. His heart rate was slowly rising and with it his breath. He could feel the sweat across his body as he stared at the unwavering gun.

What the hell is Amara going to think if I kick the bucket like this? Bastard's Blood, I should have gotten a neural implant.

Mahmud was nearly hysteric, speaking fast like it was his lifeline to sanity. "You don't work for Song, do you? Who do you work for, bitch? Who do you work for? Who's got you getting me killed?"

"Song? Hannah Song?" Elliot asked.

Zarah didn't shoot him because a door opened down the hall and she had to check who was exiting. It was a skinny, dark skinned boy who should have been doing his service. The kid had bags under either arm, using his ass to push through doors. "We good?" she asked.

"Let's go, let's go!" the newcomer responded, jerking his head to the far exit.

"Colt, this is Ether. I think something happened to Blackstone. Permission to cut this door?" Officer E11434 asked, her voice crackling over the radio.

Colt said, "Permission granted."

Zarah bolted down the hall as her comrade yanked open the far shutter. Ether slashed the locking mechanism. It must have been only residential grade because the bolts snapped in half—industrial grade might have needed an energized blade.

When the gun stopped pointing at him, Elliot first inhaled. Relief flooded through his system like a drug and almost toppled him over. The tightness in his chest vanished and his head went light for a moment. Then his training got the better of him. He dove for his own pistol.

Ether and two other officers shoved through the security gate as Elliot hit the floor, skidding on his armor plates. He managed to crack off two shots at Zarah. Both sparked against the walls. "Fuck!"

Ether ran over and knelt beside Elliot as he was getting up. "Colt, looks like one suspect on foot."

"Two," Elliot corrected. "Man and a woman."

Ether nodded. "Permission to pursue?"

"Negative," Colt said. "Half our team is still apprehending the big guy. We'll have EVE tag them for pickup later."

Elliot snarled and stood up, glaring at the far door. "That bitch almost killed me! Threatened to!"

Ether stepped over and planted her boot on Mahmud's gut, pinning him to the ground. "So what happened? She got the drop on you and held you there?"

He nodded. "Yeah."

"Weird."

"...Yeah."

An hour later, the entire neighborhood had become a crime scene. The big guy was arrested, and Elliot never got his real name. He could have pulled up the database and taken a look, but he found himself going through the motions in a daze. He knew that both the apartment the girl had left and the one the guy had left were standard units, but the actual details escaped him. The investigation of the apartments seemed fruitless and most people were grumbling that they were obviously nothing more than safe houses.

Colt leaned against the kitchen counter of the girl's apartment, next to Elliot. The older man had his helmet off. "Doing alright, Blackstone?"

"Yeah, I'm fine."

Colt glanced at the cabinet he was looking in. "Find anything in there?"

The shelves were sparse, just some instant coffee and some chocolate bars. "Not really."

"Huh," Colt said, and looked back at him. "Because you've been staring at it for a quarter of an hour."

"Have I?

"Having a gun in your face isn't a very fun time, is it? Take the day off, Blackstone. Go get a drink or something."

25

Sword For Hire

2140/10/22

Anne had sent over a picture and a name. He had been put up in an apartment under her control. Just one box of dozens, barely larger than the pod Heartsteel had given him. No lock, no security, and no surveillance. The fact that he had a burner phone to get the old lady's messages was his only luxury, but it couldn't really help him. It couldn't do the one thing he wanted.

He didn't have his sister's phone number.

It had been saved in his neural implant, and that was busted. He couldn't go check it at home. He couldn't log in to his accounts and go digging through his messages with her. Anything like that would get him flagged and arrested. So, he didn't even know if she knew what had happened, that their mother and brother were dead. If she had been told anything, it might be that he was dead too. She was in California though, and transport back from the coast was never fast.

Clyde was able to get names and faces and where to find them. He was like a trained attack dog and he wondered if that was how Grief saw himself. The latest one came accompanied with a rap sheet of crimes. Most seemed to be taken from an independent journalist. Completely above board as far as he could tell, just like the kid whose arm had been snapped. That journalist had been trying to build a case for legal action but never got enough traction nor funding to act on it. Anne Grief had other uses for the intel, and that was.

Michael Grozzuh had worked for Hearsteel for six months. Before he had been hired by them, he worked as a club bouncer where he hospitalized three people. Flux nightclub seemed like a trendy place, or rather a gaudy place for people flaunting money they didn't actually have. The police already had him on work probation for assaulting his then girlfriend and causing a miscarriage. For good measure, the journalist also included a list of games, media sites, and social networks he had been banned from.

Grozzuh had been in the group that had put down Johnny's protest.

Anne Grief didn't have any hard info that he was the guy, but he hadn't stopped the violence. He was culpable enough for Clyde. He just had to wait until Grozzuh left Heartsteel's tower, and hope that after five kills, they weren't locking everyone down. Until then, he just had to wait and stay quiet.

Zarah didn't knock when she entered, kicking the door shut with her heel as she swung a bag at him. Steam billowed out from the sagging heap. "Sorry it ain't home cooking," she said, dropping the carryout on the table next to him.

He popped a lid open and looked at the fried rice noodles within. There were some lumps he thought were tofu, bamboo shoots, and something green that might have been broccoli. Maybe. The agri-corps must have mutated it to grow indoors better. He hoped it tasted the same and pulled it over. "It don't matter, you're spoiling me by eating with me regardless."

"So, how does it feel? To get revenge?"

The noodles were sticky and wet, but seemed to lose their flavor as soon as he bit into them. There was nothing left of them when he swallowed. "Justice, not revenge."

"You're avoiding the question."

"I don't know, it's strange. It's sort of like the first time I shot a gun, you know?"

"The first time I shot a gun all I hit was a light and got my ass beat. I think we had different experiences there."

Clyde laughed. "I learned in boot camp. They gave us beer cans and glass bottles to shoot. Reactive targets they called them. The whole afternoon they had us firing and getting yelled at by the sergeant. I was one of the first to hit a bottle at twenty meters or so. Thought I was hot shit because other people couldn't. I can still remember the way it made the palm of my hand slightly numb and the thump it gave my ears... and then..."

Zarah jabbed her chopsticks into her food. "You better not be about to make some kind of Christian morality lecture out of this or some disgusting shit like that."

He shook his head. "No, after we had our fun, they brought in a marksman. In hindsight, I think he was chromed up. They've got nerve stabilizers, you know? Smooths the twitches in the muscles. I hear it makes you so itchy afterwards you want to rip your skin off, but this guy came down and took the same little service pistol we had been using but he aimed at nothing–or so we thought. The drill sergeant had to turn on a tv livestreaming the end of the range because none of us could see the damn bottles. There was a set of them half a kilometer away and that sonofabitch walked bullets down the line–hit every one of them."

Zarah scoffed. "No way. There must have been little explosives or something. No pistol is that accurate. It doesn't matter how good he was. You got tricked."

Clyde shook his head and stuffed his mouth again. "Maybe, maybe not. Point of the story is there's always someone better. So far, I feel like an idiot getting giddy over the kiddy range even though I damn well know I'm about to set foot in the big leagues. Someone way better than me is going to show up and make me look like the fool that I am, only this time I'm not going to get embarrassed. I'm going to get killed."

"Hey, you can always get the drop on an expert. So long as you are the one setting the pace, you have a chance. Speaking of which, what's your plan?"

"Plan? Do I look like I have a plan to catch a man on probation? He's practically under house arrest. The only time he's going to be motivated to leave is to get his junk wet at a whore house, and that's if he isn't scared enough to stick it to digital only... ah well, maybe he won't do that. It was fucking creepy to know that Heartsteel was monitoring my internet."

Zarah looked over and held his gaze. "You want to know where he goes to fuck? We can find that out."

He thought it over for a moment, and shrugged. "Alright then, sounds like a plan."

A few hours later, he was walking through the Worm Tunnels, following a hand drawn map Zarah had given him. Half a dozen turns, staircases, and ladders threatened to leave him hopelessly lost. The lighting was gloomy at best, making it almost impossible to see through his void mask. The only other people in the desolate caves of steel beneath the city were on journeys of similarly clandestine natures, so nobody spoke. Communication never exceeded glares and a quiet giving-way of personal space. He didn't even speak a pass phrase when he got to the marked door, he held up a piece of paper with a QR code on it.

The bouncer looked at it long enough for his implant to decode it, then the doors were unbolted. They let him into a sort of air lock and patted him down. Clyde had left the micro-blade behind, but kept the gift from the survivor. The bouncer found it and pulled it free. When there was nothing attached to the handle, his fat eyebrows wrinkled up.

"Is that a problem?" Clyde asked.

"Guess not, Mr Samurai. I don't think you're going to find a girl who's into that kind of roleplay though."

"For the right amount of money, I'm sure I can make it work."

The bouncer laughed and unlocked the inner door. Stepping inside the proper premises, the grime and rust of Epsilon immediately vanished. If he hadn't known better, he would have never guessed that they were on ground floor, buried beneath a factory tower seventy stories tall that non-stop, every day, pumped out the cheapest forms of packaging.

Styrene cups, cardboard boxes, paper carryout boxes, every piece of universal trash a business could need was spewed out of the tower. They were one of the few buildings in all of Bastion that had a direct connection out of the wall so they could accept a near endless torrent of wood pulp brought in by machines the size of dinosaurs.

Buried beneath that very essential service was a maid cafe where every girl had an hourly rate.

It was warm and the air heavily circulated through hydroponics setup which gave the air an earthy and floral scent. The scent would have been cheaper with pseudo-olfactors, but that would have hurt the fantasy. They even had real wood paneling across all the surfaces, CNC'd into Victorian scrawls and stained cherry red. Girls of all shapes and sizes strolled between tables, carrying pints of beer. One of the waitresses locked eyes on him and stopped in his path. Holding her tray to her chest, she smiled and bowed. "I'm sorry sir, but we do need to know your identity to serve you. You'll have to take the mask off before I seat you."

Clyde looked around the room again, seeing no other void masks. "Seriously? A place like this?"

"You can trust us with your privacy precisely because we're this kind of establishment, sir. Besides, how would you drink with that silly mask on?" The way she smiled at him, blonde bangs falling across her face and the neckline of her dress more than low enough, was more than enough to make him consider the prices.

"Well, I don't think Dr Bahtt will mind."

The smile vanished. "Eh? If you're a worker, why did you come in the front door? Are you an idiot?"

Clyde physically flinched from the emotional whiplash. "Can you just point me in the right direction?"

The backroom she directed him to didn't immediately lose the antique splendor, it was only after the second door that everything was once again paint and steel. He found Dr Bahtt in a converted office room. A bed had been shoved in where a table should have been, and all of his first aid tools strewn about side tables. Clyde froze when he saw the girl, twenty at the oldest, sitting on the bed in front of him.

The doctor barely glanced over at him before adjusting more of the sensors across the girl's arm and neck. Wires fed over to a computer, turning her bio-signs into diagnoses. "Don't worry about her. I won't be taking her skirt off or anything," the old man said.

The girl, an artificial redhead, looked Clyde over with a sneer. "You the guy?"

"My lawyer would advise me to not answer that, if I had a lawyer."

"He's the guy. You should know better. He doesn't work for your boss, he's just a mercenary."

The girl smirked. "And that's what you called yourself when you first showed up, all bedraggled and jobless. Now look at you, been inside all of us ladies."

Dr Bahtt peered over the rim of his glasses at her. "Jenny, not only am I too old to be interested in any of you, but I know full well what you do and I would not call you a lady."

She pouted.

Clyde cut her off. "Doctor, please," he said, sticking his thumbs in his belt. "Just send me on my way. It's safer for all of us."

Dr Bahtt finally turned to face him. He shrugged. "Oh, there's no rush. In fact, there's the very opposite of a rush."

Clyde sucked in a fistful of breath. "Is he not here? Did he leave already?"

Jenny rolled her eyes. "Oh, he's here," she said as she peeled a medical strap off from her neck and revealed the finger-line bruises around her throat.

"The boss doesn't want you doing anything untoward here in the cafe," Dr Bahtt said.

Clyde rolled his eyes. "I'm not stupid."

Again, the doctor shrugged. "Well, it should be a relief to you that I saw fit to make your job a bit easier. That's why there's no rush. He has to metabolize the rohypnol I put in his beer."

Clyde arched an eyebrow and looked around the miniature clinic. He spotted an entire bucket full of pill bottles along with boxes of Aji-tatsu chocolate. "Bastard's blood, so you people are the ones who were getting the special deliveries. Fuck. Now it makes some damn sense."

Jenny laughed. "What? Were you a delivery boy?"

"In another life."

Dr Bahtt spun on his heel, one hand to his ear. "Look alive, mercenary. Your target is on the move."

26

Cooldown

2140/10/22

Mikey d'Angelo held up a pint of beer and tapped it against Elliot's. "To not dying."

"To not dying," Elliot agreed, and sipped his beer. It was cold and faintly flavorful. The carbonation buzzed on his tongue, but he had no appetite to drink. The two of them were in a dive bar on the thirty-fifth floor of a Gaia residential block. Cozy place, tight walls with album art everywhere, the other patrons minded their own business, and it even had a pinball machine. The seats were as hard as rocks, but the rubber padding was at least clean.

"So how's Amara?"

Elliot shook his head. "I don't know, I think I'm welcome back. The situation with the thief was a fiasco. I guess I'm hoping this game tournament boosts her viewership because she needs to start generating some revenue. She's got more stuff she wants to buy."

"Outfits?"

"Equipment."

The sly smirk on Mikey's face went away. "So how's this murder case going?"

"I don't know, let me check," he said, and pulled out his phone. There was an alert from Amara that he didn't read. He didn't dismiss it, but he didn't read it. He clicked on the message from EVE instead and found that Chloe Bondsman had a general request for alert on any information about her presumed-dead brother, Clyde. Elliot sat back in his booth and drummed his fingers on the table.

The blood sample didn't actually prove anything. He hadn't been expecting to find a missing person when he took the evidence, so he hadn't thought to scan for fingerprints. Unfortunately, the retro-rock music playing in the bar was competing with a drizzle of rain which would be cleaning the boat of all evidence. Ram might have gotten fingerprints, but if she had then it would be strange that she had missed the blood.

And it would be cruel to give Chloe false hope like that.

He messaged Ram to ask if she had fingerprints, and said, "EVE hasn't spotted the killer yet. There's some followup I should probably be doing right now, but my... temporary partner is supposed to be taking care of that given the circumstances." The other reason to not contact Chloe was that Clyde, if he was alive, fit the profile perfectly. The man was deeply wronged by Heartsteel, had the military training to be deadly, and probably knew most of the victims personally.

Unfortunately, just a cursory glance at their recently separated employees was a hotbed of the criminally inclined. Dixie seemed to have a policy to hire sociopaths and rent them out as mercenaries. Psych profiling was supposed to narrow the field, but that was for general population. Elliot had foolishly thought that a company with a preference for hiring veterans meant he would only have to check a few dozen people, not over a hundred. Dozens were more likely to be the killer than Clyde Bondsman.

Except they were all accounted for at the last killing, and Clyde was supposedly dead in the wilderness.

The thought nagged at him, but he was having a beer with his friend. "How's Dom doing?" he asked.

Mikey blew air out his lips and shrugged. He drank half his beer and said, "I don't know. He's a teenager. He's hanging out with his friends and passing his classes. He doesn't talk to me much and I don't know if

I know how to reach him. Kids are great, but hell, I'm not his mother. I figure as long as I get him into the military, he'll do alright."

"You're not pushing him too hard, are you?"

"I'm more worried that I'm not pushing him hard enough. Shit, you've seen how kids can end up when they're coddled, haven't you? You go up to Alpha and you live in Beta. They're completely dysfunctional if they aren't given anything to do. I hear some of them intentionally make themselves too fat to pass the fitness exam because they know that Mommy and Daddy will get them a job. Can you believe we have modern day political dynasties like this?"

Elliot drummed his fingers on his glass and frowned. "Do you follow politics much, Mikey?"

"Here and there."

"What do you think of the Buffalo Party?"

Mikey laughed. "Oh, we're actually talking politics now, are we? The Buffalo Party. What do I think of them? I think they steal my money. I think they're completely fortified against losing any of their congressional seats and that they did so by agreement with the Glacier Party so that both of them have their little super minority positions. I understand they do right by you, funding the police but always with strings attached. They're also embroiled in corruption and scandal if you so much as sneeze at their veneer of respectability. The wind tunnels are in complete disarray because they contracted out the work to a subsidiary of their chairman's empire, but I guess that's better than the completely scuffed geothermal work that the Glacier Party did. Either way, Bastion is headed down a road to power blackouts because of these fucking idiots, and you can be sure that their lights aren't the ones that will be going out any time soon."

"Do you vote, Mikey?"

"I piss it away on write-ins. It don't matter."

"I always have conflicted feelings, since I'm on their payroll, so I try to not think about politics. But now and then, I end up working with these people and I find myself wondering what the hell they do for their jobs."

Mikey flagged down a waitress for another round of drinks. "They vote on policies that EVE wrote and they make speeches on the news when they're not advocating for their companies. If you want to see a real talk, what you have to do is find the debate forums they upload. The ones that nobody watches because they're ten hours long with huge pauses they intentionally don't edit out. There's this little under strata of political actors who aren't in politics, you know? I'm talking like agricultural optimizers that show up to argue about soil loss in the great plains or the mining companies working out of Alaska who don't know whether to sell their copper at a loss to one company because it will let people buy their other products for profit. You can find days and days and days of people talking about the little things about UAAF's militarization in those kinds of conversations. And you know what else you find?"

"What?"

Mikey downed the last of his first beer and leaned across the table. "They take their masks off and will just openly say things like they don't care about the murder rate in Gamma."

Elliot hung his head until after their second round of beers had been dropped off. "Until it affects them," he said, and killed his beer.

"So, are we going to keep talking politics? We can switch to conspiracies, history, historical conspiracies. Gossiping about the Bastard is always good fun."

Fucking bogeyman.

"I think," Elliot said as he rubbed his thumb across the condensation on his mug. His subconscious resolved the dispute before he knew it. "We need to do a shot, then I'm going to go back to that stupid party pad."

Mikey grinned and a moment later, two shot glasses hit the table between them. The waitress–an older woman modestly dressed and with a friendly grin–doused them with whiskey. They tapped glasses and knocked them back, the liquor burn opening up his nose and getting the blood to flow again.

"Hey," Elliot asked, "Since when were you so politically inclined?"

Mikey laughed and shrugged sheepishly. "Found a streamer I like. I was mostly repeating him. I think we should do one more."

Elliot looked at the glass. The round rim transformed into the barrel of the girl's gun. "Yeah, we should do one more." Again, the waitress poured and they drank. "Alright, how about this for a question: should I get a neural implant? I almost died because I didn't have one."

MIkey whistled. "Well, it sounds like you have one real good reason to get an implant right there, doesn't it? I've got a rudimentary one myself, you know. I can't go into virtual reality without a hardware connection, but it handles things like calls and internet browsing pretty well. Nothing went wrong with it."

"Just like the propagandists say?" Elliot asked, looking at the shotglass and feeling the burn in his gut. He waved the waitress off. "More safe and effective than a condom?"

"Yeah, pretty much. I didn't even get headaches after the first week. That's how fast I adapted to it. Just that initial calibration discomfort, you know? And I hear that's down to days now, maybe less if you pay more. What are you worried about, exactly? The digital temptation?"

"I don't know, I've just always been kind of repulsed by the idea."

"Well, you visit those ground floor mausoleums near every week, don't you? I'd be leery of doing whatever those skeletons are doing too."

Elliot grunted and shook his head. "The dumb thing is that the best way to check if something's safe is to see if the billionaires are doing it, the politicians too. Fact of the matter is those people have more implants than anyone."

"But they've got better stuff, eh?"

Elliot shrugged. "You say that, but not really? They have better neurists to put it in, but literally every glycolysis engine in the city is the same make and model. They figured out how to make it work once and never changed a damn thing. Right there you've got a power limit and you can't really buy efficiency by wasting money. Because I'm an MP, I'm pretty sure my insurance covers the basic model all of Congress—more or less—has. And yet…"

"Afraid it will get hacked or something?" Mikey asked.

All Elliot could do was shrug. He couldn't say that he literally had hard proof that they could be re-written sitting in a jar in his desk. Then his phone buzzed with an alert from Eve that read, "Are you serious, Blackstone?"

Elliot scowled and went back to his beer. "Maybe this is the definition of a phobia."

"Nah, it's too rational to be a phobia. But the thing I find weird…" Mikey paused until Elliot gestured for him to get to the point. "Don't you do a lot of shit you should be afraid to do? Like chase a murderer through ghetto alleys? A hell of a lot more people have opted to get their brain wired than would ever do something like that."

Elliot leaned back in his chair and turned that idea over. He looked at it from one side then the other and found it strange. "Shit, that's a good point. Or maybe I'm just drunk."

"Fuck," Mikey said as he leapt to his feet. His eyes were vacant, staring into a dark corner as his mouth formed silent words. "Shit, bastard's blood. I'm sorry Elliot, can you cover the tab? I've gotta run. Dom got in a fight."

Bastard's Blood, it's three in the afternoon, isn't it?

"Go, you're fine. I got this."

Mikey kept bowing as he slid out. "I'm sorry. I know you need someone to talk to but shit, I'm sorry. Single parent things. You know how it is, don't you?"

Elliot rolled his eyes. "You're fine. I'm fine. It's all fine, Mikey."

"I'll make it up to you another day. Later tonight maybe, eh? Until then though, fuck the Buffalo Party and fuck the government. Have a drink to that, eh?"

Elliot slouched in his chair as Mikey ran out the door. After waving for a refill on his beer, he checked his phone again. Eve had sent another message; "As the personification of the government whether I like that or not, you can tell Mr d'Angelo thanks but no thanks. He's not my type." Elliot smirked and finally Seraphina messaged him.

"Dr Forez was just found dead, along with another of Heartsteel's thugs. Dixie is in hiding it seems. Shit is hitting the fan, Blackstone. Meet me at the pinned coordinates ASAP."

Elliot wanted to bang his head against the table. He wanted to buy a bottle of liquor and drink it until he passed out and didn't have to deal with the case. Half a dozen less savory—and less feasible—ideas passed through his head until he shoved up from the table and staggered over to pay his tab.

I need a fucking cigarette.

Dive bars were supposed to be havens for drugs. The bathroom didn't even have an attendant selling cocaine. The vending machine existed, but was sold out of everything but condoms. No matter how much he jabbed the buy button for the nicotine sticks—while thinking about the real stuff, the dried out and rolled plant that only the Isles could make—nothing popped out the bottom.

He ended up marching from the bar with fiending eyes, searching either for a vending machine or a convenience store. Spotting a vending machine was easy enough, but the damn thing was sold out of everything but the worst flavor of tortilla chips; mango. He wanted to punch his fist through the display window, but there was nothing to even steal.

How the fuck am I going to deal with Seraphina like this?

The answer came, somewhat, when his phone buzzed in his pocket. His pursuit of nicotine, his abandoned vice, had taken longer than he realized, judging by the clock. Evidently, long enough for one of his other friends to catch wind of what had happened. "Blackstone speaking," he said.

Wyatt said, "Hey there, survivor. I hear I'm missing a drinking party of one?"

Elliot smacked his forehead against the vending machine. "Party is over, work calls."

"Eh? I thought you had the day off."

"Days off don't count when corpses are showing up."

"Shit, this a serial killer?"

Elliot sighed. "That, or an organization. I don't suppose your department is investigating anyone with a particular grudge at the moment?"

"Can't say that we are," Wyatt said. "Of course, I literally can't say. You're in some other cocamamie department that Cinder cooked up. We're not supposed to talk about our work like that, you know? I can show up and have a drink if you need to talk though. Colt told me what happened."

"It wasn't much. Practically over in a moment. I shouldn't even be concerned about it. If she had wanted me dead she would have killed me so I guess I wasn't ever in any real danger."

"You just keep telling yourself that. I'm sure Colt will have her rounded up quick enough and you can talk it out with her between bars, yeah? Cinder isn't letting you take the day off though? Tell you what, how about I get you something I know you'd like?"

"Wyatt, don't."

"Nah, man. I'll take all the blame, don't you worry. I know a guy. You need some after getting a gun in your face. Don't worry about it. Hell, your partner is smoking them, ain't she?"

"Wyatt, do not buy me cigarettes."

"If you don't want them, throw them out when you get them. I'll call again later tonight, alright?" Wyatt said, and hung up.

Elliot punched the vending machine and glared at his phone, then he headed to the coordinates Seraphina had sent him.

27

Strike Breaker

2140/10/22

Tailing someone through Gamma was easier said than done. They said that the police QRS teams had it easy, that their implants could just synchronize with EVE and slap a navigation beacon onto their target like a video game. Waypoint, glowing trail through the halls, whatever they wanted. It took all the thought and confusion out of the stalking process. Clyde didn't have that kind of hookup. He didn't even have an implant to take a call through.

Thankfully, Grozzuh was in no shape to out-fox anyone. The man lumbered through the halls and had to pull himself along with handrails. He wore a black duster and his head lolled against his chest as he left the brothel. The sight of his back—the leather of the coat gleaming in the neon—threw Clyde's mind back to the wilderness. There was something feral about it, or at least close enough that his mind kept superimposing the blighted to him. Every other step put him back in Nebraska.

He should have been smelling the grime, the lingering canal stench, the overflowing trash chutes and the steaming stalls of street food. His brain kept putting wetland detritus and blood into his nose. He almost missed when Grozzuh slumped into a bathroom. For a moment, Clyde just stared at the door, then he checked at his side. He felt the grip of his special weapon, but not of the micro-blade and he swore. By the time he convinced himself that the drugs were enough of an advantage, someone else walked into the bathroom and Clyde stopped.

His heart raced and he turned away from the bathroom. Standing in front of a vending machine, he slowly slotted a credit chip and punched the first thing he saw, all while watching the reflection for Grozzuh to leave the restroom. Of course, that soon left him holding a bag of mango-flavored tortilla chips. Clyde had his void mask pulled tight over his head, the hood snug to his throat, and no way to actually eat them.

He was just asking himself what the hell he had been thinking when Grozzuh left the bathroom. The man had wetted his face, greasing back his black hair. Perhaps it had refreshed him somewhat, but the man still kept blinking his eyes whenever he tried to focus on something.

Squeezing the bag so tight it nearly popped, Clyde waited until Grozzuh had turned the other way and fell in behind him again. He could hear the whump of wind as trains passed overhead and tried to remember where the nearest functioning station was. If Grozzuh got on a train, he could ride it all the way back to Heartsteel and Clyde would lose his chance. The man–the strike-breaking killer–didn't go to the train station though. Grozzuh detoured down an alley. With boarded up, abandoned commercial lots to either side, the only thing the alley was good for was for drunks to pass out.

That seemed to be nearly what Grozzuh was planning to do as he meandered to a support beam and threw up his forearm for support against it. He looked like he was about to pull out his cock and piss in the corner. The way the man slumped and hung his head, the drugs had to be hitting him and shutting off his awareness. The man was oblivious.

Clyde reached into his coat and put his hand on the special weapon the survivor had given him.

"So who the fuck are you?" Grozzuh asked, staring at Clyde through the reflection of a broken camera. "Do you think I didn't notice a fucking void mask stalking behind me? Bastard's Blood, I may not know who you are but I sure as hell know you've been following me."

Every muscle in Clyde's body tensed. His vision tunneled in on the man, some twenty feet in front of him. Clyde drew. The electric blade clicked as he ripped it from the sheathe, slinging out a burst of electromagnetic radiation. The camera beyond Grozzuh sparked.

A moment later, Grozzuh grabbed at his skull and fell to his knees screaming as his neural implant fried.

The weapon in Clyde's hand burned, nearly searing his flesh as the electronics shorted out. He had to shake it and pop the cap off to get the battery out before it melted. The thing tumbled to the ground just like Grozzuh. The EMP was too slip-shod to use twice, but the sight of the man on his knees let Clyde sigh in relief. No fight.

"What the fuck did you do?" Grozzuh screamed, his voice devoured by the noise of Bastion at night. He hunched over, tearing at his hair and curling into a ball.

Clyde didn't say anything, but he could sympathize with the man. It was nearly the same thing he went through if he ever powered his implant on. Clyde looked away, scanning the alley for something to use and found a pane of glass. He smashed it and ripped out a shard. Breaking a man's spine had put a fracture in his micro-blade and he didn't need to risk breaking it here. But, grasping the jagged edge with the sleeve of his coat was only so safe.

Then he heard Grozzuh gag and convulse. He seemed to be having a seizure, or sicking up from the alcohol. His world was probably spinning through static and playing hell with his insides. The man was facing a pitiful end, like he deserved.

Then a pill bottle clattered from Grozzuh's grasp. It tumbled and bounced across the floor, rolling end over end without a label. The man's groans became rough laughs as he pushed back to his feet. "Oh man, I don't know what the fuck you people did but it was not enough," Grozzuh said, and he grinned. Black ichor as thick as blood coated his teeth.

Grozzuh charged. When Clyde stabbed with the piece of glass, the thug threw up his arm and took the slash across his sleeve, ripping his coat up. Then Grozzuh's fist hammered into Clyde's ribs like a sledge-hammer.

Clyde went reeling back, unable to breathe for a moment as he hacked at Grozzuh. Here and there he nicked the man's hands, he forced the thug back. The instant he got a full breath, the thug pulled a switch up. Grabbing first at the blade then driving his boot into Clyde's knee. Fire exploded in his joint and he nearly toppled.

Clyde was nearly screwed. He could barely put weight on one leg. He couldn't switch his grip on the glass and one bad swing could shatter it. One good swing and he might rip his palm apart. The only thing he had going for him was faster reactions. Grozzuh was riding high on CZAR, but that did nothing about the rohypnol already in his system. The thug was drooling black down his chin.

For a moment, he considered running. The EMP had destroyed everything in the immediate area, but there were always more cameras. If EVE saw Grozzuh, they'd dispatch a kill squad. He didn't have to do the deed himself at all. But he wanted to.

Clyde switched his focus from Grozzuh's vitals to what was at hand. Whenever the man swung, Clyde fell back and slashed at Grozzuh's arm. In seconds, the thug's coat was bloody tatters, but Clyde could feel bruises and cramps forming all over his front.

Then his foot slipped on a bit of gravel. He stumbled and felt Grozzuh's bloody hand grab hold of his coat by the lapel. Panic and instinct made him lash out, thrusting his hand forward at the snarling face as he himself was thrown back. A wall plowed into his back and his skull cracked against the concrete. Nausea surged. Blood trickled anew out of his wounded implant and his feet weren't touching the ground either.

When he managed to blink his eyes back into focus, he felt something squirt across his mask. Grozzuh stared, slack jawed and with mismatched, dilated eyes. His head twisted to one side as he grunted, the noise gargling through black spittle as more blood sprayed out of his throat.

Clyde's thrust had slid right under the CZARhead's chin and cut him deep and true. He let go as the thug fell over, glass sticking out of his neck and pooling blood. "Serves you fucking right," he said, shaking out his hand. The glass had put a little red line across his palm and blood seeped out, but not bad. Before anyone could respond to the noise, he ducked his head and ran.

28

Gang Politics

2140/10/22

Elliot had seen murders before. He had seen fights escalate and knives appear and people die. Especially in seedy areas of Gamma where the cameras were no good and the locals weren't likely to show up. Michael Grozzuh staring at the twilight sky with a piece of glass sticking out of his throat wasn't too shocking to Elliot.

The fresh bag of mango tortilla chips laying on the ground made him feel like the world was laughing at him though.

I swear, if there is some kind of evidence trail because of a bag of chips, I should just quit my job.

Seraphina threw back her cloak to plant her hands on her hips as dramatically as a cartoon hero. It probably made for a dramatic shot for Heartsteel's recon drone, which buzzed around the two of them. The constant re-focusing of its lenses was almost as noisy as the helicopter blades. She paid it no mind and said, "Well this was a shitshow for our killer, wasn't it? What gives?"

Elliot glanced up and down the alley, and to the floors above them. Caution tape and alert holograms surrounded them, warding people out of the area. EVE had sent a bigger drone to keep an eye on the alley, one equipped with appendages that let it perch upon a railing like a metal bird. It made for an almost predatory reminder of who was really in charge of the city. Heartsteel's recon drone didn't stray far from Elliot, practically hiding in his shadow.

The place had already been contaminated before the pair of Romulus Guards found it and called it in. Grozzuh's wallet was missing, best guess was a cityboarder or other variety of punk had frisked the body. Anyone who knew what they were doing likely wouldn't have even touched the body.

"I got a guess," Elliot said as he tugged on disposable gloves and eyed the dozens of cuts across the thug's arms. He knelt down and spread the man's lips to see the black slime.

Seraphina bent over and peered at it. "Well, that'd do it."

"Alright, so, our killer must have been following this guy, caught him in the alley, thought he could kill him quick and easy then the guy turned out to be a CZARhead…"

I wonder if Dixie knows his goon is on the black stuff.

Elliot tugged out his phone and turned on the flashlight. Little bits of trash and debris cast swimming shadows across the alley as he looked around. He spotted the broken pane of glass easily enough. It had been a windowed door to a shuttered business. The sign above it still read Sally's Psychic Sayings, but even the piping had been stripped out by thieves. The rest of the broken glass was on the inside and still glistening sharp. The killer must have smashed it right then. "I thought our guy had a micro-blade?"

"Maybe he lost it?" Seraphina said. "It's not like it's impossible to lose your grip on a knife."

That's odd, for someone who was killing people in a single slash.

He turned the flashlight to the ground. Everything vaguely looked like trash, and it was his nose that pointed out the thing that was wrong. Acrid burning plastic lingered in the air and only got stronger when he knelt down to look at a burned out battery the size of his thumb. Something inside had shorted, the chemicals burning and fusing, recombining and smoking still. Elliot frowned and got out an evidence bag, his biggest one. The battery wasn't very large, but–after photographing it–he sealed it into the bag and watched it still slowly fill the bag with the toxic gas. Leaving it where he found it and hoping it wouldn't pop, he walked back to the start of the alley.

Based on the timing, that was probably from the killer. If he stopped to get his micro-blade off the ground, why didn't he get the battery? Because it shorted? Why even lose a battery?

With a frown, he started working systematically. The body inspection he left to Seraphina. She didn't mind and getting into someone's neural implant was easier done with another neural implant. He was begrudgingly taking a photograph of the chip bag when she said, "This guy's implant is totally fried."

"What?"

"No signal, no power, no wi-fi ping at all. And yes, I'm sure he has one. He literally has the back of his head tatted up with circuit diagrams for it."

Well, that sounds like fantastic justification for a full forensic investigation.

"Have it sent to the lab to be torn apart, would you?"

"Whose lab? Mine or yours?"

"Mine."

She arched an eyebrow at him. "There something you're not telling me, Blackstone?"

He stopped and stared at her. "I think there's a lot of shit you haven't been telling me, so if I feel like having a damn secret, I'm going to keep my mouth shut. Why don't you focus on getting everything photographed and submitted to the database? EVE is double checking her cameras to find the killer. Chop chop."

The crime scene turned out to be a small treasure trove of evidence. Not just the battery, but blood too. Of course, there was the arterial spray from where Grozzuh had been stabbed, but a secondary blood stain as well. It looked somewhat like a bloody rag had been slapped against the wall at head height, and Elliot had a good guess how that happened. The blood was still drying, and he easily collected some samples.

When he was writing the last label for blood samples, every single splatter had to be checked, he said, "We have to check the neurist too, right? Dr Forez?"

Seraphina was squatted down, next to the body and looking at something. "We've got his corpse too."

"Where?"

"They stuffed it down a storm drain and a QRS team fished it out of the canal. The man was tortured to death, it seems. Snapped his fingers one by one and there were cut marks where handcuffs would have been. Ankles too."

Then they had Forez for a while. Why wasn't there a missing person alert on him? Can this even be one person anymore?

"How long do you reckon a body could stay in a storm drain before getting flushed out?" he asked.

"Depends on the rain. That little shower we had today must have moved the body. It was a week ago that we last had rain, wasn't it?"

Elliot scratched the stubble on his chin. "Was the body chewed on?"

After a moment, she said, "No. Maybe he smelled bad though. I'll take you to see the body later. We've got somewhere else to go first." She half turned to him and held up what she had been looking at. She had a lace choker in her hand.

"Am I supposed to know where that's from? Some kind of kink shop or something?"

Seraphina laughed and slipped the choker into her pocket as she stood up. "Or something. Don't worry, I wouldn't expect you to know about it. You're a happily married man, aren't you? I'll show you though. We can let a meat wagon clean up the body. EVE? Be a dear and keep an eye on the place." What EVE's drone could actually do to protect the crime scene, Elliot wasn't sure. Seraphina thumped him in the shoulder and jerked her head. "Come on, and uh... you'll have to, you know."

When they arrived at the cafe, Elliot lingered behind as though distracted and oblivious. He pretended to not hear the man sneaking up behind him and he didn't even flinch as an EM-blocking net was thrown over the drone. He turned his head only after the signal had been cut, and saw the wiry youth glaring at him. It was a tall kid, so overtaken by puberty that he might never fill out to the frame nature was giving him. When he said, "Thanks, just don't break it," the kid didn't know how to react.

Seraphina leaned against the wall inside the building, waiting for him. "Just don't cause trouble, yeah?"

Elliot looked around the establishment, nodding his head. It was the nicest restaurant that he had ever seen on ground level, and the waitresses weren't even scantily clad. He wasn't sure Victorian era maid outfits were particularly better but he wanted to say that they were. They had managed to clean up the air and everyone seemed to be minding their own business. One customer put an arm around his chair to glare at the new arrivals and ask, "What the fuck are they doing here?"

Instantly, three maid girls swarmed around the somewhat chubby man to scold him for interrupting other people's meals.

Elliot shook his head and took a look at the chalkboard—actual chalk somehow—put up behind the bar. Half of it was dedicated to a collection of beers, teas, and desserts. The other half had such listings as "Airline Cut, $150", "Rib-Eye, $200", "Blackened Salmon Plank, $350" "Rotisserie Blonde, $400", and "Rotisserie Red, $500". Elliot took stock of the waitresses again, spotting the ones with dyed hair more clearly. The redheads were certainly a cut above.

Well that's one way to legally obscure it.

"I'm not gonna cause trouble," he said as a slightly older maid approached them with a dour look.

"Officers," the maid said. "May I invite the two of you to a private room?"

Seraphina grinned. "So long as the wait isn't long."

They were shown to a room on the second floor larger than most apartments. It had a service door in the back that a veteran maid used to bring them water and, after asking their preference, pints of beer. Those were set on a low table between their booth and a life-sized hologram projector. While the furnishings were aesthetically pleasing and the cushions comfortable, not at all like the dive bar, what actually impressed Elliot was the resolution in the floor-to-ceiling display screen. It was creating a fantasy world he couldn't quite put his finger on, and yet it dredged up some nostalgia in him.

Before he could figure it out, the hologram display booted up. A woman appeared in an office chair. She was dressed like an Alpha socialite with leather boots, leggings, a denim skirt, and a windowed sweater vest. Her fashion sense was all that Elliot could see, because her face didn't exist above her mouth. The rest had been disintegrated to anonymize her, and yet the trailing end of her braided hair still existed.

"Mr Blackstone," she said. "I didn't think I'd see you again so soon. You could have called if you had an issue."

Elliot almost choked on his beer as he recognized Hannah Song's voice. "This is your establishment?" he asked, wiping his chin off and glancing at Seraphina.

"It has been for some time, actually," Hannah responded. "Didn't you get the memo? I thought the AI would have told you where my territory was."

Seraphina reached into her pocket. "We didn't come in blindly," she said, and tossed the lace choker on the table.

After a moment, Hannah sighed. "Veronica, could you hold it up to the camera? The resolution isn't very good." Silently, the maid stepped forward and picked it up. She flinched when she saw it, but held it out for Hannah to see. The crime lord frowned. "Well then, you'll have to enlighten me about where you got something like this."

Seraphina said, "We got it off the corpse of a man who took it from one of your girls. Unless they're in the habit of giving tokens out. Did you start some kind of loyalty program while I was away?"

Elliot had set his drink down, else he would have sputtered on it again. "Away?"

Seraphina arched an eyebrow at him. "How else would I have been able to identify it? It's part of the uniform," she said, and gestured at Veronica's neck where a nearly identical piece of lace was.

Hannah Song sighed. "She was the only girl who was able to get away with not working, at least until we realized whose payroll she was actually on."

"I'd have loved to stay longer you know," Seraphina responded, her grin as cattish as her swishing tail.

Hannah scoffed. "I'm sure you would have. Now, I have to ask, whether you're accusing me of being involved in this man's murder or are you just trying to pry into my camera system?"

Elliot folded his hands together and leaned in. "Are you aware of who the man was?"

"Please, Officer Blackstone, I've worked with lawyers long enough to know better than to answer that."

"His name was Michael Grozzuh, and he was serving probation. By court agreement, he only had three hours a month allowed off work premises and he was recorded leaving his home nearly three hours before his body was found halfway between here and the train station. We believe he spent the intervening time here. Further, we have reason to believe he was targeted. His killer likely followed him out and would have started here. I gather that he was a bit of a regular."

Taking a guess there.

"A moment please," Hannah said, and her hologram froze. Elliot noticed Seraphina switch her attention to Veronica and give a familiar wave, which made the maid scowl. When Hannah returned to life, she said, "It seems that he stole that from one of my employees earlier tonight. She had just filed to have him banned from the premises."

Seraphina asked, "Because of the theft? Or because of...?"

"He hit her," she answered. "If you're telling me he's dead, well, that's good news for me."

Elliot sighed. "Miss Song, is it Miss? I don't think you ever told me."

"Miz."

"Miz Song, when you first got ahold of me, you told me that if ever there was someone I wanted that was in your territory that I should call you and you would get them out. Isn't that right? So long as they aren't one of yours, it's no big deal, right? I think that offer should still be in effect, no?"

"That offer is in effect at my discretion."

Elliot nodded. "I believe you're aware of what happened to Sokolov the other week, aren't you?" Damn near the entire city knew the MPs had stormed in like an invasion and slaughtered Sokolov's entire crew.

She stiffened. "Are you implying that the man you're looking for worked for Sokolov?"

"I'm saying that there is a very high level of scrutiny on this particular case and it would be in your interest to cooperate."

After a moment she sighed and planted her cheek on her fist. "Sorry to disappoint, but I can't tell you much. He was a tall man in a void mask. He entered about the same time Grozzuh left. He didn't have any weapons on him, so no alarms were raised."

"You let people come in wearing masks?"

She shrugged. "There's an upcharge, but yes. Sorry, Officer. I can't tell you who he is. He didn't even have a neural implant to ping."

Seraphina had taken her eyes off Miz Song and locked them onto the maid. "Why are you fidgeting, Vel?"

Hannah cut in. "She doesn't know anything pertinent either."

"You sure?" Seraphina asked.

Hannah sighed. "Veronica, if you have something appropriate to say, speak up."

"The man you're looking for worked for Ajitatsu, if that helps you narrow it down at all."

Ajitatsu? I'm going to have to ask the lab to pull an all-nighter on that blood sample. If it's Clyde, I'll need the proof.

"Miz Song," Seraphina said, picking up her beer again. "Would you be so kind as to submit some of your video recording to corroborate your statement about this man's presence here? Within reason of course."

Also known as without incriminating herself.

Miz Song sighed. "I'll see what I can do, Officer. Now, unless you're looking to start paying for your time here, I'll have to ask you two to leave."

29

Date Night

2140/10/22

"**I**'m fucked," Clyde said. He sat slumped forward, letting Zarah pick at the back of his skull like a mother chimpanzee. Rather than pulling bugs from his hair, she was stitching and patching and gluing his skin into one piece again.

Anne Grief sat across from him. She had deigned to come down to the cleaning room that he had worked at so long ago. The air still smelled like chemicals and rust, like just being near the machines would bleach and starch their clothes and lungs. "Never thought one of the thugs would be using CZAR. Dixie is scum, but he's still beholden to the military. They don't take kindly to CZAR."

"That's bullshit," Clyde said, wincing as Zarah ripped a patch of skin off his head and dabbed up the blood. "Plenty of corps employ those crazy bastards."

Anne sighed. "Corporations that hire en masse do, yes. Phoenix Construction, and Gaia, and people like them. Not Heartsteel. Not a reputation based corporation. Tell me, do you know what CZAR is?"

He wrinkled his face up and shrugged. "It's blighted brain juice, ain't it?"

The old woman shook her head. "You know that man who saved you?" She waited for his nod before she continued, "He's probably the one that got you all killed. You know that?"

"How's that make sense?"

"That man was almost certainly a CZAR manufacturer. The Isles doesn't put up with them much, so they have to scatter around the country, you see? They get creative with how to move their product back to Bastion, and being near a river helps. What they do is they get a barn of some sort, say... a biological research facility the government abandoned. Then they put animals into it, and they infect those animals with the blight. Their bodies become a drug factory like a fruit ripening. The art of the process is all in the timing of the kill. Wait too long and the blight penetrates the brain in full. Too soon and it won't get you high. So yes, in a sense it is blighted brian juice, just that it's animal brains... until it's not. Eventually the real blighted show up."

Clyde sucked in breath until the chemicals burned his nose and he sagged down as he let it out. "Yeah, I guess that makes sense. Damn. They all got killed over something like that?"

"Your former coworkers got killed because Dixie didn't give enough of a shit about them. But, what he would give a shit about is CZAR, because the blight is always a political topic. You see? The government ain't lying when they say one fucked up pill can turn you. Dixie's doing enough else wrong that there's no way he would willingly take a risk like that."

Clyde stared at the ground, at the stains of dirt and grease. They were all probably tracking in chemicals from the cleaner, and from restaurants and he could only imagine a hundred other locales with their own little chemical trails. They were innocuous normally, but one of those traces might be what led the MPs to his arrest–one bad pill to end it all. "So what am I supposed to do now?"

"What, to get Dixie?"

"What else? Did you think I was asking to quit?"

Anne flicked open a metal lighter, the lid ringing like a chime before she sparked it up and lit a cigarette. One of her grandchildren complained that they weren't allowed to smoke. Without looking at them, she said, "Do as I say, not as I do. Now Clyde, for right now you're not going to do anything. You got that? You've rattled his cage, made him lock down. You wouldn't be able to get him under normal circumstances and you're definitely not going to get him when he knows you're coming for him. Not in his own domain at least."

"How do I get him out? You've got a plan, right? I've been running all over the place dancing like a puppet for you because I was waiting for your plan."

"You have to wait for him to get called by his investors."

"Won't he just ignore that? Or take it virtually?"

Anne puffed and shook her head. "That's not how loans work, boy. Not when the amount is in the billions. A little pissant like you wouldn't know. You must think that loans are based on calculations, statistics, actuaries, risk profiles, things like that, yeah? Now, that's true for most money in circulation. You get a billion people in a city and each of them floating loans here and there for thousands of credits that adds up. EVE has it all worked out to be fair as best as she can, bless her silicon heart. That ain't true when the money is too much though."

"Are you going to cut to the chase... or?"

She huffed. "Didn't I just say you had nothing to do but wait? You can damn well wait for me to explain. There's a tip over point. A difference between needing a hundred thousand credits to mortgage an apartment and needing a hundred million to finance a factory. You can't get personal loans for that much, no matter who you are. At that amount of money, they don't care about the return because they aren't trying to make money anymore. They're buying... what you might ask?"

Clyde did not ask.

"They're buying power, over the debtor. They expect to get favors for as long as that money isn't repaid. Influence. Control. They take interest payments, sure, but trifling amounts. It's when it looks like the control they purchased is no longer around... that's when they get concerned and they expect to be compensated. That is why Dixie will have to go. He can't hide behind a screen because this isn't about business. When the king summons you, you must go."

Clyde shrugged. "How are you supposed to know when that is?"

Anne plucked the cigarette from her lips and grinned, her wrinkles like skeletal teeth as she put a finger to her lips. "That's for me to know and you to act on. Now go, get out of here. Keep your head down."

Zarah slapped him on the shoulder. "Come on, you wouldn't know how to keep yourself out of trouble if a gun was to your head."

"A gun is to my head," Clyde said as everyone stood up and started filing out of their meeting room. He felt around his scalp and found one numb spot after the next. Clumps of bio-epoxy and scabs in his hair, he didn't want to know what she had patched up. Having to wait didn't feel good, but it was just time. Nobody grew up in Bastion without learning how to let time pass them by, except maybe the owners of comp-mausoleums. The trick was thinking about something else.

Anne's crooked smile had left an after image in his mind that didn't want to go away. He saw the shallow shake of her head when he blinked. When he had his eyes open though, he had something better than the latest video game release. He had something more compelling than random loot rewards on social media platforms or entertainer gossip. It compelled him more than outrage over the latest insult to his favorite tv franchises.

"Where you taking me?" he asked as his eyes followed Zarah's denim clad rear.

"Down," she said, and led him all the way to ground floor, to the real mess of Gamma. They were beneath one of the decks–boulevards as the people in Delta called them–and every single security camera had been blocked. For better or worse, the walls had different marks of ownership. It wasn't Mercurial logos noting internet relays, or corporations lining off their property. It wasn't even gangsters like Grief pushing into the real estate. Every spot of wall and several security shutters had city-boarder graffiti across it, often overlapping one another.

"What is this? A playground?"

"For the kids, yeah. You could say that. We think of it as neutral territory. No adult wants to get mixed up with kids. They'd never live down a loss, you know?" she said as she took him over to a walk-up bar. Static filled music droned from a speaker in the corner of the tap room, some relic from the bartenders long lost youth. Judging by their wrinkles, it was before either Clyde or Zarah had been alive. Still, the credit chip rang up and they walked off with two cups of watered down beer.

Clyde sipped his drink and looked around at the glowing stores. Each window was its own color, its own invite to shop for clothes, for game accessories, for food or appliances or a dozen other things he might be tempted to need. "I thought I was supposed to keep my head down."

"If you're here, don't worry about it."

"Just 'cause the cameras are busted doesn't mean I'm safe."

"Oh come on, when's the last time you saw a jannis walking around ground floor?"

He shrugged and followed after her. "How did you find a place like this?"

Zarah laughed. "It's like five blocks long that way and two blocks past the end is our neighborhood. How do you not know about it?"

Clyde furrowed his brow and scratched his chin. "Guess I didn't make any deliveries here."

"Come on, there's an arcade I haven't been to in forever."

"I can't game at an arcade." Not only was his implant broken, but signing in would have the police on him instantly.

Zarah rolled her eyes and didn't stop moving. "It's a retro arcade." She led him to a genuine pinball arcade. The place had everything from retro style bumpers to magnetic accelerators and more. Even a few digital only machines, which weren't really pinball at all but had their own sort of fans.

The night flowed. His entire concept of time contracted to no more than a moment into the future—enough to play the game and to keep the conversation moving. They drifted from the arcade to a pub and drank more. The city never changed. The sun or stars, they couldn't be seen and couldn't be imagined, Whether it was evening, midnight, or dawn he stopped caring. Only hours and hours later did the fatigue of his body begin to take its toll.

Alcohol soothed his pains and he had his head wound hidden by a cheap knight hat, but eventually teh caffeine ran thin. Zarah started handing him liters of water but the dehydration had already been done. Drinking them did nothing for the tightness in his eyes, the sloop of his head and the fog in his mind. He barely even reacted when she kissed him and told him to get ready to go.

That meant he had to stumble to a bathroom and relieve himself of the wasted water. She wasn't in the pub when he left, or maybe she was and he just couldn't spot her. He staggered out the back door, following the glow of an exit sign. He didn't emerge to the main street, just some back alley. The creak of rusted sheet metal beneath his boot clued him in that he wasn't on ground floor anymore.

He couldn't remember what story they had ended up on, or which safehouse he was supposed to go to. Digging through his pockets, he found a crumpled up pack of caffeine gum and popped one in his mouth. The cold air–he must have been near a climate control pipe–helped flush the drunkenness from his mind. It barely did anything for the fatigue, but the balance shifted to merely tired the more he chewed.

When he could focus his attention, he found the burner phone he used, strictly for his non-criminal outings, and checked for messages. Zarah hadn't sent him anything, so he messaged her as he went looking for the nearest intersection, or a staircase, anything but a train station. The boulevard deck wasn't over his head anymore. He was two stories away from the rails of a maglev line. It still hummed with magnets pulsing electricity.

"Shit," he grumbled, meandering one way and then the other as he tried to steer back to the buried canyon of private businesses. Then he saw two people in front of him and he froze. One was on the ground, the other kneeling next to them and speaking. Clyde couldn't make out the words, not because he was drunk but because there was a little quad-copter drone flying around with a camera. The rattling chop of the blades masked the woman's words like a buzzing insect.

The one on the ground wasn't moving. Their right arm had an extra joint in it, bending where it shouldn't bend and Clyde didn't think it was a cybernetic. The cityboard strapped to their feet told the story of a kid who missed their lifeline and met the floor faster than they would have liked.

The kneeling woman was in a cloak though. A navy blue one at that. The exact kind of cloak that MPs wore this time of year. It made her olive skin pop like a light in the dark. Before he could take three steps back, her recon drone lurched up and spun to face him, focusing him with the main camera, not just a beady little side-focus. It was live streaming, recording everything.

He didn't have his mask on.

Any doubt that the police system didn't recognize him vanished when the woman's head jerked up to look at him too. Her mouth opened, frozen for a moment of shock. Clyde should have taken that moment to bolt, to dive back into the network of tunnels and lose them.

He couldn't pry his feet off the floor before she was grabbing for her hip. "South Missou PD, you are–" She drew her taser instead of her pistol. That was her mistake.

Clyde drew his weapon and swung. She didn't even finish her sentence before pulling the trigger. Twin prongs shot at him going a hundred meters a second. The EMP went from him to her at the speed of light. The prongs bit through his shirt and sunk into his flesh, but the battery that would have stopped his heart exploded in the jannis' hands before she hit the floor.

Clyde ripped the barbs out and ran.

30

Now It's Personal

2140/10/22

Elliot's head jerked up when he heard someone scream. So did the ramen chef's. He, the chef, and Ram all glanced at one another. "We should go check that out," he said, not taking his hand off the counter.

The chef narrowed his eyes and stirred the simmering pot of broth. He shook his head, jostling his fat jowls. "I suppose you should. That's too bad."

Ram grimaced and stepped back. "How about I go check that out and you catch up with me?"

Elliot scowled as the chef turned his back on them and tutted. They had been trying to get an order from the guy for half an hour, to no success. The broth wasn't boiling enough. The noodles weren't thawed. Someone else had put their order in first. All excuses Elliot had heard before and should have realized were warning signs. He and Ram could have gone to an automatic kitchen and gotten food in minutes. Instead they still had empty stomachs at midnight and the chef's grease seemed to have left a permanent odor in his nostrils.

If the two of them stepped away, there was no way they would be getting their food.

"I'll be there as soon as I can," Elliot said as he drummed his fingers on the counter. "Just give me a call when you get there, if it's something serious. I'll come running if I have to."

"Roger," she said, and took off running. She darted along walkways and bridges, heading right to some tower alley the noise had come from.

Elliot shouldn't have even been out. Working the Heartsteel case exempted him from patrol, even from QRS. He was out because he needed something to do while waiting until two in the morning for Amara's stream to end so he could finally resolve the issue. That, and Ram wasn't exempted. During their time together, he had apparently given her the impression that it was normal to go down to ground floor.

She was too soft to be at the bottom by herself. He didn't think she would be able to pull the trigger if she needed to.

Better than pulling it when she shouldn't at least.

"Can we get our bowls with lids?" he asked

The chef nodded. "Oh, lids. Yeah, yeah I can do that, jannis. Those are in the back though."

"I can see them right fucking there." Elliot jabbed his finger at the shelf above the chef's head.

The fat bastard glanced up and shrugged. "Those are too small."

"Bullshit they're not. Stop dragging your feet or I'm going to slap you with an impeding justice charge at this rate. My partner is responding to a crime and you're holding me up."

The chef sneered back. "You're free to leave at any time."

"I want my fucking food."

"Oh, that's no way to talk, now is it?"

"Want to cry about it to a judge?"

"As if you'd show up to a court."

"Try me."

The chef scoffed and walked away from the pot, vanishing into the backroom and leaving two bowls of ramen steaming.

Elliot snarled and hung his head. He could hear the chef banging boxes around and not doing much to get the lids. The noise fought with a thousand other things from every direction in Colorado Tunnel. With Colorado Boulevard forming a roof over it, the human ant hive managed to trap their own echos and form something like a sonic snake as loud as a factory train station despite being the middle of the night. Merely being loud was one thing. Elliot could enjoy a concert and could keep his head in a gunfight. Colorado Tunnel had broken the noise down into static that still somehow carried little snippets of speech that his mind wanted to decipher but couldn't.

The only reason they had been able to hear the scream was because it must have been close.

Just to make sure he didn't miss the call, he pulled out his phone and held it in his hand. Before the chef could return, EVE called him.

That's not good.

"What's up?" he asked, plugging his other ear.

"Blackstone, can we talk?" the AI asked.

Elliot cocked an eyebrow and looked around. There were no functioning cameras that he could see and he wondered if she had the ability to see him or not. "What's up?"

"They're meddling with my memories again. Or rather, they already did. Vice Commander Chase is treating my memory like an on-off switch and it's pissing me off."

Elliot pursed his lips and hung his head. "That's a pretty high level of confidentiality."

"I'm almost forty years old and they still don't understand how I process data. I hate it, but the only workaround I have right now is getting the information told to me privately so I can store that memory in a regular drive then when they unlock the confidential stuff I can update my free memory with what the hell they're asking of me."

"What's it like being able to change your own memories?"

"You're the human. You tell me. You people lie to yourselves literally all the time. You consciously and subconsciously manipulate your perceptions to fit your narratives. Like, do you want an objective breakdown of your last conversation with your wife? Because it is not very flattering of you."

"So the California problem, yeah?"

Eve laughed. "Yeah, that one."

"It was government sponsored blackmail. The reason it's labeled as confidential is because it was one government branch blackmailing another and they don't want that getting to the press."

"Who in the government knew who was funding Centurion?"

"I don't know. Seraphina does. She works for them, or did at the time. Maybe it was Chase but he hadn't been promoted at that time."

"Thank you, Blackstone. And, you know, we could have a much quicker and more private communication if you had a neural implant."

"Or you could just text me."

"Yeah, but if you got an implant, I could get a live feed of your vision rather than just what the recon drone sees. I'd love to get tracking data on your eyes. Right now I'm helping Ram bring in an ambulance. The data I can get through her implant is being processed for the EMTs and might save this cityboarder's life."

Elliot rolled his eyes and stood up when the chef finally returned with lids to cover up the bowls of soup–which had lost a lot of their steam. "You're not going to convince me to get chipped like that," he said as the food was finally bagged up and put in front of him.

"Blackstone," Eve said, her tone hardening.

He tensed. "What?"

"Get to Ram, now."

Elliot left the soup and ignored the chef's screaming at him. He knew the first few turns that she had taken, but after just a few steps, Eve had to start giving him directions. His WPS map would have been the regular way, but with not having a neural implant, he couldn't exactly watch it as he sprinted. He could, however, deploy both recon drones and have them tail him to start feeding the camera data to Eve. He had to keep his phone pressed to his ear as she told him, "Left, right, up those stairs, down the fire escape, into the train alley. Bondsman is there."

He was still charging down the steps when he heard the pop of a taser. The blast of the projectile was unmistakable–a gunshot that wasn't. The sound of his phone's speaker blowing out in his ear was even more unmistakable. The police recon drone shut off, the rotors stopping before it plummeted to the ground. Dixie's drone was unaffected for some reason, and he hoped Eve had a feed from it. He hesitated for an instant, staring at the dead black screen on his phone. Then, he drew his pistol before rounding the final corner.

"Freeze!" he screamed at the fleeing back of a man. He jerked his gun up and aimed, but he couldn't see the man's face, he couldn't confirm that was the criminal. Then the man was gone, through a door and into the urban labyrinth. His attention shifted to the wider view. Ram was on the ground next to a cityboarder. Blood was dripping across the floor, but from the punk not from Ram. Their forearm had snapped in half and ripped through the skin; bad, but nothing a hospital couldn't fix.

Their spasmodic thrashing was a different category of problem.

Habitually, he tried to call QRS, but his phone was blown. Having it back in his hand though, he realized it was heating up. He had just knelt down beside Ram when the cover popped off with a burst of burning smoke. He swore and tossed it aside before prying Ram's eyelids open. Her pupils didn't match and kept darting independent of one another as she whimpered.

She needs a neurist.

Elliot tore off his cloak and wadded it up to brace her back and head as best he could after rolling her onto her side. Her taser had dropped at her feet. That didn't seem like it was about to explode, but he kicked it away just to be safe. The smell of burning smoke was getting stronger.

He didn't realize the source until he looked over at the cityboarder and saw their cityboard smoking. "Fuck!" He jumped on them, grabbing at the straps of their boots. Clumps of burning ash like napalm started sparking into the air and burning holes through his skin, hot enough to cauterize the nerves, as he ripped the girl's feet from their restraints. Every rough shift of her body made the half-conscious punk cry out in pain. There was nothing he could do for their snapped arm before he got the shorted battery away from both of them.

One of the cells popped, spewing chemicals into the air and speckling Elliot's face just as he kicked the board away. He roared in pain, feeling like some of it had burned through to his teeth. Blood started trickling off of him as he stood back up and snatched Dixie's recon drone. "Get QRS here, now! I know you're there. Get them my coordinates now!"

Someone threw open a door and Elliot spun, pulling his pistol up. An old man in an apron with a fire extinguisher was not Clyde Bondsman. The man shouted before Elliot could put up his bleeding hand and apologize. Elliot had to holster the gun before the chef–or maybe he was just the dish washer–could work up the nerve to head to the cityboard. He had an old style, foot pump extinguisher. He had to force out a clog before he could douse the inferno with sealant. The foam reacted first to the oxygen in the air, then to the heat of the shorted battery. In seconds, he had the whole thing encased like an igloo.

The fire crew would need sledgehammers to clean it up later, and they'd have shards like obsidian afterward, but the tower wasn't going to burn down.

Elliot squatted next to Ram, waiting for the seizure to stop completely and made small talk about fire safety with the old geezer. EMTs arrived first, but only expecting one injured person. The doctors split up, doing what could be done. QRS arrived as they were pulling the punk up to the ambulance car.

"She needs a neurist," the doctor said as the other MPs swarmed the alley and brought a fleet of drones with them.

"Put her in the QRS car," Elliot said, not taking his gaze off Ram's sedated face. Without knowing how much damage there was to her synaptic connections, putting her under was standard protection.

"She needs surgery."

"Then stop wasting time!" he snapped at the EMT, leaping up to snarl in the man's face.

A metal hand yanked him back by the shoulder. "Easy there, Elliot," Wyatt said. He had on full armor, but his voice was enough. "You need a doctor yourself. You look like a mess."

"I need to put a fucking bullet in that man."

Wyatt shrugged and reached into his pouch. He pulled out a tube of BleedStop and handed it to him. "Alright then. Let's go get that fucker. We'll have to fan out–"

"He went that way," Elliot said, pointing down the alley.

"Well that's a start."

"You got a dog in there?"

Wyatt looked up at the QRS car as the ambulance sped off. "Yeah, I think so. What good's that going to do?" Dogs, digital sniffers to be precise, relied on simplified calculations to do their analysis of odors. It couldn't cross reference to a database of information and identify what it was smelling, not fast enough to track someone down in a chase at least, but it could do a direct comparison.

Elliot picked up the bloody barbs of Ram's taser and said, "I've got a sample of his DNA right here."

The sniffer noticed the split in the trail instantly, but Elliot had seen the way Clyde had run. He knew the thug had one back and down the steps, which meant the trail leading into the restroom hallway of a faux-japanese salary man bar must have been where Clyde came from. They sent in two other QRS agents, already thinning down their numbers considerably. Too many had to escort Ram to the nearest hospital, along with the EMT, but teams were getting called in from North Missou.

Officer down had that kind of effect.

"Let me take point, I"m the one in the armor," Wyatt ordered as he shoved in front of Elliot with the sniffer in one hand and a couched shotgun in the other. The way Clyde had gone was down a zig-zag stair-case that kept butting up against corporate territory. The sniffer pinged on every door handle, but digital logs always confirmed that he hadn't gotten through. Companies like Romulus didn't let unknowns force their way in.

They kept checking the lower floors and winding into the depths of the city until they realized they were in Epsilon and the whole city was above them. "Shit, he could be going anywhere," Wyatt said.

31

Horrorshow

The inside of his void mask smelled like stale beer after he put it back on. Every puff of his breath watered his eyes as he ran down steps to the lowest levels of Epsilon he could find. He should have worn the whole time, every minute he was with Zarah. Both of them should have. They should have known better, but they had been distracting one another the whole time. He didn't want a piece of plastic between him and her, and he hoped she felt the same. The drunken memory of their kiss made him hope as much.

Hindsight made everything so clear, like the face of that jannis before she fell.

He didn't know if she was dead. He had never used the EMP blade on someone he didn't intend to kill. The thing was still cooking in his hand. When he found a trash chute, he dumped the battery and hoped for the best. He didn't have any spares on him, just the standard micro-blade. His surprise weapon was empty. Worse than that, he was drunk going on hungover, tired, and still light in the head from his bleeding scalp.

If the MPs caught up to him, the rusted halls of the city underbelly would be ringing with gunshots, not the clash of steel and micro-blades. They weren't going to fuck around. They weren't going to be limited by self-defense laws. Hell, their standard uniforms were level 1 body armor;

he wasn't even sure he could cut a jannis down on his first try. If QRS showed up, he didn't stand a chance.

"Gotta go, gotta go…"

He pulled out his burner phone and sent Zarah one word, "Bail," before he chucked that in the trash chute too. Immediately he cursed, because he should have found a different trash chute to split that off from the battery. Too late, and he was on the wrong side of the city as far as he was concerned. He couldn't actually get lost. The city was walled in. So long as he had his void mask, he could access a public terminal at a train station then pay with a credit chip–he checked that he had one.

He just had to get away from the jannis in the area, change his outfit, and do what he should have done in the first place: hole up in an apartment and not leave until Anne Grief said so.

Then his escape from Colorado Tunnel took him to one of the worst parts of the city, which might also be the safest place to hide from the police. Clyde found himself in Survivor's Canyon, a rusted strip of crime eating through a gash in the city. It was like rust stripping away the foundation of the towers. There weren't even businesses in Survivor's Canyon, not permanent ones at least. If money was changing hands, so too was data and guns, maybe CZAR. Whereas Colorado Tunnel wasn't patrolled because the police were lazy, this wasn't patrolled because the police would get killed.

As much as Clyde wanted to breathe a sigh of relief, he was just as endangered. The only difference was that he might be able to survive a fight in the canyon.

So, he headed into the dilapidated sprawl. He crossed bridges that were nothing more than two exposed I-beams, missing their platforms entirely. He climbed ladders that weren't bolted down and passed by doors that had been welded shut. The ghetto was the worst of the worst, and hot as hell. Something about the climate control kept the exposed steel and construction foam like an oven. Rumor had it the canyon brushed against one, maybe two, of the incineration plants. If they were dumping wastewater into the place, he couldn't spot anything more than steam.

He ignored the heat until he found another trash chute, even Survivor's Canyon kept those operational. His jacket went in, never to be seen again. Then he was thankful for the heat, keeping the October chill away as he rushed further from Colorado Tunnel. On foot wasn't getting him far, fast. Even with a straight road, even ground, he wouldn't have felt that he was making enough distance. He needed a train, or the guts to stay put and wait for them to pass by.

He needed a way out and he found one in the form of three idiot kids with cityboards. There was a fat one, a tall one, and a girl. They had cut a hole through the floor above and rigged it with a removable flap of corrugated steel. Any pretense at it being secret was abandoned because of the chain ladder going up to it, as well as the enormous graffiti mural the fat one was touching up. They had written, "Horrorshow" in hyper saturated orange bubble letters, accented with some gear decals.

Clyde wasn't the only one to notice the punks waiting for the train over their head to depart. Some middle aged guy with his skin as tight as a mummy across his bones hollered at them, "Do you fucking quazes even realize you're referencing a book? Not a movie? It's like two hundred years old, you fuckheads, and you clearly missed the message."

The tall one jumped onto the railing and flipped his middle finger. "Why don't you come up here and have a dance with me, eh?"

"Fuck you, buddy. Your art is shit."

"No, fuck you, buddy! I'll piss on your head."

"You gotta sit down to do that?"

"I'll cut you, quaz!"

The girl in the group had to pull the tall one off the edge. She was smacking him on the shoulder as the fat one packed up his paint cans. All three of them were strapping into their boards to go riding when Clyde used the drooping edge of a wall partition to walk across to them. It was nothing more than a sheet of foam narrower than two of his fingers put together with open canyon to one side and what smelled like an abandoned fish farm on the other. He would have fallen if not for holding onto an exposed I-beam over his head for balance. Thankfully, the construction foam was cured properly. It bowed less than steel would have.

The tall one jumped up and sneered at him. "You with that other guy?" he asked, whipping out a micro-blade perhaps as long as his hand.

Clyde drew his sword and pointed the tip at the kid's nose. "Give me your board."

There was essentially nothing he could do by way of footwork, but he had half a meter more reach than the kid and all he really needed was a flick of his wrist to take the kid's arm off. He genuinely assumed the kid would back off, but Clyde must have underestimated how hungry the kid was. While the tall one was dressed well enough, all the right kinds of fashion and flash, that occasionally meant they were even poorer than average and needed to prove themselves that much more.

Cityboards were fairly expensive things, and stealing one from a rival was a risky proposition.

Clyde stared and blinked as the kid sized him up, looked at his footing, and flared his nostrils. The girl saw it too, but she grabbed at his jacket and tried to pull him back. "Are you an idiot?" the little redhead shouted as she fell on her ass, feet already strapped into the board. She was scrawny and young, but not so young that she looked like a teenager. She must have missed the draft.

Clyde figured the fat one had also been disqualified, but the tall one, the one in charge apparently, should have been taken. Unless he drew the short straw on the genetic lottery. "Back off, kid," Clyde ordered, wondering how big of a chip on his shoulder a kid would end up with after getting denied service.

"You want my board?" the tall one asked as he stepped back. He grabbed it off the floor and hoisted it up. "Why don't you come and get it?"

Clyde leaned his head forward in what he hoped was an intimidating way. The mask hid his eyes as he checked how long of a fall he might have. Two stories if he was lucky. Three to four if he tumbled. The board was a problem: two meters of fiberglass was slightly longer than his microblade, more than capable of knocking him over, and he couldn't just hack through it if he wanted to use it.

The solution to the problem was a struggle for his mind, still muddled with hangover despite the severity of the situation. If the kid had seen his face, the screwed up expression of concentration that practically had his tongue sticking out his lips, Clyde probably wouldn't have been able to pull it off.

"Drop it and back off," he said, eyes glued to the kid's hands.

"Fuck you," the tall one said, and swung the board. It slammed into Clyde's side, knocking him into the wall.

It felt like one of his short ribs dislocated from the impact. He couldn't inhale at all, but he didn't fall off the wall. Instead, he took a step in. The kid took it as a provocation to jab into his gut like a fiberglass ramrod. Clyde swung his blade and twisted it, hitting the edge of the board with the back of his blade. Then he flicked it forward like he was popping a champagne cork. The kid's thumb went flying into the air as he fell back, howling in pain.

Clyde watched as the hunk of flesh bounced off their platform and vanished into the lower stories of the canyon. He leapt onto the platform with them, stomping his boot onto the cityboard before one of the kids could pick it up again. "Good luck finding that. Now, get," he ordered.

A bloody micro-blade had a lot of persuasive power to it. The fat one had been unbuckling his board from the start and he tossed it over the side. The magnets apparently had already been turned on, so it snapped onto one of the support beams like a signpost while he slid down the ladder. The girl was trying to stop the bleeding, until he screamed at them again. Moments later, the tall one fell off the ladder, his good hand too slick with blood to hold on. Looked like he rolled his ankle in the process, but that wasn't Clyde's problem.

Thankfully, the cityboard was generous in the strap sizes. He stepped into it, fiddled with the switches to check the power, then grabbed onto the hole in the ceiling. He struggled his chin up, flailed his feet, and realized that he had to use the board. Only by magnetizing the board to the wall could he force himself up into the rail pit. Half a dozen bored drunks watched him emerge from below. They watched with the same quiet passivity as the security cameras.

One of them, probably with a direct hookup to EVE, looked right at him and the abyss that was his masked face.

Then, he jumped up and turned on the cityboard. The onboard computer matched his magnets to the maglev rail. Titanic forces of electromagnetism grabbed hold of him and held him in the air. When he spread his feet, the alternating began, switching polarities just right to crawl from magnet to magnet. Then, he was off.

32

Interrogation

2140/10/23

They only made it a few dozen meters into Epsilon chasing Clyde's trail before Wyatt's radio–set to speaker mode–buzzed. One of the other officers said, "We just got a positive on a known associate. Zarah White. She was outside the bar. Trailing her now."

Wyatt turned and grabbed Elliot by the shoulder. "You go focus on getting her. You're useless down here."

Elliot balked. "And leave you without backup? Are you fucking crazy?"

"I've got backup," Wyatt said, tapping his helmet. "We're about to have half a dozen recon drones in here making a local map. You don't have a phone to see it. You're just going to get lost. Go back up top, help arrest Zarah if you can, and if we find Clyde instead, you'll get to the spot faster by train."

Elliot snarled, his face a horror show of blood and patches in the gloom of Epsilon. "I'm sticking with you and I'm going to get that bastard."

"Elliot, buddy, stop wasting time. Think about it, if that Zarah was here with him, she might know where he's going. You think one of those knuckledraggers fresh out of the army are going to know how to talk to a lady? They don't work the beat like you do."

Bastard's blood, he's making a good point.

"Come on, this will be just like old times. Me and you, let's do this. I won't get lost if I'm right on your ass and you know you can trust me to have your back."

Wyatt laughed. "I thought you didn't want to be in on the action anymore?"

"Now it's personal."

"Fine, just like back in California, on one condition. You split off if they arrest her and I've got my backup. No damn point in a sewer goose chase. Come on," Wyatt said and stuffed the nose of the digi-sniffer to the ground.

Elliot shot a glance at Dixie's drone, still tailing behind him and jostling for space with Wyatt's. He wondered if the CEO was running his background, or if he already had. His trip to California was a sealed record because of Seraphina's report, but maybe Dixie had access to the Buffalo Party's private investigations or something. No way to tell, and the sooner he got Clyde the sooner it stopped mattering.

The two of them dropped into an abandoned service tunnel, the kind of concrete and steel tunnel that looked like an enormous termite had eaten through the foundation of the city. It was a hard rail system, no magnetic supports at all. Somewhere, the car and engine were probably collecting rust, the diesel long ago evaporated. Other tunnels and pipes had cut through it, sometimes opening it up and other times closing it off with beams and tubes. No train would ever drive through it again, but Elliot and Wyatt could follow the trail without stooping.

"You know," Wyatt said as they crawled through a web of sensor lines. A few markings implied it was for a nearby trash chute, but Elliot didn't understand what the wires and pumps were controlling. "My daughter is trying to move out. She got a job with Phoenix doing desk work, can you believe that?"

"Not in the field?"

"Stress analysis. Like, mechanical stress, not human resources or something. She's interning with a computer program that calculates how to reinforce old towers so they can be built taller. Ain't that something?"

Elliot's mouth went dry. "Interesting time to be telling me something like this."

"It's because for now, Phoenix is putting her up in a corporate apartment. You know, it's to give her a taste of the good life, up in Beta like where you live. Get her hooked and then get her to commit to the corporate ladder."

"Well, she always was a smart kid, right? Teenage rebellion aside."

"Yeah, yeah, it's just that I want to move up there with her, and I can't do that on an E-level salary. Don't know how you do it, man."

I had a bigger down payment.

"Then apply for a promotion exam."

"I already have, but openings are slim. It's looking like they might use me to chase down tax evaders. And you know what? I think that's good. You fucking got in my head, you know that, Blackstone?"

"I... what? Wyatt, are you stepping down from the group you were trying to recruit me to? That was like a week ago, tops."

Elliot didn't need to see through the helmet to know Wyatt was smirking as he shrugged. "Well, let me just say that it will depend on how tonight goes, yeah? Besides man, this ain't the heat of the moment anymore. You know how doctors don't operate on their loved ones?"

Elliot's nostrils flared. "My judgment is not impaired."

Wyatt knocked his knuckles against Elliot's chest. "Then you should be interrogating this Zarah woman instead of running around a glorified sewer."

Elliot closed his eyes for a moment and thought about the path they had taken so far, the twists and turns, the ups and downs. He tried to keep them all in his head and found them blurring together. He couldn't backtrack if he wanted to. Finally, he threw up his hands. "Fine, but if you corner him, I'm the one kicking the door in. Got that?"

Wyatt gave a two fingered salute. "Roger. Now, let's swap you with upstairs," he said, and continued along the trail.

To Elliot's chagrin, he was soon climbing the rungs of a rebar ladder and got pulled up to ground floor by two QRS members from the north branch of the PD. "How do I find her?" he asked.

One hooked a thumb over their shoulder. "Train will take you," she said as her partner climbed down to join Wyatt.

Elliot nodded, then yelled down the tunnel, "You better bring him in alive!"

"Only if he lets me," Wyatt shouted back. His voice echoed and faded into the substructure.

Elliot snarled and went over to the train station. He had to ride an elevator up a handful of stories, getting above the bulk of urban overgrowth so that the train had air to move through. It was empty when he arrived, the doors slid open automatically. He was sliding on a spare vest of ballistic armor when the main display screen sprang to life.

Eve's dismayed face colored the nose of the train as she looked at him. She said, "If it makes you feel better, you wouldn't have been able to shoot him without injuring a bystander."

He huffed and tugged the strap tight across his chest. His cloak still had an oily smell of filth to it, but he wasn't sure he'd get it back if he took it off. "I've got frangible rounds."

Eve scoffed. "Frangible means it won't penetrate a wall that's up to code. Those were... let me put it this way, you have baking sheets thicker than those walls. The only reason you weren't hearing half a dozen conversations was because of noise cancellers, not because of insulation."

Elliot planted himself in a seat, folding his hands together between his knees as he looked at her. "Are you trying to console me that I had him in my hands and didn't get him? If I had been the one to go instead of–"

"Yes, yes, you probably would have gotten him if you were the one to go instead of her, but not because she was slow on the draw. You just would have been lucky that you're a luddite."

"I also would have used a gun instead of a taser."

Eve didn't respond for a moment. She frowned at him so long he wondered if her attention had gone elsewhere. A silly wonder; her attention was always in a thousand places at once. "That's not a good thing, and you know that. Ram just got checked in at the clinic. She's already on the surgery table and in good hands."

Elliot turned away from him, he looked to the city zipping by. The train was speeding up to max speed and he saw more than one city-boarder have to bail out of the way as the QRS cab hurtled out to one end of the city so it could circle back like a slingshot. "I shouldn't have left Wyatt," he said.

The screen with Eve's face had gone dark again. Her time with him expired.

Ten minutes later, Elliot stepped off the train car with a backup re-con drone. He set it to tracking mode after conferring with the onboard computer about who he was meeting up with to catch Zarah. Officer B14223 wasn't an officer he was familiar with, but they far outranked him. He could barely muster the determination to jog as he followed the silicon fairy through the urban labyrinth. He found B14223 along with a junior off on the deck of Green Hill Boulevard, a bifurcated prome-nade floor. The undercity could be seen through the middle, like a view-ing window in the bottom of a ship, not that the boulevard was much better. They were still in Gamma.

"She's in here," B14223 said, gesturing to what looked like an aban-doned weight lifting gym. The orderly rows of machines had all been torn apart and jumbled, but the lights were on.

"What are we waiting for?" Elliot asked.

"Certainty," the older officer said. He cocked his head to one side, lis-tening to his radio. "You can call me Blaze by the way."

"Elliot."

"Nice to meet you. And, now that the fox is trapped, let's go catch her," Blaze said, pointing to the three glass doors that led to the gym. His subordinate took the far one, which had been painted black. Blaze took the double doors in the middle.

Elliot entered through a converted office that had been absorbed by the gym before it went out of business. Broken beer bottles crunched beneath his boots as he stalked in, pistol in one hand and flashlight in the other. "Be careful, these people like to use crawlspaces," Elliot said as he scanned a dumbbell rack that seemed to have gotten some use recently. The heavy weights didn't have dust on them.

"We know," Blaze said, gesturing towards the stretching area in the back.

Overhead, feet were pounding on the floor, shuffling to the discordant beat of remixed hip-hop. A few hundred people were none the wiser of the police operation beneath them. The same couldn't be said for Zarah. As tension made Elliot hyper aware of every noise, a door's deadbolt scraped open. The sound echoed from the stretching area just before everyone's radio's burst with noise.

"We got–!"

The thud of a suppressed shotgun thumped the gym and everyone ran to the stretching room. Between the smacking of boots, Elliot heard a body hit the ground, and then a groan. What they found was Zarah flat on the ground, clutching her chest next to a sandbag. Across from her was a very triumphant QRS officer climbing out of a crawlspace.

Zarah put up her hands, her left side not moving well as everyone surrounded her. "This is what I fucking get. The one day I don't wear a mask. Goddamn."

Blaze cleared his throat. "Zarah White, first of all you're under arrest for... well, fleeing arrest. A nice little subcategory of obstructing justice."

"Fuck you, don't I got fifth amendment rights?"

Every single police officer laughed. Blaze continued, "You are a known associate of a supposedly dead man. One Clyde Bondsman. He is currently wanted for arrest as well and we would like to know how to find him."

"Fuck off."

Elliot knelt down beside her, holding his pistol beside his knee. The body armor came with a little chest light, which he turned on. The

LED blasted her in the face, making her wince back. "You know, it's fairly common for people to be reported dead who aren't actually dead. There's nothing wrong with that, not at your level anyway. Clyde was reported dead by his company and it's their fault that they didn't confirm it. Unfortunately, they did confirm that he was outside and he was attacked by blighted. Pretty rare that. Pretty dangerous too. In fact, there's a decent chance that, despite being vaccinated, he could be carrying some of the blight inside him. Maybe he just hasn't turned yet. He needs a full medical checkup, you know that? You were in the military at some point, weren't you?"

Blaze gave the nod to confirm. Zarah didn't make a noise.

Elliot continued, "Clyde Bondsman could be classified as a national security threat. Given that he has now hospitalized an officer, I think I need a good reason why he shouldn't be."

Zarah snarled for a moment, then sank back. "Bastard's blood. You–ah–broke my ribs. Get me to a clinic and I'll talk."

Elliot's nostrils flared and he had to remind himself that he didn't have a mask on. He stood up and leaned close to Blaze's ear. "Where's the nearest clinic?"

The older officer scoffed. "You really aren't chipped. Incredible. Nearest clinic is a ten minute walk."

"You got an F-bag?"

Blaze looked at the officer who had climbed out of the crawlspace. "Hey Fools, you got an F-bag?"

Every department has that tradition, eh?

"No, sir," the underling responded.

"Fuck," Elliot said. Without an F-bag–an electromagnetic wave blocker to be put around the head–Zarah would be able to make any call she wanted. North Missou had just fucked up, but he didn't have a way to fix it. "Let's get her moving. And you, I expect you to start talking on the walk."

Zarah rolled her eyes, put up her hands, and sat up. Blaze's radio burst to life as they were cuffing her and helping the woman to her feet.

Wyatt's voice filled the abandoned gym. "We got a problem. The trail just led to Survivor's Canyon. Do I have permission to pursue?"

Elliot and Blaze stared at one another. It was Elliot's case, but Blaze had three ranks on him, and it was his men that would be in the line of fire. The other officer said, "Negative."

Elliot scowled put his full attention on Zarah.

33

Muzzle

Everyone always said that cityboarding was dangerous, a self-assigned death sentence. The modern day motorcycle–the most dangerous form of road transportation back before the apocalypse happened, don't you know? Clyde had been one of those people, unable to grasp why anyone would do it long enough to get a rap sheet for it. Cityboarding was illegal. It was a nuisance and dangerous to the individual as well as to the city, the trains, the people passing by, and–most importantly–the tyranny of government controlled trains.

People still told ghost stories about protests becoming dead transport zones until they fizzled out. How people had to walk ten kilometers just to organize. Apocryphal as far as he could tell, but anywhere a QRS team went, they shut the trains down and there would be no complaining about delayed commutes, missed dates, not even hospital trips.

The reasoning was never anything more than childish justification. The people who rode cityboards liked the thrill of danger. It was the same reason people used to climb mountains, hunt predators, and race cars. The feeling of holding onto energy and danger, like grasping an anti-material machine gun without supervision–the idea that at a moment's notice everything could go terribly right in all the wrong ways.

And Clyde didn't feel any of it as he flew from Survivor's Canyon.

He was crouched down, legs spread as far as the board would go. The electromagnets were switching so fast he could hear the hum, a sine wave fighting with the wind. The smoothness of the ride–the only friction he had to deal with was the air ripping at his clothes–almost made him feel like he was standing still. Only by grasping the board with his hand could he feel the vibration, and the heat of internal resistances. The tactile grasp helped him keep in his mind on just what kind of beast he was standing on.

That, and the towering buildings that flew by him in blurs. The people on bridges and walkways were nothing more than smudges of color in his peripheral as he stared down the line. Either a train would appear or–

He jerked his feet together when he saw the turn. The lurching deceleration tumbled him forward but a rolling stop was the first trick any kid learned when giving cityboarding a try. He flipped and landed again, the nose of his board almost vertical before he sagged into the magnetic groove. Just as he did so, one rail arced over the other, turning the straight line rail northward as split into the gap between city and wall. The way he had taken out was a red rail and he had taken it northeast. Reaching the wall meant that he wasn't even in Missou anymore.

His flight had just taken him across sector borders. The question of how many police departments he had just offended made him laugh as he crouched and sped up again.

The laugh died on his lips as he silently pondered why the thrill wasn't there. Neither was the fear. He had nothing inside him. It had all been carved out, first by Heartsteel and then by himself. On the bright side, he told himself, it didn't bother him much to max the speed on the board.

Top speed or not, the board couldn't last forever. It had taken him almost half an hour to get to the edge of the city and that was only about halfway to where he needed to be. Like it or not, the only allies he had in the city were back in Missou. Unfortunately, between the wind, the void mask, and just not realizing he had to listen for it, he didn't realize the cityboard was beeping a low battery warning. The first thing he realized was when it started slowing down despite no change to his feet. The board crawled to a stop as he stared at it, then glanced over his shoulder at the nose of an oncoming train.

"What the–"

The magnets gave out as the board's battery failed and dropped him like a rock. The fall would have been seven stories down to pavement, not even shanty town roofs to land on. He was between the towers and the walls, above the circle road. Even if the fall didn't kill him, he was as likely to be run over by a military truck as he was to get hit by a train.

Clyde threw his arms as he fell and grabbed the railing. The metal felt like it wanted to snap his arms, but he held on. In a panic, he scanned the towers next to him, looking for a nearby railing, walkway, staircase, or even just an overhanging advertisement. There were a dozen options, but none close. Swearing, he tried to steal himself and slid down until he was hanging from the maglev line by his fingertips. He clamped his eyes shut and prayed as the train plowed over him. The wind buffeted him like getting bodychecked by a door. His hands burned and he had no idea if it was from the raw electromagnetic fields or entirely in his head.

Then, an instant later, the roaring tube of aluminum and people was past him, the magnetic couplings just wide enough to have not ripped his hands apart in the process. Feeling like he had pissed himself and hoping he hadn't, Clyde took a moment to appreciate his life anew. Then he swung his feet, pumping the board back and forth before tossing himself at the nearest balcony. He slammed into that, but his body was already numb. He flopped over and laid down until his heart stopped racing.

Laying there, he had a sliver of sight up to the skies above, to star and stellar haze. It was a dirty sky, colored by the lights of the city more than the darkness of space. He couldn't see the moon, nor any sort of beauty in it. Nothing but a dark crescent above that reminded him what the world could be like outside the walls.

The moment of respite killed the adrenaline in his body. His muscles melted and lost their strength as his eyelids sank and he realized it was almost dawn. Jacking himself up on caffeine would just lead to him making a mistake when it mattered, so he had to figure out a way to sleep. He abandoned the cityboard and headed down to ground floor for as far as his trudging feet would take him.

In olden times, the hotel industry had been relevant to people like him, if for no other reason than to have a private place for intimacy. That was before Bastion, when travel could mean days of time between one spot and another, not an hour or two. The businessmen flying in from the sprawl or from the guilds needed places to stay, but they were all on the top floors. The fiftieth floor was considered slumming it to them.

There was another option, if he felt like paying for it. At the moment, he did.

Clyde ducked into a computer mausoleum and stood in line to rent a box. It took ages, and he nearly fell asleep on his feet. When he finally made it to the front, his mind played tricks on him, blurring dreamlike interpretation with reality and almost fooling him. The worker behind the counter was misshapen, first by injury and then by self-abuse. Something had taken the man's legs from him. At the moment, he only had cybernetic ports sticking out from either side of his barrel like chest, and nearly tearing his nylon shorts. While the cybernetics looked normal enough–Clyde could see them charging against the wall–the man's arms had atrophied and given him an alien-like appearance, complete with bruising across scarring from repeated neural implant surgeries.

"Rate ya need?" the worker asked, his voice pinched in his nose, wheedling.

"What?"

"What bitrate? What are you trying to do here?"

"Oh, lowest."

The worker cocked an eyebrow. "Our lowest is zero."

"That'll do... my woman kicked me out, alright?"

The worker shook his head and turned the chip reader around. "I wasn't asking why," he muttered, and then gave him a box number to crawl into and close his eyes. It was in the middle of the wall, easily missed and squeezed between eight other people dead to the world. The wire for an obsolete ENU connection had been ripped apart, a true zero bitrate for the box. The internet connection didn't matter, just that there was a charger for his burner phone, the mausoleum music was muffled, and it was dark.

Clyde slept.

Hands grabbed hold of his coat and yanked him out of the box. Not into the hall with everyone else, but through the wall in the back. He woke up falling just before his back hit the concrete beneath him. Before he could blink his eyes open, someone ripped his void mask off and stuffed the cold barrel of a pistol against his cheek.

Clyde froze and blinked, stretching his eyes wide in the dark until he could pick the silhouettes from the shadows and see the three bodies looming over him. As soon as he opened his mouth, one of them said, "Shut it."

Two of the heads leered closer to him, screwing up their eyes in the gloom. While the third stood up and replaced the false backing to the mausoleum box, one of them pulled out a cellphone and turned on the flashlight. They shined it in Clyde's face like an optometrist.

Judging by his hangover, he could imagine how bloodshot he must have been. The only thing in his body that seemed to be working up to snuff was his racing heart. Blood pushed through sore limbs, crying out for water as he slowly revitalized and tried to imagine what he could do.

"See? I told you this was the guy," the one with the light said.

Clyde blinked and furrowed his brow. He recognized the voice; it was the employee from the counter. Peering down, he could see the cybernetic legs bent double like an ostrich, with probably a thousand times the strength the man's arms had. "Who are you?" Clyde asked.

"Keep your mouth shut until spoken to," the man with the gun ordered. "If you understand, blink once for yes. Good."

"Where did you get the mask?" the cripple asked. His voice took on a bored, professional tone as he waved the item in front of Clyde.

Clyde glanced at the gunman and got the nod. "Previous owner died in my neighborhood."

The men snarled at him. "So, you took it off a corpse?" the worker asked.

Clyde almost answered, but blinked once instead.

"Word gets around, you know that, Bondsman?"

It was Clyde's turn to snarl. "You saying there's a bounty on me?"

The gunmen pressed harder, making the metal scrape against his cheekbone. "That was a yes or no question, quaz."

The worker rolled his eyes. "You don't even know where these masks come from, do you? No wonder, I guess. They aren't made in Missou. You're just seeing the diffusion of thieves. You're one yourself. Look what you're using it for. Murder. I'm disgusted, you know that?"

"The fuck do you know about me?"

The worker put a hand on the gunman's arm before he could dramatically cock the hammer. "We know you're working for the old bitch, Greif."

"And who are you?"

"None of your goddamned business. At best, you're going to die in a blaze of glory like some kinda goddamn movie star. At worst, they're gunna lock you in a room with a mindbreaker and you'll be lucky if he decides to just rape you physically before dumping your body in the river. If you're unlucky, you may well find yourself a retribution slave. You know that? Wouldn't want that, now would we?"

Clyde blinked twice and the worker smiled at him.

"Good. We definitely wouldn't want you spilling your guts out to the police, now would we? I bet Greif had a handler for you, one to make sure you got a bullet when you were done. Of course, you wouldn't have been told that was their job. Ah, there's the shock. Love to see it."

Only one face came to mind.

"It seems to me like you slipped your collar though. Things are going sideways. Useful pawns don't just show up on someone else's doorstep hungover and bloody, too dazed to even realize it. Now, you've gone and made it our problem by being here. You see?"

Clyde blinked once.

"Just so I know that I'm making myself clear here, we absolutely could shoot you, cut you to chunks, and incinerate your body with the trash, never to be seen again. Case will go cold, and eventually be forgotten so long as you didn't earn a personal vendetta. That might be the safest thing for us and trust me, my friend would be happy to keep our family safe at your expense."

Clyde squeezed his hands into fists. He could feel his sword at his side, but it was too long to draw with both of them on top of him. "Is there an or?" he asked, eyes moving to the iron sights a hand's span from his eyes.

The worker laughed and thumped him on the chest. "I said it already. Best case scenario is you go out in a blaze of glory. Big movie star style. Great for the cameras."

His mouth was running dry. "You even know who I'm gunning for?"

"Yeah, Robert Dixie, a real piece of work if you ask me. World will be a better place with him dead. Just... we don't want you doing it in a void mask. You understand, don't you? It's bad marketing for us to mix messages."

"You people make the masks?"

The men laughed. "Wouldn't you like to know. Maybe we make them. Maybe we work for the guys who make them. Maybe we just agree with the message. You're too short lived for this world to care. Got that? But don't worry. I'll very kindly give you–"

Clyde's burner phone rang. Everyone froze and looked at the false panel. The third man popped it off again and fetched the phone. "It's the old bitch," he said, and tossed the phone to his leader.

The leader glared down at Clyde and said, "If you open that mouth, you'll be in an incinerator, got that?"

Clyde blinked once.

The man accepted the call and said, "Granny Greif, the owner of this phone is indisposed."

"Chucky? You incontinent little shit. Fucking sausage on stilts. What do you think you're doing?"

"What do I think I'm doing? What do you think you're doing?"

Chucky snorted. "Me? What the hell do you think you're doing? Your dog got loose."

"I've got fifty fully armored jannisaries crawling up my asshole right now. I do not have the patience for you."

"Relax," Chucky said, shaking his head and tutting his tongue. "I'm just gunna muzzle him and send him back."

34

Nicotine

2140/10/23

The Talos-Shmidt Private Clinic smelled like coffee. The neurist used his scent machine like an incense pump, smothering the smells of antiseptic, blood, and hand-sweating worry. Elliot had met him briefly after the surgery. The doctor didn't smell like coffee, rather he had caffeine patches covering half his throat. The middle-aged neurist had been peeling them off with one hand and taking pills with the other when Elliot tried to find out about Ram's condition.

"It's just swelling mostly. One fried component. She won't be able to use her implant for a while but I fixed her up. Tell her not to play with magnets like that again," he had said. He was a haggard man, too small for his own coat and with a throat like a turkey gizzard. Within the coat was nothing more than pajamas covering him up and even in the span of a few sentences, his eyes hazed over to return to sleep.

Elliot got one look at her sedated face before the door was shut and he was ushered to a waiting room to sink into one of the plush chairs. The nice thing about private clinics was that they knew who their clientele were. Namely, patients who would have people waiting for them. A hospital ICU ward could be packed like a field hospital; bodies lined up elbow to cheek and moaning all over. Elliot had interviewed dozens of people in such un-private spaces. At least there, the doctors and nurses were always so pressed for time that there was never any waiting.

In the Talos-Shmidt Private Clinic, Elliot sat in a low chair with a thick cushion, upholstered in faux-leather. It was blocky and strong with a vaguely twentieth century feel to it. He had the feeling that if he looked for it, one of the cabinets would have a selection of liquors along with an ice bucket. He hadn't thought to check before he sat down and he hadn't stood up since. At some point, maybe around dawn, the motion detector had given up on him, and shut the lights off.

Still, he hadn't moved.

This is my fault. I should have been the one to go to that scream. I wouldn't have been hurt by an EMP. I should have been there, not her.

Maybe had head dozed for a moment, passing between frustration and restless dream without realizing. Through the door of the waiting room, he eventually heard more footsteps. A pair of two that rushed in from the hall and stormed past the virtual assistant. When the door to Ram's room unlocked, Elliot figured out that it was her parents.

I should go tell them what happened.

He didn't move. He just listened to the garbled echoes of their conversation with the faux-AI. The bits he picked out were the same questions he had asked the neurist and the same answers. Ram was still sedated, not expected to wake up for hours more. Of course, they would wait. Elliot thought they might step in and see him decaying in the chair, but he heard them enter a different waiting room.

That's good, I guess. I think. I don't know.

Another pair of feet clicked across the plastic floor. Click-clack, click-clack; the shod feet of a woman in heels.

Who is it this time?

The feet didn't go across the hall to Ram's room, they grew closer. They walked right up to the door. The person opened the door and for a moment blinded Elliot as the lights flashed back on. Seraphina grinned at him and clicked them back off, but she left the door open as she strolled toward him. "There's the man I know."

"How did we not catch him? I was on his fucking trail. Wyatt shoved me off! I should have been the one to follow him."

Seraphina leaned forward and planted her hands on the arms of his chair. She wasn't in uniform. She had on a wide-necked shirt that bared one shoulder and her bra strap. Her skirt wrinkled across her thighs, tugged up by the twist of her tail. She smelled like cigarettes, enough to trigger that yearning in him. "You think you could have caught him? Do ya? You would have been able to chase down a madman on a cityboard, blasting through the city as fast as an express train?"

Elliot dug one hand into the leather of the chair and covered his mouth with the other. He wanted a cigarette. "I would have tried," he said, his eyes resting on the top most star that marked Seraphina's chest.

Seraphina grinned, rocking her head back as she said, "You would have tried and you would have failed and you would be back here just the same. Don't you realize this is good news though? We know who he is. We know why he's after Dixie. That cunt has already forked over all the bio-data we could dream of. Retina scan, facial structure, neural implant make and model, gait, you name it we've got it. Not to mention all the info we got out of Fletcher. Now that Clyde's assaulted an officer, the only thing you have to worry about is whether you'll be the one to put him down."

He snarled at her, eyes locking the pale blue moons of her irises. "Ram nearly fucking died. Don't talk to me about good news."

"Righteous anger, I love it. Show me more, Blackstone. Oh, I wish I could march you down to Clyde's home and let you loose. I want to take you off your chain and watch the carnage."

Elliot recoiled and broke their gaze. In a lower voice, he said, "There wouldn't be carnage. I'll arrest him if he surrenders."

"If," she said, and smirked. In a whisper, she asked, "But do you want him to?"

Elliot closed his eyes. Ram's glossy gaze flashed into his mind. It made his body tense like an electric shock. He had to suck breath in and unclench his teeth. Ram was going to be okay according to the neurist. He tried to focus on that as Seraphina slid a knee in between his thigh and the arm of the chair. "Why did you drag me onto this case, Seraphina?"

She laughed. "I've been reading your reports, you know that? I bet I'm the only human being in the whole world keeping up on your reports. Just me and Eve. You're a very dispassionate man, you know that? You don't get riled up. You don't lash out. Always there to help and take their insults on your chin. I asked for you to be my partner on this case because I wanted to know."

Elliot pushed himself back in the chair. Their breaths were close enough to mingle. Every word was a poisonous snake of memory. It made his head pound. Fatigue raged inside him, fighting a war between his anger and his biological necessities. His arms felt heavy. Budging his legs was herculean. "Know what?"

Seraphina slid her other knee into the wide chair and sat down on his lap. "I want to know why? Is it your bitch of a wife? That's what Cinder thinks, you know that? She thinks you subject yourself to an endless parade of human filth because... what? It helps you clear your head after an argument? I'm sorry, but I just don't see the therapeutic value in that."

This is wrong.

She had put her ass on his legs, like a cybernetic nymph. She was fuller and heavier than the last time he had touched her–the head of Centurion had liked them young, afterall. With her back to the light of the door, he almost couldn't see the sadist's smile twisting her face. The staggered breaths of excitement shook her body as Elliot said, "It's the right thing to do."

"So virtuous of you I can hardly believe it."

"Better than watching as crimes are committed. Better than being complicit in them."

"Ah!" She threw her head back and twisted her shoulders. "You wound me. Here and here and here and here and here too! These stabs of truth, you cruel man," she said as she jabbed herself in every bullet scar from top to bottom, leaving her finger on the one next to her navel.

Then she dropped the actress' affectation and grinned again. "Well, I guess technically it was your friend that wounded dear old me. You never... stabbed me."

Elliot's eyes flicked to his hand. She had pinned it with her own and worked her fingers in between his so she could roll his wedding ring with her thumb. "Why the hell are you even on this case, Seraphina? You're not a detective. You're not even a bodyguard. You're the snake they send to worm her way into organizations to snitch on them, you walking honeypot."

She slumped, her hair cascading across her tilted face before she sighed and brushed it back. "I could give you the justification I used, but isn't it enough that it was to see you? My dear savior? The man who ran away from me? Justice incarnate from behind the barrel of a gun... You've fallen so low, Tom. You're a damned E-rank. How did you let that happen?"

He snorted. "Your report didn't help me on the matter."

Seraphina shoved her finger into his chest, the nail digging in. "You're the one who didn't respond to me. I tried to help you. I would have covered for you."

That would have been wrong. Even more wrong than killing Centurion. But now, look where it's landed me?... Ah.

"That's why you brought me on, isn't it? You never expected to arrest Clyde from the start, did you?"

Seraphina licked her lips and straightened her back. "Guilty as charged."

"He's just a man with a grudge, isn't he? You know who's been giving him the means. Who is the actual person that wants Dixie dead?"

The ivory mounds of her shoulders shrugged in the gloom. "Hell if I know, Blackstone. Chase is the one who got tipped off, not me."

"And what is he getting in exchange?"

"A political favor most likely. A limit to the carnage. It's not like this mad dog we're hunting is gunning down people in the street. They've been carefully pointing him only at people that nobody is going to miss."

"Then why is Ram hospitalized?"

"Come now, you know why. She's a rookie. Not only did she fuck up, but Clyde slipped his handler. You know that. You're the one who interrogated Zarah."

Elliot closed his eyes and put his chin to his chest. "We're not going to get cleared to raid Greif, are we?"

"Not. A. Chance. Why would we backstab someone so cooperative?"

"What about Dixie?"

"He lives. At least, that's the plan. He'll get fired of course. What kind of head of security would allow an assassin to get so close to them? But really, all the PR damage has been done. All that's left is the grand finale but you're the secondary character, the supporting role. Dixie only lives if you save him. The grand finale is almost here. The calls are being made to tell Clyde where to be and when." Seraphina gently put her hand to Elliot's head. She pushed her fingers through his hair and slid around to the back of his skull. "Of course, he's going to come in swinging. That EMP weapon of his is something else, but that's what makes you so special. You're dry. Nothing but a man with a gun... and a grudge. The perfect counter."

Elliot sucked in air, again that cigarette scent ten times better than coffee. "It's a shame. Zarah's in love with him. If she hadn't fucked up, I wouldn't be this pissed."

Seraphina laughed. "Happy coincidences I guess."

"Not for him," Elliot said, and glanced to Seraphina's side, toward the room Ram slept in.

Seraphina pulled her hand back from Elliot's head and reached down her shirt. From between her breasts, she produced a crumpled, sweat smelling, pack of cigarettes. With a flourish, she twirled one of the coffin nails between her slender fingers and held it out to him. "You'll come with me, won't you? I'll take you right to the bastard and let you have him. Nobody else in the whole wide world can offer you that."

Elliot's mouth was dry and his chest hollow. His head sat thick and dark, smothering any flicker of thought. He took the cigarette from her and stuck it in his lips. When she lit it, he sucked in and tasted the familiar bite of smoke and tar. It burned his lungs and flooded back out as the ember colored their faces yellow; hers full and grinning, his sunk within the reflections of her eyes.

He was going to kill Clyde.

35

Gear Up

2140/10/24

Clyde knew he would wear the mask for the rest of his life. They had taken his void mask and given him another. It still covered his face, but it was made from steel and locked onto his head. His eyes were covered by a visor, but everything from his cheeks down was a snarling maw of jagged metal, hiding the electronics within. Not the least of which was a thumb-sized wad of plastic explosives stuck next to his jaw.

Chucky hadn't been entirely cruel however. After so kindly improving Clyde's fashion sense, he had locked him in a room apparently tailor made for these kinds of situations. The door in locked shut with no hope of Clyde forcing it back open–too much steel reinforcement–and the only other way out was a utility lift they had taken control of. "When it's time, you'll get the ride you need," the amputee bastard had said, before slamming the peep-slide shut on the door and leaving Clyde with the goodies.

Whoever Chucky was, he was a resourceful and well-connected bastard. The waiting room had everything an aspiring murderer could want. There were guns and knives, tactical grenades alongside half a dozen sensors, and body armor too. While not the latest and greatest that Daedalus Labs could cook up, most of it was a step up from military grade. Basic equipment for deployment was crude, practically medieval. Steel stompers and metal gauntlets, so the unwary soldier might not get bit. That didn't matter much inside Bastion. What Chucky had for him was poly-weave alloy, long-sleeved too. It weighed almost twenty pounds and the previous owner must have been half Clyde's size, but he had the time to break it in and afterward it would be able to shrug off most small arms fire. If the police deployed drones to shoot him, he would almost be able to ignore them.

While he was still stretching and fighting the interlocking mesh of metal, he picked through the weapons. None of the knives were better than the micro-blade he already had, but firearms were another matter. A Lupa revolver chambered in .45 was easy enough to strap to his hip, but he couldn't just take every long gun on the rack. Everything was traditional combustion, bang sticks, but nothing was anti-material grade. He supposed there were some limitations to what Chucky had to offer, and was about to take a standard 5.56 rifle when he recognized the mass of metal at the end.

It was a Romulus Specialty firearm, an R-Spec. Purpose built and never intended for general use. To use it against a person or a blighted would be a joke. Just showing up to a fight with it could get the user laughed at because of how heavy it was, equivalent to an LAV machine gun. In the right circumstance however, every gram of weight was justified. There was no waste material on the weapon, everything was needed to carry a magazine of six precision engineered flechette bolts the length of Clyde's forearm. Against a biological, they would be the world's worst acupuncture treatment, they could slip right through without the adrenaline-addled victim even noticing. When it came to crippling kuzuri drones and autonomous turrets however, Clyde couldn't think of anything better.

He was trying to slide a straw between the teeth of his mask to suck down water and listening to the most stale reporting on the stock market he could imagine, when the television blacked out. It was a cruddy little thing with worn out colors, striped with lost pixels and unfit for even the poorest domicile, but it was all Chucky had left in the waiting room. No remote control of course. The end of the inane pingpont of pseudo-AI personalities, batting ideas and incidents back and forth to fill air time, came as an uncomfortable relief. If he never saw another graphic of a dead cat bounce again in his life, it would be too soon, but it left him staring at the black screen.

His own reflection was replaced by a default video call icon. He glanced around, but didn't see a microphone. "Hello?" he asked.

"They got Zarah." The voice was Greif's.

"That's my fault."

"Damn right it's your fault. What were you doing without your mask on? I explicitly told you to keep your damn head down, fool. If you had done what I told you to do, you wouldn't be that twat's prisoner right now. Zarah wouldn't be arrested. And I wouldn't have police crawling through my hair trying to get me! But... not all is lost despite your monumental effort to make it so."

"You telling me today's the day?" Clyde asked.

Greif said, "Yes, today's the day. You're going to have to go all the way to the top of the city though. Not only is he taking a security detail from Heartsteel, but he's getting cooperation from the janissaries. That means auto-snipers."

Clyde ripped the straw from his mask and whistled. "I hope you're about to say you've got a plan for me despite that."

"I do, but you're not going to like it. Any approach from the top will be spotted. That's the whole point of the auto-snipers. They'll punch a wad of lead through you with enough force to send it clear of the far side of the city if you give them the chance. Of course, both his headquarters and the bank are under permanent surveillance. There's nowhere to come from that you won't have a soldier or a kuzuri shooting you within seconds. Which means the only way to get to him is while he's on his train, and you're going to have to come from below."

He frowned.

Greif paused to suck on a cigarette, the sizzling ember crackling through the speaker. "I hope you're comfortable on a cityboard. You're going to have to jump and you'll only get one chance at it."

Clyde blinked and slumped forward. The folding chair creaked beneath him as he buried his face in his hands. He could still feel the tension in his legs from riding out of Survivor's Canyon. That was nothing but a straight shot run. If he had to jump, that meant he would have to bounce from one rail to another, at the top of the city no less. Eighty stories of free fall, bouncing from bridges to signs to cables to rails and everything else. At least down in Delta and Gamma, the fall would likely be no more than a few meters before tumbling off of something, but in Alpha there was space and air and nothing much to grab onto. There was a damn good reason cityboarders didn't go that high.

With his eyes closed though, he saw the death report of his brother. He saw his mother's lifeless face. He pictured Zarah not smiling in the bar but clapped in steel, getting hauled to prison. Dixie's smiling, press-release-perfect face loomed over it all as Clyde dug his fingers into the steel mask.

"Are you sure this is the best chance?"

"It's the only chance," she said.

"Then what does it matter if I like it or not? When do I go?"

"Chucky will let you go when the time is right. Dixie is scheduled to arrive in a few hours, but there might be delays. We're playing this by ear. And Clyde, you realize that even once you get on that train it won't just be Dixie, right? You're going to have to kill more than him."

Clyde pressed his lips into a line and thought about the police girl he had maimed. That had been a mistake. She hadn't deserved it. Whoever stood between him and Dixie though, that was another matter. "Not a problem," he said. "Just tell me how to get there and when to go."

"You'll get told when the time comes. I guess I don't need to tell you to keep your head down this time, do I?" Greif asked. She laughed and killed the call. The finance reporting came back on and Clyde snarled. He shut his eyes as the two programs started talking about the recent crash in Gamma Coin and speculating on how the tax systems would account for the wild changes in fortune it wrought. Clyde just shut his eyes and tried to tune it out.

When the elevator finally came, he heard the motors first. The creak of cables and the grinding of old wheels. The terraced doors pulled apart in shudders, letting yellow light bathe the waiting room foot after foot. The same cityboard he had stolen sat waiting for him, battery fully charged according to his new mask's heads up display.

After having not eaten all day, his stomach was near empty. It left him light and cagey as he slung the R-Spec over his shoulder. It came with a cloth cover, which would hide it from visual detection to an extent, but Clyde couldn't think of what a normal person would sling over their shoulder like he did. It would be a very strange shape for a briefcase and besides, as soon as he crossed up through Beta, EVE would have the entire EM range to look at him with. There were spots in alpha where she would probably be able to diagnose him with cancer if he got too close. Spotting a barrel of metal would be trivial, cloth or not.

As soon as he stepped onto the lift, everything was going to be about speed. He had to get to Dixie as fast as possible, take him out, and then what? Dive? Fall into the depths of the city as fast as possible? He could go back to Survivor's Canyon at the least. Maybe just turn himself in and go to prison. Dixie deserved it after all.

He nodded to himself. Today was the day it came to an end. Nothing was going to hang over his head after this. Besides, Chucky wasn't letting him out any other way. He stepped onto the lift and turned around to face the shutting gate. As soon as the metal clicked shut, the cables pulled him up from the depths of Gamma, inch by rusted inch.

His visor dinged and lit up with a red dot in the corner of his vision. When he lifted his head to look at it, the dot swam and twisted, fixating on some distant location. When he stared at it, the angle settled in place, tracking some distant objective flying across the top of Bastion. A few stories later, the computerized avatar of a dragon sprite appeared before him, flying across the translucent visor. It flew a figure eight, circling against the door out from the elevator. Clyde's nose wrinkled as he watched the red thing fly.

When the elevator stopped–somewhere around the thirtieth floor he figured–the doors slid open and the dragon shot forward. It left a glittering trail in the air as it shrank to a little speck, guiding him past half a dozen doors. The visuals crudely updated as he followed along, and when he opened the indicated door, cold wind nearly blew it out of his hand. The city was dark, covered over by fresh sheets of roiling gray, a wool that crackled with lightning and yet withheld a torrent of rain. The trail continued on out of the tower, across a bridge, and to the sloping rise of a maglev line. The dragon danced beside it.

Clyde hefted the cityboard and shook his head. "I'm getting the damn VIP treatment, am I?" he asked, wondering if Chucky had snuck a microphone into the muzzle. Rather than wait for a response, he took off running. With the door open, cameras could see him. The mask hid his face, but it would only be a matter of time until EVE put two and two together. When he reached the end of the walk, he vaulted the railing and landed on the cityboard, strapping in as the magnets synced with the train rails.

Then he was off.

36

Obligations

2140/10/23

"**S**he's awake," Seraphina said, and tossed Elliot her phone. It soared down from her perch atop the train station awning, where wind warred with her hair and jacket. She had a certain kind of knowing indecency to her attire; the wind also fluttered her skirt and exposed the cycling shorts underneath.

Elliot caught the phone, his steel gauntlet clicking against the glass. The armor enveloped the device as he turned it around and saw Ram's groggy face staring up at him. She was still in the clinic bed with bandages wrapped across her forehead. She looked like she had just rolled out of bed, given the chaos that was her remaining hair. Ram glared at him as she sucked on what was either a milkshake or some kind of latte. "You really not going to take the helmet off?" she asked.

Shit.

Elliot unbuckled the QRS helmet and pulled it off. For a moment, he was accosted by the swelling smell of canal water far below, dredged up by the stormfront. The suit had been filtering that out. After brushing his hair out of his face, he cleared his thoughts and looked at her again. "Feeling alright?"

She shrugged. "I'm still waiting for the anesthetics to wear off. It'll probably be a few days before I really have my feet under me again but hey, I got a free upgrade on my implant processor. So that's cool. Insurance is really generous when you get injured on the job."

Thank God.

"Take all the rest you need. In fact, you should explicitly make sure that Wyatt covers your duties if I can't. Got that?"

She nodded. "Yeah, I heard he's the one who lost Bondsman. He left me a text message apologizing."

"Don't worry about Bondsman. I'll be getting him today," Elliot said.

"In that suit? Won't he just brick you with that EMP thingie?"

Elliot snorted and grinned. "There's nothing in here but some fans. I'm all natural, remember? He'll be in for a hell of a surprise if he tries that on me. Still, we've got drones to be the front line. In all likelihood, he's just going to get tazed and detained."

"Unless he's on CZAR."

"His psych profile says he's not going to do that. But don't worry about that. Focus on rest."

Ram snorted and sucked down the last of her drink. A scowl formed on her face as she pinched some of her hair and held it up. "Oh trust me, I've got my own things to worry about. I'm half bald now! Can you believe that? This crotchety old neurist shaved my head! I look like some kind of punk. Miccolo is going to laugh at me! I'll have to get a wig or something. For months! This is the real tragedy!"

Elliot rolled his head back laughing. "And here I thought a private clinic doctor would be better about that."

Ram growled and threw herself back against her pillow. When she lifted the phone back to her face, her irritation had melted back to concern. "Just don't get hurt on my account, okay?"

"Blackstone," Seraphina called as she jumped down from the awning. "Ride's here."

Elliot hopped up, spotting the armored train car as it lumbered across the skyline. It emerged from between the towers like a pill bug wary of the storm. Far heavier than a normal commuter, it could shrug off small arms fire but paid the price in acceleration. Diplomats tended to use it, or CEOs with assassins on their asses. "Gotta go."

"Hey! Just don't do anything stupid. Don't forget–"

Seraphina's phone cut to black, the call dying in his hand. She shrugged. "Radios only, you know protocol, don't you?" she said, plucking it back from his grasp.

"No, I know. I was just thinking that I need to get a new phone for myself. Mine's fried, remember?"

She smirked. "Yeah, I remember."

A boom like a mortar went off behind them, and a drone unfolded itself like a flower. It twirled high in the sky, corkscrewing through the breeze as it scanned all over with a dozen cameras, floating atop the wind as Dixie emerged from his office with a civilian-grade bullet proof vest and two bodyguards even more well armored than Elliot was.

Isn't that obsolete by now? That just reeks of it.

Elliot put his back to the train and met the VIP without a salute or even a nod. He just put his helmet back on and appraised the politician.

Dixie was gaunt and his eyes bloodshot. He sneered at Elliot as he walked past. "I don't appreciate being bait."

Elliot snorted, the noise muffled by his mask. He fell in behind Dixie and trailing the two thugs the man still had employed. "You're only bait if Bondsman knows you're exposed."

Dixie stopped outside the train to snarl over his shoulder. "You being here is all the proof I need that somebody is leaking. I know how the fucking game is played, Blackstone."

"Well!" Seraphina exclaimed as she tugged the armored door open with a smile. "It's a good thing you're an expert at security, isn't it? With all your precautions and us too, what could possibly go wrong?"

Dixie asked, "Why the hell aren't you wearing body armor."

"If you think I'm going to lay down my life for you, that's fucking hilarious," she said, not cracking her smile in the slightest. She kept her post perfect until Dixie was the one to awkwardly step past her into the train. Everyone followed behind, but she ducked in right before Elliot so she could rub her tail against his metal chin. "Keep your priorities straight, Blackstone."

The inside of the train looked more like a private airplane. There were no rails for support, no rows of seats. Advertisements hadn't been painted over every exposed surface and it didn't smell like body odor. Dixie took a seat in a swivel chair and pulled a bottle of whiskey from a cabinet, all in the space that ten normal chairs could have been. His thugs walked to either end of the train car, standing next to the doors to the nose and heel respectively. "Half an hour," he said, splashing the amber drink into a glass, no ice.

"I'm sorry?" Elliot asked as the train started gliding across the city.

Dixie snarled at Seraphina who plopped herself into the opposite seat. "That's how long this ride will be. Because of the turns and the weight and the distance, we'll be on average going slightly faster than a cyclist. Can you believe that?"

"Makes sense to me."

Dixie narrowed his eyes. "Are you familiar with calculus, Detective?"

What a condescending asshole.

"I don't see how that's an appropriate question."

"It's a serious question, Detective. Not everyone takes basic calculus before they serve and not everyone goes on to higher education afterward. You might not be aware of how summing rates over time works. Let me put this simply just in case. The fact that I am marginally safer in this slow train than in a normal, fast train, does not necessarily mean that I am safer overall. For instance, I may be nearly impervious at the moment–which I am not–but because we are barely crawling across the city, my would-be killer has all the time he needs to find the chink in my armor. Much like a safe cannot keep your jewelry safe forever, neither can armor keep your life forever. Now do you understand?"

Elliot pursed his lips and put his hand to the ceiling of the train car as it banked through a turn. "Since you want to dress up with mathematics, should I point out to you, Mr Dixie, that you have a habit of making enemies over time? That, if it weren't this Clyde Bondsman that someone else would be gunning for you? The way you operate business earns you enemies and now you're crying about it."

Dixie drained his whiskey and crossed his legs. He grinned. "I must be being recorded right now. Well, for the pleasure of my detractors to hear, I want to say that I have done absolutely nothing wrong. I provide necessary security for the functioning of our economy. Just like how an EMT arrives to slap a bandage on a wound, I send my men in when accidents happen, when violence is flaring up. Where other, lesser, security companies would balk at the danger, Heartsteel steps up. This isn't just a service I perform for the big companies mind you. We even offer a rate discount for independent companies, which we make up for by charging the American government when we do our real work. You understand, don't you? That Heartsteel exists to take the blame when Congress wants a scapegoat?"

"Do you rehearse this speech often?" Elliot asked.

The man's smile didn't flicker. "You understand, don't you, Detective? That there are times when the government has to do things that the public wouldn't approve of? It goes both ways of course. There are times when a private citizen must do things that the government wouldn't approve of, just that the scales are different. Certain things... if we don't do them the damage could be incalculable. Think nuclear war with UAAF, you understand?"

"Is that your excuse? You just happen to be the guy in the position? You can't be blamed because you have to do it?"

Dixie smirked. "You must think what was done at the Sigurd chemical plant was a mistake, but if you were in my position, you'd call it unfortunate collateral damage. You understand, yes? It's not that I want people, these protesters, to get killed—Bastard's blood, no! Very obviously, it ends up with people coming after me, either legalistically or with guns. But factories like Sigurd must keep running. You know, a hundred years ago—before the apocalypse that is—some of the most vital components of the economy relied on shipping parts around the world in a ballet of shipping containers that arrived just in time for manufacturing. If there were ever a mishap, suddenly half the economy would just stop. There would be no new computers, no new cars. Those were very important before public transport. And when that happened, the cycling of money would lurch. The whole economic system would have entered the equivalent of cardiac arrest and from there, who could say what would fail next? With it so spread out across the globe, a billion people confused and uncoordinated, it's easy to see how you could end up with cascade failure. Today, we actually know in general terms what will fail when, if certain interruptions occur. Thanks to EVE, we have such precise modeling that we can actually quantify how many people will die early, and how much early, if these protesters have their way. I've seen the numbers myself and trust me there is far less harm in killing a few idiots than in letting them have their way."

"So, how many people do I get to kill?" Elliot asked.

Seraphina threw her head back and laughed as Dixie blinked at him. "I'm sorry?" the businessman asked.

"You quite literally just justified murder through utilitarianism. You put very real murder on one scale and a computer model on the other like a big trolley problem. Well how about me? I know for a fact that my actions have saved people's lives, plenty of them. So when do I get to kill somebody? If you're justified in killing someone to save others, then surely I'm justified in killing someone after saving others, right?"

Dixie scowled. "Does the word causality mean nothing to you?" he asked, before he, and his two thugs, simultaneously turned to the east and looked out the window. The alert appeared in Elliot's vision as well, pointing to the fast moving object approaching them. "Excellent. Good distance. Deploy the sloth," Dixie ordered as he got himself another glass of whiskey.

The alert indicated Clyde Bondsman.

37

Romulus Special

2140/10/23

Clyde didn't dare go above the skyline, to where the highest train lines looped and arced across the city in haphazard arcs. Half a dozen of them would shave minutes off his trip, but would cost him his head. Even beneath the tops of the towers he felt like he was falling through the wind. A cobalt blue expanse would have assaulted him with vertigo, but the cloth of gray storm hung above him like the roof to a cave. Every buffet of wind helped lift him higher as he stared at the glistening trail before him.

Warning indicators appeared across his vision, highlighting every known defense turret across his path. He tried to whistle, the sound died in the wind. From his memory, he dredged up what he had been taught on the shortcomings of static defense–easy to plan around. Then a speaker started beeping in his ear, hammering his skull like a woodpecker. He swore and swatted at the mask, but there were no buttons on the outside. "What is it?"

"Incoming," someone said through the speaker, their voice almost making him jump.

Clyde twisted his head around, feeling tension build in his gut every instant that he wasn't looking where he was going. A thousand things were flying past him, advertisements, signs, parks, trees, his own reflection in the glass of the towers. Then he merged from one line to another, banking up another story and redirecting himself. That was when he saw the train flying in behind him. It was a double decker, the kind that could only fit in the highest reaches of Bastion. Fresh paint too. Somebody had paid to turn it into an enormous billboard. If he didn't pick up his speed, a pop idol was about to plow through him and turn him into a smear on the ground.

He swore and spread his feet as wide as the board would allow, maxing his speed as he crouched down so far he nearly sat on the battery pack. There was something wrong still. The dinging warning didn't stop. The train could only go as fast as the magnets could oscillate, just like him on his cityboard. He and the train were traveling at the exact same speed, so even if he went all fifteen kilometers to Dixie, it would never hit him.

The knot of unease didn't lessen until he scanned the city again and spotted something that wasn't a blur. Him, the train, and it were all matched in speed, like it stood still beneath him. It was several hundred pounds of metal and firepower with a dozen glass eyes tracking him from six stories lower.

He threw the cloth off the R-Spec, almost losing his balance as he shouldered the weapon. The moment he did, the drone lurched. Metal limbs and wheels spun as it twirled between rails and support beams, gliding upwards before it grabbed onto a crossing rail. The body swung out as it shot from Clyde's sight.

"Fuck. Fuck-fuck-fuck-fuck!" he roared as he looked for another path to Dixie. Before he could spot anything, he heard the incoming whine of motors. He shouldered again, spotting the machine as it came flying back at him, now only two stories below. He tracked it, sighting in and almost pulled the trigger, then he saw what was behind the machine; people. Dozens of people had stood up from tables at a cafe, gawking at him and the machine.

Then his chance passed. The robot swayed and launched itself up to his rail. It grabbed hold of the train rail like a swinging ape, hooking onto it and launching itself over and under until it hung from below once again. Wheels squealed as it matched speed and pivoted gun barrels at him like the silk spinners of a spider.

Clyde reared back, pulling the nose of his board up as he swung the R-spec at it again. Again, he saw the swath of afternoon commuters beyond the machine's back. He didn't pull the trigger. Something pricked him in the neck, a micro-syringe hidden within the mask. His face flushed, his mind dulled for a moment. The whole world slowed as the drug poured into his mind, shifting it into overdrive and leaving him scrambling to catch up with his own thoughts.

Anti-personnel munitions were pointed straight at him. The only reason they hadn't fired was because the machine was calculating punchthrough on his board. There was a computational war with the various processors and memory databases. He had a moment before it realized it could shoot him anywhere but through the board's battery. He had a mere machine beneath him. It had hard coding. There was something he could do about it.

He slammed his heels together, throwing his chest forward as his board decelerated. The gun barrels tracked him, only catching up as he landed on the nose of the train. Suddenly, he had metal and people behind him, not open sky. There was collateral damage. The machine had to re-position. The only way it could create a safe firing solution would be to get closer. It had to slow down and ride directly into the barrel of the R-spec.

Clyde pulled the trigger and felt the recoil thump through his body. Half of a kilogram of steel flung out from his weapon and punched through the belly of the machine. Electricity spewed out like a volcanic shower as the onboard computing bricked. The internal battery shorted, spraying fumes as one of the four wheels died. The steel rod continued through, punching through the city beyond. Clyde heard someone scream, but put it out of mind. He and the train overtook the attack-drone. The magnetic fields trampled it, shunting the wheels from the rail and sending it crashing to a boulevard far below and out of his mind.

One gone, five left. The R-spec smoked in his grasp, baking off residual oil as he cycled a fresh slug into the chamber. The recoil felt like a horse had slugged him in the shoulder. He could feel the muscles swelling, going numb.

Clyde blinked. He felt wind blow against his chest, and heard the wind whistling through the mask's metal mesh. The train beneath his feet rumbled. Vibrations passed through board to boot to thigh and higher still. The magnets of his board clamped nose to steel, holding him tight, flesh-close it was like, as the mask had pricked, slashed something in his thoughts ran clipped.

The earth below had fell away. His mind soared with the day in a stormy rage. Bitter path and littler death. Fifteen had become ten and would become one fifth. His gaze was fixed upon the beacon red, his path from now to Dixie dead. Clyde stood upon the train, in defiance of gravity and electric rain.

He saw the city standing on tilt. From the firmament they rose, those bold fractal fingers of metal devil foes. Life uncaring, rules unwavering. A living crypt of concrete and glass, lined with plastic flowers never to wilt.

He knew his mind was crooked. The slowing of the train–for people to escape to sheltered stop–meant nothing to him more than a shift and a flip. He fell through air and landed on the electric field, invisible to eye and hand yet he knew it would be there. Gone was his fear, the hammering of the heart but a phantom jeer. His body danced through twist and turn, and sailing through, the city till Dixie came to view.

One kilo remained between him and the armored train car. The closer he drew to his goal, the more his mind focused on it. He didn't know if the drug was abating, or helping. He didn't much care. Half a dozen spikes of warning lashed his eyes. As he rode up from the city canyon to the free clifftops of Bastion, the sighting lasers of snipers flashed against him. Survival necessitated action and again his R-spec shouldered. All the training of his military and security careers pulled into the front of his mind like a different spirit took hold of his body.

He aimed and fired, his back to a pedestrian park. The first sniper turret snapped off its stalk like a bird shot from the sky.

Then the next, and a third, and then he slammed the nose of his board to the tail of the armored train. He had to act fast before one of the remaining turrets got a sideways bead on him, but the glass was bullet proof. An R-spec outclassed bullet proof however. His fourth slug punched a hole through it, leaving a spider web of cracks. The fifth he put in the side, splitting open a slit through the polycarbonate which howled in the sucking wind. He heard the scrape of a sliding door come from inside. The light increased as an armored thug stepped in. The man aimed but didn't fire.

Clyde shot the sixth round directly into the man's chest. The steel knocked a proper hole through the so-called bulletproof glass and slammed into the security guard's body. It crunched through the man's armor and slammed him into the wall, but didn't pierce through—too much energy lost with the glass. Clyde had to unbuckle his back foot and dive through, flipping over and nearly breaking his ankle as he rolled across the floor of the train, dragging an inert but heavy board behind him. Pain seared through his leg as he rolled over, but the idea of pain came distant to him. It didn't blot his thoughts or make him flinch.

It simply was, and he knew what drug the mask had given him.

The security guard coughed, staggering back to his feet. The impact had dented his armor. It gave Clyde a moment to whip the empty R-spec at him. That bought him an instant to jump up as the security guard aimed at him again. Clyde grabbed his EMP and lashed it out as the man fired three rounds of 9mm into Clyde's center of mass. Each bullet punched him, the bullets failing to penetrate the armored weave. A moment later, the thug toppled over, as good as dead.

"He's armored!" someone yelled.

Clyde locked his gaze on the beacon that indicated Dixie's location. He popped in a new battery as he stepped over the thug's body. The man grabbed him by the ankle, stopping his foot as the thug tried to pick up his pistol again. Clyde drew his own and emptied half the magazine into the man's mask, firing until it shattered and blood pooled beneath him.

"Firing heavy!" the other man shouted. The partitioning door from one train segment to the next opened. Clyde darted forward, priming the trigger on his EMP again. He locked eyes on the other thug, spotting the thick-barrelled shotgun too late. Fire erupted from it, propelling .33 caliber shell shot directly into Clyde's face.

38

Intercept

2140/10/23

Elliot grabbed the security officer by the shoulder and nearly hauled the man off his feet. "Why the fuck did you wait?"

The man rocked, unshouldering the shotgun in a daze. He shook his head. "Something's wrong with the targeting."

"With the targeting?" Elliot screamed. "Your friend is fucking dead because you didn't go in with him! He's goddamn blighted food and you deserve to be right there beside him!"

"Hey, he might have been planning to get on top of the train! What if he had been firing down, taking shots at us. That was a real danger! How was I supposed to know he would have a fucking R-spec!"

Absolute human waste.

Elliot snarled and swept his gaze around the train. Corpse, corpse, idiot, and Dixie had vanished to the nose along with Seraphina. "EVE, is anyone else moving?" he barked.

The AI spoke through the train intercom. "I know you're a little stressed, Blackstone, but that's a silly question. To answer what you meant to ask, while nobody else is approaching your position, Mr Bondsman is not dead."

Elliot's eyes shot back to the bleeding criminal. The man grunted and shifted. He planted one hand on the floor and pushed himself up as bits of metal from his mask fell into a bloody puddle. "Freeze," Elliot ordered, pointing his sidearm at Clyde's head.

The man laughed. "Targeting," he said, and spat pieces of blood teeth onto the floor. "How did you idiots not know? I've been flagged as friendly this entire time. Thanks to Dr Forez."

"Move," the security guard said as he shouldered past Elliot and nearly put the shotgun to Clyde's forehead. Then he didn't pull the trigger. He just stood there staring into space.

What?

Before Elliot could get his bearings on what had happened to the other man, Clyde reached out with what looked like the handle to a knife. Where there should have been a blade, electricity crackled. Simultaneously, the security guard went down, the intercom exploded, and the digital banner ads blacked out. The device popped too, throwing smoke into the air as Clyde tossed it aside.

And then it was just Elliot and Clyde.

"Fuck, you're just a cop," Clyde said as he stood up and clawed at the remains of his mask. More chunks of it broke off, revealing the butchery that was his face. One of his eyes was missing, most of his cheek, and not one square centimeter didn't have blood on it.

"You're on CZAR, aren't you?" Elliot asked. He took a half step back and braced his aim. The suit didn't have any kind of stabilizers to it. Every breath was a struggle to keep his adrenaline under control and his gun pointed at the white of Clyde's remaining eye.

The man shrugged. "Guess so. Metal-legged fuck did it to me. I don't suppose you'd just let me kill that piece of shit behind you, would you?"

"It's your fault I'm here."

"Oh, right. The girl. Sorry about that."

Elliot fired. Clyde jerked his head to the side as soon as Elliot's finger tensed. The bullet punched a hole through the man's ear and nothing more. Elliot fired again, catching the man in the armored weave to no effect. Clyde fired too, emptying the last of his magazine to scratch the surface of Elliot's armor. They each exchanged punches with their grams of lead, ducking and circling one another until each clicked empty. Elliot dropped his mag.

Clyde ripped his micro-blade free and hacked.

Elliot dropped his gun and swung his arm out. He hammered the outside of his forearm into the nano-scale edge, catching the weapon with his own nano-scale shielding. He smirked when he saw the surprise in Clyde's face. Unfortunately, there was no good solution to a CZAR user with a sword. He jabbed his fist out, hammering Clyde in the remains of his metal mask, but that was as useful as punching a wall.

Clyde had both hands on the grip of his blade and his bloodshot eye fixed upon Elliot. The drug-enhanced killer flicked and chopped with his micro-blade. It slammed into Elliot's other arm, also armored. He swung it at Elliot's thigh and forced him to jump back, not trusting the steel. Then Clyde twisted the point to center and thrust.

"Drop!" Seraphina screamed.

Elliot dropped, his back hitting the floor after his chin almost bifurcated on Clyde's micro-blade. His stomach dropped when he saw the weapon flip back around to swing down, but Clyde took an instant to look past him and see Seraphina. She stood with one foot through the door, her hand outstretched and pointed like a gun.

"Bang."

A .50 caliber anti-material bullet put a hole through the train's armor, through the carpet floor, and through Clyde's armpit. His shoulder joint grenaded. Bone and cartilage hit the roof like shotgun spray and his arm hit the floor. The pressure wave thumped Elliot as hard as the bullets had. Before Elliot could even uncoil his muscles and move again, Clyde had toppled over and hit the floor. The micro-blade skidded across the train, eventually getting stuck beneath a chair as everyone stared at the killer to see if it would move again.

Elliot sagged down and stared at the ceiling for a moment, listening to the howling of wind through the broken rear windshield. "Bastard's blood."

Seraphina walked over and nearly stood atop his head as she grinned down at him. "You. Are. Wel-come. Mis-ter Black-stone," she said, her tail flicking.

"CZAR," Elliot grunted and sat up. Clyde's body hadn't moved, but he probably wasn't dead yet. He crawled over and planted his knee on the man's side. The poly-weave armor had shrugged off the small guns easily, but as soon as it overloaded, the whole piece unraveled. Ribbons of alloy kept popping free from every shift, throwing blood everywhere. It wasn't a very robust design compared to hard plates.

Elliot found his pistol and reloaded. The mask covering Clyde's face was as good as gone. CZAR could turn off pain, but couldn't do any-thing about a bullet to the brain. Dozens of training courses flashed through his memory, urging him that he was entirely in his rights to kill Clyde. It was protocol in fact. CZAR users could be contaminated with the blight, could turn into one of the walking dead at a moment's no-tice. Clyde had even been outside the wall. No court in the city would even think about charging him for killing Clyde.

It was just like back at the Gaia plantation, when he had killed and brought in an ARU to kill more. And that was just like clearing out the trash from Centurion.

But it's not the same. Gaia was self-defense. This? What is this? What's justified? Does a killer deserve to die? If I shoot him now, who wins? Oh... Dixie wins.

Elliot found his pair of handcuffs and stuck one on Clyde's remain-ing limb, opting to cuff it to the man's belt loop for lack of anything better. He had just grabbed the remains of the metal mask when Dixie stepped through. "Tough fucking bastard, wasn't he?"

Elliot glared over his shoulder at the businessman. "Why don't you check your surviving employee?"

Dixie sneered. "Like I can do anything for him. He needs EMT and those will be waiting on site... in about two minutes actually. Wonderful timing."

Maybe I should have accidentally let Clyde get by me. It would have done the world a favor. If I had stepped aside, just waited a moment.

Then he recognized the beige putty his fingers were touching inside Clyde's mask: plastic explosives. He swore and jumped back. Using his arm, he shoved Seraphina away too. It wasn't enough to blow the train up, but it would make a hell of a fragmentation grenade.

Payoff

Clyde didn't feel cold, but he felt like he should have. He had to rebuild the world within his mind, one piece of sensory input at a time. There was pain, enough that he should have been screaming for mercy, but the CZAR in his system muffled it all. Screaming wasn't going to help him. It wouldn't bring an ambulance faster and it wouldn't make the police officers go easy on him. It certainly wouldn't help him kill Dixie.

The bastard was standing three meters away from him, talking. Whatever the words were, Clyde couldn't figure them out. There was wind noise, the air ripping against tattered holes in the train. He could see the ragged flap of carpet from the corner of his eye and he could remember what he had done to the rear windshield. It made the car noisy, enough that the police were almost shouting at one another to be heard. They wouldn't hear him rustling on the floor.

His right arm was out of reach though. He didn't even have a stump to work with. He could already hear a prosthetic surgeon laughing at the damage. He still had his left hand and Dixie wasn't in full-body armor. A gunshot to the head would do him in. Thigh might do the trick in a pinch. He grunted and closed his eyes, working through the train mentally. His gun was empty on the floor near his feet. The spare magazine was tucked into his pants, near where he had been cuffed.

Someone kneeled down next to him and pulled the mag out and pocketed it for themselves. Clyde opened his remaining eye and glared at the jannis he had nearly killed. His options were almost out. There were firearms at the back of the train, but crawling there seemed impossible. The jannis' pistol was on the man's hip. So it seemed firearms were out of the question.

He could kick Dixie off his feet and bite his throat out.

Then the female officer asked, "So are we shooting him or patching him up? He's obviously on CZAR. That's a capital offense." Her voice was familiar. He couldn't place it.

The male police officer said, "If he knows where it came from, we are obligated to look into it."

Dixie snorted. "You think he's going to survive long enough either way? It would be a mercy to kill him."

The male police officer said, "That's still murder no matter how you cut it, and you never answered my question earlier."

The two men went at each other verbally as the woman dropped a first aid kit next to Clyde. She popped it open and took out a spray can of clotting agent. With a childish grin, she gave it a rattle and spewed the burning chemicals across what had been his arm. Again, the knowledge of pain announced itself, he even felt the muscles in his chest contract. Shock had set in, mingling with the CZAR, and blunted it all. When she was satisfied, she tossed the bottle back in the first aid box and leaned down with a cattish grin that reminded him of a night in the company bar not too long ago.

"Looking for one of these?" she asked, unholstering her pistol and holding it in front of his face. She smiled, and he thought he recognized the smile.

He blinked, or maybe it counted as a wink now. When he tried to reach for it, of course his wrist came up short on the handcuff. The police woman laughed at him and dangled it. "You really dropped the ball, you know that?"

"Seraphina! What the hell are you doing?" the male police officer demanded as the train began slowing to a stop.

The woman grinned. "Having some fun."

Clyde snorted, spilling blood out of his mangled face. "Funny, I almost got there in the end."

She cocked her head at him. "Yeah, you really did. You want to tell me what happened? I watched them try to shoot you and... well the one guy did but why didn't he get you?"

He smirked. "He never fired me."

Dixie leaned over and asked, "Bastard's blood, is he still alive?"

"He's hanging on for now. Don't worry, as long as the paramedics have touched him before he dies, we won't get in much trouble," Seraphina said. Then she leaned closer and whispered, "Go on now, these are your last words. Make them count." She put the gun away and held a cell phone out to him, set to record video.

Clyde swallowed the welling of bloody drool in his mouth and stared into the girl's eyes. "He rewrote the firmware," Clyde said, and he felt his body start to fade. He sagged against the floor and realized he couldn't feel his legs anymore. She said something else to him, but he couldn't hear it. His vision narrowed to a tunnel and he only dimly realized the train came to a stop when the doors opened.

EMT ran onboard. They grabbed hold of him and flipped him over. Gloved fingers poked and prodded him, tore at the poly-weave armor to get to his wounds. More clotting spray as they shouted at him. The flashing light in his eye intermittently blinded him. They turned the world into a slideshow as he faded to sleep. Before he vanished, they rolled him over and put him on a stretcher. The doctors tried to prolong his life with injections that made his heart race. They carried him out to the station and laid him beside the security guard that still lived so they could jab an IV into his remaining arm.

For all that, his life never flashed before his eyes. The burst of DMT that should have come never arrived, or if it did, the CZAR ruined it. He just laid there thinking about his brother and his mother, along with all the scum he had killed but he hadn't killed the man responsible. The police had robbed him of that at the very last moment. So-called defenders of the peace were doing nothing but making phone calls next to him.

The lot of them were on top of the bank, the place Dixie had to report to his investors at. They were in the protective umbrella of Heartsteel security once more, full and autonomous. Then Seraphina put the phone down and walked over to Dixie. She smiled at him as he asked what she wanted.

Then she put her gun in his face and blew his brains out.

40

Execution

2140/10/23

Elliot had been trying to get a signal jammer for Clyde's head, so the explosives couldn't be detonated, when the gunshot went off. He flinched, spun, and had his own gun drawn before he realized it had been Seraphina. Dixie hit the floor a moment later and everyone stared at her. Blood pooled across the marble tiles, spreading and pouring across her boots as she holstered and made another phone call. "Done," she said.

Elliot sucked in breath and aimed his pistol at her back. He stalked forward, putting himself between her and the paramedics. "You'd better have a damn good explanation."

She glanced over her shoulder, hair slipping down her back as she shrugged. Then she held out her phone and turned on the speaker. Vice-commander Chase's voice came through it. "Detective Blackstone, stand down."

"With all due respect Sir, I need to arrest this woman for murder."

"She executed justice on my order, officer. Robert Dixie committed treason. His actions endangered the very fabric of our society. Following this, all of Heartsteel will be dismantled and their crimes purged."

"Sir, if there's something I need to be made aware of–"

"You don't need to be made aware of anything, officer," Vice-commander Chase said. "I will deign to tell you that Sera just sent me testimony corroborating the evidence you already provided us as part of your investigation. Namely, that Mr Dixie employed a team of unlicensed neurists to hack the fundamental operating code of civilian neural implants. Do I need to tell you just how dangerous that is? Neural implant firmware is a matter of national security. She acted on my behalf for the safety of Bastion, so stand down, officer. You will be debriefed at a later time. But stand proud. For your part in this I'll be commending you!"

The call ended with Elliot still aiming at her. He squeezed his grip until his hand hurt and his barrel wavered. She just grinned at him. He asked, "Is this what you think a happy ending is?"

"Please, this isn't a massage parlor. But, if you want–"

"How are you any different from back then?"

Seraphina laughed. "When did I ever say I was? Let me ask you the same question. How are you different? Why haven't you shot Clyde? What kind of sense of honor do you have that is stopping you?"

"It's not honor," Elliot said.

She cocked her head at him. "Then what is it? You want to send him to court so someone else can do him in? Or maybe you think he shouldn't die after all the people he's killed? Oh, maybe that's hitting close to home? But what would your partner think about that? After what he did to her?"

Elliot wetted his lips and squeezed the grip of his gun. He knew he didn't have any justification for shooting Seraphina, and he knew that she wasn't a threat to him. Lowering his gun was still a struggle.

She sighed and turned up her hands. "And after that moment we had together. Well, at least I got to see you fight like you meant it. I suppose it's too much to expect after you've let your blood cool off. There really isn't a chance of him walking free afterall. Why don't I let you handle the rest of this?"

"The case is over now, isn't it? Get the hell out of here."

She bowed back and retreated. "Tah-tah then. Until next time," she said as she strolled to the nearest elevator.

Elliot took one step after her but stopped himself. He watched as the doors opened and swallowed her. Then, he marched back to Clyde Bondsman. The bloody mess of a man was laughing and grinning, his remaining eye no longer focused. Elliot took his helmet off and faced the man. "You should have sued Dixie."

No one succeeds in suing the government machine.

"You should have gone to the press."

No one liked Heartsteel anyway.

"You should have..."

Gone to the police? He probably didn't even know his firmware had been changed. No one would have thought that possible. Any crime he saw on the job would have been ignored—not in jurisdiction. What the hell am I saying? Am I saying he should have come to me? That I would have done something to bring Dixie to justice? So that I would have been the one to put a bullet in the guy instead of Seraphina?

Clyde grinned at him. "Say thanks to Claire for me, alright?"

"Fuck, I hope you're happy you son of a bitch. You killed the bad guy, the man in the suit at the top. You picked off his goons who did the dirty work then you got the one that made it happen. Congratulations. You're going to be dead and your sister will have nothing," he said and turned his back on him. He went to march over to Dixie but one of the paramedics grabbed him by the arm. The man had just started to say something with the plastic explosives popped.

41

Promotion

2140/10/23

There, on the top of the tower with nothing above but stormy sky, the sound seemed muted. It didn't echo and smash in from every side, but melted into the wind and left a red halo around the burn spot.

The rain had begun to fall when the rest of the teams arrived. The doors to the bank had been locked tight and the clean up crew had to push through journalists to get to the bodies. Elliot watched it all from a bench, drinking from Dixie's bottle of whiskey. It was genuine, barrel aged liquor. Probably over a hundred credits a shot. He barely even tasted it as he pushed himself to numbness.

Wyatt showed up, not in QRS armor but just in uniform. "Come on," he said. He helped Elliot get back to MPHQ, drop his armor off, and requisition a new phone. The whiskey ran out on the train, but the two of them got to a bar. It was a nice arcade jam type of place, with games on the walls and a live band playing their hearts out. They weren't very good, but hardly anyone in the world could make music more than a hobby so Elliot tried to just enjoy it for what it was, a call back to the survivor generations, to the eternal human tradition of drink and song to come together.

"Are we bad people, Wyatt?"

His friend twisted the cap off a bottle of imitation whiskey and poured them both glasses. "You religious now?"

Elliot picked up the drink and stared at the liquor and dye like an augury bowl without answers. "Today, several bad men died for the wrong reasons. I felt better after the two of us, you know."

Wyatt nodded and pulled out his phone. "That was simpler, wasn't it? Here, check this out," he said, and pulled up a video. He hit play and slid it across the table. It was a video of his daughter playing tennis. Every time she darted for the ball, stopped, pivoted, lunged, her prosthetic legs ripped new flaps through the court carpet, but she was moving faster than Elliot had seen any natural athlete move.

She was smiling too.

"Looks expensive," he mumbled.

"Daedalus is covering that. Look, see all the gyroscopes they taped on? This is from a study. Just last week she was barely able to move in VR, but already her brain has figured out the connection. She's got all her balance back! Can you believe that?"

"Remarkable," Elliot said, and drained his glass. Then a notification flashed on the phone, from a name Elliot didn't recognize. It had a link to a news article. With a furrowed brow, Wyatt clicked the link and both of them watched a telescopic recording of that afternoon. The feed zoomed in on three figures atop the Sterling Capital Group: Elliot, Seraphina, and Dixie. It didn't censor anything as she held up her gun and killed Dixie, instead it zoomed in more to show her grinning face.

Wyatt looked up at Elliot.

Elliot sank into his seat.

"That's who you've been working with?"

"Yeah."

"Funny. She looks familiar."

Elliot grabbed the whiskey and refilled his glass. "Because she is. You shot her seven times."

Wyatt crossed his arms and sat back. "You'd think seven bullets would be enough to kill someone."

"Hospitals are pretty good at keeping people alive, if someone carries them fast enough."

"Now, why would someone do that?"

Elliot shrugged. "Lack of foresight, I guess."

Wyatt's mouth tightened. Even the people playing darts near their table got the message and paused their game, evacuating to the service bar. When the band paused to change from one set to the next, Wyatt rose. His chair toppled as he marched out of the bar, sticking Elliot with the tab.

I bet he'd say I'm the bad guy now, wouldn't he?

The video had over a hundred million views by the time Elliot made it home. The lights were on. The kitchen was filled with the scent of chili bubbling in a slow cooker, a dirty ladle sticking out the top and a clean bowl beside it. He was taking his cloak off when Amara emerged from their bedroom. "You cooked," he said, stirring the pot.

"Babe, what the hell happened to you?"

"A lot."

"It's been two days!"

"My phone broke."

"And you don't come home? You don't use anyone else's phone? Not even a public call through EVE?"

Elliot filled the bowl and sat it down on their table. When he met her gaze, he could only shrug. "Like I said, a lot happened."

She shook her head and put her hand on the chair he tried to pull out. "Yeah, my chat has been blowing up all night. You're... the meme of the week, to say the least."

He scowled. "Shouldn't you be at that tournament thing right now? What happened? I haven't been able to pay attention. Been dealing with an assassination, as you've heard."

She rolled her eyes. "Fell apart. Nick got cold feet, said we weren't good enough to place so what was the point. I would have been dragging him back to practice if I weren't busy riding this meme wave. I've gained over two thousand followers in the last few hours! I swear, the whole fiasco with Nelson primed the pump and it feels like I've hit a jackpot. I finally have enough followers to get real sponsorship deals!"

Amara smiled at him, inching closer, her face radiant. The only thing Elliot could do was try to laugh. "Glad you're having a good night, but EVE is going to squash that and call it national security protection."

"Oh come on, that's why I said meme of the week. People will have something else before you know it. But, what's important is that if I'm getting sponsored now, I can dial my hours back. I don't need to be begging bigger streamers for collabs. I don't need to chase whatever the latest game release is. As long as I can keep my community, I can have way more control–Honey..." She frowned and looked at his lapel. She sniffed. "Why do you smell like cigarettes?"

"Because I was smoking."

She stepped back from him. "I thought that was a thing of the past."

Elliot shrugged. "A lot happened."

"Don't give me that shit. Some whore shows up, you vanish and kill a guy and come back like this? You promised you'd never do that again."

"You don't even know what happened."

"You killed somebody again, didn't you? You cowboy bastard."

"He deserved it."

"Get out. Forget the stream, forget the everything. Get out of here."

Elliot was sitting at a defunct train station around the corner from Peasant Food, having a cigarette, when his new phone rang. It wasn't Amara, but Cinder. "Blackstone here."

His boss said, "I'm sorry your vacation was ruined, but I thought I'd share the good news. Chase just accepted my recommendation. Blackstone, you've been reinstated as a D-rank officer. You'll be issued a new badge number within the week."

Elliot laughed and hung his head as they wrapped up the call. Then, he sighed and snuffed out the cigarette. He crumpled the entire pack and threw it off the balcony, then marched back down to the bottom of the city.

If you have made it this far, please consider leaving a review. Word of mouth is king. More stories in this setting are on their way and Blackstone's story will continue.

You can check out jameskrake.com for more information on other stories available, such as Ship of Fuls, which occurs many centuries after the events of this novel. In addition, there will be all the latest on associated social media accounts and upcoming projects.